THE FOREVER OF
ELLA AND MICHA

Ella and Micha have been through tragedy, heartbreak, and love; now they are thousands of miles apart. Ella continues to go to school and tries to deal with her past, desperate for Micha to be by her side, but she refuses to let her problems get in the way of his dreams. Micha spends his days travelling the country with the band. He wants Ella closer to him — but he won't ask her to leave college. The few moments they do spend together are fleeting, intense, and filled with passion. They know they want to be together, but is wanting something enough to get them to their forever?

Books by Jessica Sorensen
Published by The House of Ulverscroft:

THE SECRET OF ELLA AND MICHA

would like to help support the Foundation or
require further information, please contact:

THE ULVERSCROFT FOUNDATION
The Green, Bradgate Road, Anstey
Leicester LE7 7FU, England
Tel: (0116) 236 4325

website: www.foundation.ulverscroft.com

Jessica Sorensen lives in Wyoming with her husband and three children. She is the author of numerous romance novels; her first new adult novel, *The Secret of Ella and Micha*, was a *New York Times* bestseller.

JESSICA SORENSEN

◆

THE
FOREVER OF
ELLA AND MICHA

Complete and Unabridged

ULVERSCROFT
Leicester

First published in Great Britain in 2013 by
Sphere
An imprint of
Little, Brown Book Group
London

First Large Print Edition
published 2014
by arrangement with
Little, Brown Book Group
An Hachette UK Company
London

A catalogue record for this book is available
from the British Library.

ISBN 978–1–4448–2041–6

Published by
F. A. Thorpe (Publishing)
Anstey, Leicestershire

Set by Words & Graphics Ltd.
Anstey, Leicestershire
Printed and bound in Great Britain by
T. J. International Ltd., Padstow, Cornwall

This book is printed on acid-free paper

Acknowledgments

A huge thanks to my agent, Erica Silverman, and my editor, Selina McLemore, and to my very first readers, Kristin Campbell and Kristine Young. I'm forever grateful for all your help and input.

And to everyone who reads this book, an endless amount of thank-yous.

Prologue

Ella

There's something ominous about the bridge, yet I'm drawn to it by an inner compulsion. It's not as painful as it used to be, but there are still raw memories linked to it that will haunt me forever.

The sky is cloudy and the gentle breeze kisses my skin. I zip my jacket up as I gaze out at the dark water, lost in my thoughts of that terrible night when I considered jumping.

'Are you sure you're going to be okay?' Micha asks, the same question he's been asking for the last few days. His knuckles turn white as he clutches onto the railing of the bridge and peers down at the lake. 'You've been through a lot this weekend.'

I wince at the recollection of my dad's angry voice when he told me he wished I wasn't his daughter, when Dean and I had confronted him about his alcoholism. Cruel words were shouted that ripped at my heart. I keep trying to convince myself that it's the addiction talking, not him, but I don't

1

entirely believe it. My body and mind are exhausted from the drama, but I'll push through, just like I did the last time. There is no running away anymore, only dealing with it and eventually moving on.

Micha doesn't know the entire story of what happened and I want to save him from the burden. He worries about me all the time and the guilt consumes me. He should be happy, love life, do what he wants to do. He deserves it.

I frown, hating that when we walk off the bridge, he'll leave me to return to the road with his band. 'I'm a little sad you have to go.'

He releases the metal railing and his aqua eyes sparkle as he hugs me. I bury my face into his chest and breathe him in, never wanting to let him go.

'I love you, Ella May.' He kisses the top of my head.

I shut my eyes and suck back the tears. 'I love you, too.'

He presses his full lips to mine and kisses me passionately, his lip ring digging into my mouth. My skin warms as his hands explore my back and his fingers graze across my ass, begging my body closer to his. I tangle my fingers through his soft hair before securing my arms around the back of his neck. His tongue traces the inside of my mouth and he intensifies the kiss until we have to pull away to catch our breath.

My chest heaves as I gaze out at the lake one last time and the sun reflects in the water. 'It's time to go, isn't it?'

He squeezes my hand. 'It'll be okay. We have the whole twelve-hour drive ahead of us, and I'll be gone for only a couple weeks before I'm annoying the hell out of you again.'

I force a smile. 'I know and I'm looking forward to being annoyed.'

We walk hand in hand back to Lila's black Mercedes. I let him drive and he flies down the dirt road, leaving a cloud of dust behind us that quickly vanishes.

1

Two months later

Ella

Every night I have the same dream. Micha and I are standing on opposite ends of the bridge. Rain beats down violently from the dark sky and the wind kicks up debris between us.

Micha extends his hand and I walk toward him, but he slips away from me until he lands up on the railing of the bridge. He teeters in the wind and I want to save him, but my feet won't budge. A gust of wind slams into him and he falls backward, vanishing into the darkness. I wake up screaming and full of guilt.

My therapist has a theory that the nightmare signifies my fear of losing Micha, although that doesn't explain why I won't save him. When she mentioned it, my heart sped up and my palms began to sweat. I never looked far enough into the future to realize that maybe one day Micha and I may not be together.

A forever? Does such a thing exist?

With as much time as we spend together I wonder where our relationship is going. The last time we saw each other was at Grady's funeral. It was the second toughest day of my life; the first being my mother's funeral.

Micha and I had been out on the cliff that overlooked the lake, with a black jar containing Grady's ashes. The wind was blowing and all I could think about was how much death owned life. At any moment death could snatch up life and take it away, just like it had done with my mom and Grady.

'Are you ready for this?' Micha had asked, removing the lid from the jar.

Nodding, I extended my hand toward the jar. 'I'm as ready as I'll ever be.'

From behind us, the car was running and playing Grady's favorite song, 'Simple Man' by Lynyrd Skynyrd, a song that fit Grady and his lifestyle perfectly.

He moved the jar toward me and we held onto it together. 'What's that thing he used to say all the time?' Micha asked me. 'About life?'

'It isn't as important to feel great about all the things we do,' I say softly. 'But how we feel toward the end when we look back at everything we've done.'

Tears streamed from my eyes as we tipped

the jar sideways and spilled the ashes off the cliff. As we watched them float down to the lake, Micha wrapped his arm around me and took a shot of tequila. He had offered me a sip, but I had declined.

My insides shook as pain rushed through me, but I quickly repressed it. Though sunlight sparkled down on us, there was a chill in the air as I observed the lake that seemed to hold everything. It was connected to so many deep, painful memories of my past with my mom and myself.

'Earth to Ella.' Lila waves her hand in front of my face and I flinch. 'You seriously space off more than anyone else I know. Class got out like five minutes ago . . . What the heck is that drawing of? It's creepy.'

Drawn back to the present, my gaze sweeps across the empty desks in the classroom and then falls on the pen in my hand, the tip pressed to a sketch of my face, only my eyes are black and my skin looks like dry, cracked dirt.

'It's nothing.' I stuff the drawing into my bag and grab my books. Sometimes I lose track of time and it's unsettling, because so did my mother. 'It's just a doodle I was messing around with during Professor Mackman's boring lecture.'

'What's the deal with you? You've been like

super spaced out and super grumpy,' Lila asks as we walk out of the classroom and push out the doors, stepping into the sunlight.

I adjust my bag on my shoulder and pull my sunglasses down over my eyes. 'It's nothing. I'm just tired.'

She stops abruptly in the middle of the sidewalk, narrows her blue eyes at me, and puts her hands on her hips. 'Don't shut down on me now. We've been doing so well.'

I sigh, because she's right. 'It's just this dream I've been having.'

'About Micha?'

'How'd you guess?'

She elevates her eyebrows. 'How could I not guess? All of your thoughts are about him.'

'Not all of my thoughts.' I dwell in my thoughts about my dad, who's in rehab and how he won't talk to me.

We stroll down the sidewalk and she links arms with me. There's a skip to her walk, and her pink dress and blonde hair blow in the gentle fall breeze. About a year ago, Lila and I looked very similar, but then Micha cracked through my shell and I opted for a happy medium. I'm wearing a black Spill Canvas T-shirt and a pair of jeans, and my long auburn hair hangs loosely around my face.

8

'Where should we have lunch?' she asks as we reach the edge of the parking lot. 'Because our fridge is empty.'

'We need to go shopping.' I scoot over as a group of football players walk by in their scarlet and gray uniforms. 'But we also need a car to go anywhere, since you won't take the bus anymore.'

'Only because of that creeper who licked my arm,' she says, cringing. 'It was disgusting.'

'It was pretty gross,' I agree, trying not to laugh.

'My dad's such a jerk,' Lila mutters with a frown. 'He should have at least warned me when he decided to tow my car back home. It makes no sense. He doesn't want me there, yet he takes my car away because I ran out during the summer.'

'Dads tend to be jerks.' At the end of the sidewalk, I veer to the left. 'Mine won't talk to me.'

'We should make a Dads Suck Club,' she suggests sarcastically. 'I'm sure a lot of people would join.'

I strain a smile. I don't blame my dad for his negative feelings toward me. It was my choice to leave that night my mom died and now I have to deal with the consequences — it's part of moving on.

9

I stay under the shade of the trees as we head up the sidewalk toward the side section of the school. 'Let's just eat at the cafeteria. It's the easiest place to get to.'

Her nose scrunches. 'Easy, in the sense that it's close. But other than that there is nothing easy about . . . ' She trails off as her eyes stray to the side of the campus and a conniving smile expands across her face 'Here's an idea. You could ask Blake to give us a ride somewhere.'

I spot Blake walking across the campus yard toward his car. He is in my water base media class and talks to me a lot. Lila insists it's because he has a thing for me, but I disagree.

'I'm not going to just go up and ask him for a ride.' I tug on her arm. 'Let's just eat in the cafeteria — '

'Hey, Blake!' she hollers, waving her arms in the air, then giggles under her breath.

Blake's brown eyes scan the campus and a smile expands across his face as he struts across the lawn toward us.

'He knows I have a boyfriend,' I tell Lila. 'He's just nice.'

'Guys are hardly ever just nice, and I'm using his little crush on you to get us a ride out of here,' Lila whispers. 'I'm so sick of being stuck here.'

My lips part in protest, but Blake reaches us, and I cinch my jaw shut.

He has a beanie over his dark-brown hair and blue paint spots dot the front of his faded jeans and the bottom of his tan T-shirt.

'So what's up?' His thumb is hooked on to the handle of the ratty backpack slung over his shoulder and he looks at me like I'm the one who called him over.

We're almost the same height and I can easily look him directly in the eyes. 'It was nothing.'

'We need a ride.' Lila flutters her eyelashes at him as she coils a lock of her hair around her finger. 'To get some lunch.'

'You don't have to take us,' I intervene. 'Lila just really needs an off-campus fix.'

'I'd love to take you anywhere you need to go,' he offers with a genuine smile. 'I'm headed back to my apartment first, though, so if you don't mind stopping you can just come with me now.'

From inside my pocket, my phone starts ringing the tune 'Behind Blue Eyes' by The Who and my lips curve into a grin.

Lila rolls her eyes. 'Oh dear God. I thought you would have been over your giddiness by now. You two have been together for almost three months.'

I answer the phone, loving the flutters in

11

my stomach that are caused from just hearing the song play. It reminds me of how his hands feel against my skin and how he calls me by my nickname.

'Hello, beautiful,' he says charmingly and the sound of his voice sends a quiver through my body. 'How's my favorite girl in the world?'

'Well, hello to you too.' I amble toward a leafy tree in the center of the lawn. 'I'm doing great. Are you having a good day?'

'I am now.' He uses his player's voice on me. 'I'll have an even better day if you'll tell me what you're wearing.'

'Jeans and a ratty T-shirt.' I press back a smile.

'Come on, pretty girl, it's been like a month.' He laughs into the phone, a deep noise that makes my insides vibrate. 'Tell me what you're wearing underneath it.'

I roll my eyes, but tolerate him. 'A red, lacy thong and matching bra.'

'That's a really nice mental picture you painted there,' he growls in a husky voice. 'Now I'll have something to help take care of myself later.'

'Just as long as you're taking care of it yourself,' I say and there's a drawn-out pause. 'Micha, are you there?'

'You know I'd never do that to you, right?'

His tone carries heaviness. 'I love you way too much.'

'I was just joking.' Kind of. Lately, it's been bothering me that he spends so much time with Naomi, especially because a lot of his stories involve her.

'Yeah, but you always joke about it every time we talk and I worry that deep down you believe it.'

'I don't,' I insist, although the thought has crossed my mind. He's a lead singer in a band. And gorgeous. And charming. 'I know you love me.'

'Good, because I have something to tell you.' He pauses. 'We got the gig.'

My mouth instantly sinks. 'The one in New York?'

'Yeah . . . Isn't that great?'

'It's awesome . . . I'm really happy for you.'

Silence takes over. I want to say something, but the sadness has stolen my voice so I stare across the campus at a couple walking and holding hands, thinking about what it's like to have that.

'Ella May, tell me what's wrong,' he demands. 'Are you worried about me being gone? Because you know you're the only girl for me. Or is it . . . is it Grady? How are you doing with that? I never know since you won't talk to me.'

13

'It's not Grady,' I say quickly, wanting to get off that subject. 'It's just that . . . it's so far and I barely get to see you as it is.' I slump back against a tree trunk. 'You're still coming up here this weekend, right?'

He lets out a gradual breath. 'The thing is, to make it to New York in time, we have to leave tomorrow morning. And I'd drive over there tonight, just to see you, but we have a performance.'

My insides wind into knots, but I stay calm on the outside. 'How long are you going to be gone to New York?'

He takes a second to answer. 'About a month.'

My hand trembles with anger or fear . . . I'm not sure. 'So I haven't seen you in almost a month and I'm not going to be able to see you for another month?'

'You could come visit me in New York,' he proposes. 'You could fly out for, like, a week or something.'

'I have midterms.' My voice is sullen. 'And my brother's wedding's in, like, a month and all my extra money is to pay for that.'

'Ella, come on!' Lila shouts and my eyes dart to her. She motions me to come over, while Blake stands beside her with his hands stuffed into the pockets of his jeans. 'Blake's waiting on us.'

14

'Who's Blake?' Micha wonders curiously.

'Just a guy from my class,' I explain, leaving the tree and heading toward Blake and Lila. 'Look, I got to go.'

'Are you sure you're okay?'

'Yeah, Lila's just waiting on me.'

'Okay . . . I'll call you after my performance then.'

'Sounds good.' I hang up the phone, realizing I forgot to say good-bye, but the word wouldn't have left my mouth anyway. It feels like we're slipping away from each other, and he was the one thing that brought me back out of my dark place. If he leaves me, I'm not sure I can hold onto the light.

Micha

'Fuck.' I hang up the phone and kick the tire of the band's SUV, which is in the middle of a parking lot of a shitty-ass motel in the bad side of town where crack-heads walk the streets and every building has graffiti. It makes Star Grove look classy.

The sadness in Ella's voice worries me. She's still struggling with her personal demons, Grady's death, her mom's death, and won't completely open up to me about everything. There's always a thought in the

15

back of my mind that she might vanish again.

A car backfires as I walk back to the motel room. On the stairway, I weave around a man making out with a woman who's probably a hooker to get to my door.

This is what I'm choosing over Ella? Sometimes I wonder why.

'Wow, you look like you're in a pissy mood,' Naomi remarks from the bed when I slam the door of the motel room. She's painting her toenails and the room stinks like paint thinner. 'Did you have a bad day?'

Clearing my throat, I empty out the change from the pocket of my jeans and drop my wallet down on the nightstand. 'What gave it away? The door slam?'

'You're so hilarious.' She sits up and blows on her nails. 'What did Ella say to you this time?'

'She didn't say anything.' I unzip my duffel bag that's on a chair between the television and the table. 'She never does.'

'That's the problem.' Naomi likes to put her two cents in on everything and sometimes it gets on my nerves. 'That she doesn't tell you how she feels.'

I grab a pair of clean jeans and a black, long-sleeved shirt from the bag. 'I don't want to talk about this.'

'But you do when you're drunk.' She

smirks. 'In fact, I can't get you to shut up when you're wasted.'

'I talked to you about stuff once.' I walk backward toward the bathroom. 'And I was having a really shitty day.'

'Because you miss her.' She clips bracelets around her wrists. 'Here's a thought. Why don't you just bring her on the road with us?'

I pause in the doorway. 'Why would you say that?'

'Dylan, Chase and I have been talking and we think maybe you'd be a little bit more . . . ' — she hesitates — 'pleasant to be around if she was here.'

I cock an eyebrow. 'Am I that bad?'

'Sometimes.' She gets up and slips on her shoes. 'It's like you're the same as when Ella disappeared for eight months, only sometimes it's worse. You're always so down and you hardly ever go out with us.'

I rub my face with my hand, taking in what she said. 'I'm sorry if I've been acting like a douche bag, but I can't ask Ella to come with us.'

Naomi grabs the keycard from the dresser and puts it into the back pocket of her jeans. 'Why not?'

'Because she's happy,' I say, recalling the many times she chatted to me about her classes and life in an upbeat tone that made me smile. 'And I can't ask her to give that up, even though I'd love to have her here.'

Naomi shrugs and opens the door, letting in the sunlight and warm air that smells like cigarettes. 'It's your decision. I was just giving you an outsider's point of view. Do you want to come out with us tonight? Drinks are on Dylan.'

'Nah, I think I'll stay in tonight.' I wave her off and she leaves, closing the door behind her.

I pile my clothes in the stained bathroom sink and turn on the shower. The pipes squeak as the water sprays out. Raking my hands through my hair, I let out a frustrated sigh. My fingers grip the counter and my head falls forward.

My mom told me once about how she met my father. He lived in the town over from Star Grove and one day when they were both cruising, they ran into each other. *Literally*. The front end of my dad's truck slammed into the back end of my mom's car. Her car was trashed, but they ended up talking for hours after the tow truck had come and gone and my dad had offered to drive my mom home.

She said it was instant love, or at least that's how she interpreted it in her hormonal teenaged brain. She was supposed to be leaving for college at the end of the summer, but she stayed behind and married my dad instead.

She said she regretted the decision, but I'm not sure if it's because my dad turned out to be a cheating dick, or if she was just sad over the loss of her future.

I push away from the counter, coming to the conclusion to let it go for now. Ella and I are tough enough to make it through a month.

We already made it through hell and back.

2

Ella

Blake gives us a ride to lunch and then drops us off back at campus about an hour later. I try to be happy, but fail. According to my therapist, I shouldn't try to conceal my feelings because it's unhealthy. She says bottling things up and letting them eat away at me usually ends in disaster; that suffering in silence is never an option.

Lila hops out of the back of the car when Blake pulls into an empty parking space. 'Thanks for the ride, Blake.' She shuts the door and shimmies off toward the sidewalk.

'Are you okay?' Blake asks me as I unbuckle my seatbelt. 'You seem kind of quiet today.'

'I'm fine.' I start to open the door. 'I just have a lot on my mind.'

Pulling the beanie off his head and ruffling his hair, he rotates in his seat to face me. 'I'm a good listener.'

I eye him over warily. 'I'm sure you probably don't want to hear it.'

'Try me.'

'It's about my boyfriend.'

'Ah.' His eyebrows arch upward. 'The infamous Micha.'

'That would be the one,' I say. 'He's leaving . . . clear across the country.'

He wiggles the keys out of the ignition. 'And you're upset about this, I take it?'

'Well, obviously. He's leaving and he was supposed to drive out here from LA this weekend.' The more I talk about it aloud, the more panic chokes at my chest. 'But now he has to drive out to New York tomorrow. I have no idea why I'm telling you this. I'm sorry.' I climb out of the car and close the door.

He meets me at the front of the car, swings his bag over his shoulder, and pushes the lock button, the headlights blinking. We walk in silence toward the grass area that stretches over the front of the campus. Lila is underneath a tree talking to Parker, a tall guy with thick arms and sandy blond hair. He's wearing a button-down shirt and a pair of fancy jeans. It's her type of guy normally, except for Ethan. The two of them occasionally talk on the phone, although they still insist they're just friends.

'Thanks for taking us to lunch.' I step up onto the curb. 'I'm sure Lila's thankful too. She's been going crazy being stuck on campus.'

'Anytime.' He stuffs his hands into his pockets with a pensive look on his face. 'So your boyfriend's in LA right now?'

I nod unenthusiastically. 'Until tomorrow.'

He mulls over something, gazing at the parking lot. 'You know that's only, like, a four-, four-and-a-half-hour drive from here. You could probably make it there later tonight if you left soon.'

'I know that.' I force back a smile, knowing I could make it there in less time than that. 'But I don't have a car.' I point over my shoulder at his red Ford Mustang. 'Hence the ride this afternoon.'

An amused smile tugs at the corners of his lips. 'I know, but I have a car that could get you there.'

'Why would you do that?' I ask, shocked.

He shrugs, scuffing his shoes against the sidewalk. 'Because I know how hard it is to be away from the person you love.'

'Are you for real?' I ask, and he nods. 'Let me get this straight. You're going to let me borrow your car and drive it out of the state, so I can see my boyfriend for, like, a night?'

'Actually I was going to take you,' he clarifies. 'My girlfriend lives in Riverside and you could drop me off and pick me up.'

'Girlfriend?' I sputter out a laugh. 'Oh my God, you have a girlfriend?'

He tilts his head to the side with a mystified expression. 'Am I that repulsive?'

I shake my head swiftly. 'No, I'm sorry. It's just that . . . Well, Lila thought you had a thing for me and that's why you talk to me all the time.'

He tugs his beanie onto his head, pressing his lips together to suppress a laugh. 'Oh, I see. Your friend's . . . interesting.'

'She's nice, though,' I tell him, glancing over at Lila, who's running her fingers up and down Parker's arm. 'I love Lila to death.'

'I know that,' he replies. 'And for the record, I talk to you because you're an interesting person. You remind me a lot of my friends back home.'

I'm curious what his friends are like back home. 'Are you sure you want to take me? Because you don't have to.'

'I'm sure.' He tucks the car keys into the back pocket of his jeans. 'It's worth it just to keep that happy look on your face. You don't smile very much.'

I can't stop smiling. 'Well, thank you. It means a lot to me.'

'Why don't you go grab your stuff and we can meet back here in, like, an hour.' He backs down the sidewalk as I hike across the grass toward Lila.

'Sounds good,' I call over my shoulder.

'And thanks again.'

By the time I reach Lila, she's writing her phone number on Parker's hand with a red pen.

'We're going on a road trip,' I announce, interrupting the conversation.

Parker gives me a once-over and then dismisses me with his eyes. 'So I'll call you later then?' he asks Lila.

'Yeah, sure.' She waves at him and he struts toward the main entrance of the campus, high-fiving another guy standing beneath the canopy in front of the doors.

'Where and why are we going on a road trip?' Lila clicks the cap back on the pen and drops it into her bag.

My stomach flips, thinking about how I'm going to see Micha in just hours. 'To LA. Blake is giving us a ride. And before you say anything, he has a girlfriend.'

'Sure he does,' Lila says cynically. 'And he also really loves her and would never do anything to hurt her. Typical guy cop-out.'

'What . . . Are you okay?' I've never heard her say anything like this before.

'I'm fine,' she swears, shrugging it off. 'Let's go.'

★　★　★

24

Blake's a slow driver and when I ask him what he has under the hood, he has no idea. I try not to give him too much crap about it, but a few sarcastic remarks slip out.

'Aw, you like cars.' He merges the car back into the slower traffic lane.

From the backseat, Lila snort-laughs. 'Likes them. The girl's insane about them. It's actually kind of annoying.' She shoots me a grin and I flip her the middle finger.

'Is it just old cars?' He makes a careful turn down the off-ramp. 'Or is it cars in general?'

'Fast cars.' Like Micha's poor Chevelle lying in pieces in his garage back home. May it rest in peace. 'Ones that will kick ass in a race.'

He cuts me a sideways glance. 'Now I'm starting to get concerned about letting you borrow my car.'

'I won't race it.' I cross my heart with my finger. 'I swear I'll be easy on it.'

He winks at me. 'Don't worry, I trust you.'

The way he says it makes me uncomfortable and Lila gives me a knowing look in the rearview mirror.

We keep quiet for most of the drive. Blake doesn't have the air on and the black leather seats get hot and stick to the back of my legs. When we pull up to his girlfriend's house, which is in the suburbs where every house and yard looks similar, I'm sweating.

His girlfriend runs out of the house and throws her arms around him, nearly knocking him to the ground. She's petite with red streaks in her hair and a piercing through her nose. She waves at us and then Blake backtracks to the trunk. Maneuvering over the console and into the driver's seat, I pop the handle and he gets his suitcase out, before shutting it.

He walks around to the driver's-side window and waits for me to roll it down.

'Be careful,' he reminds me in a serious tone and I nod.

Flashing me a grin, he heads off to the house as Lila dives over the console and into the front seat.

'Be careful,' she says in a low, mocking voice. 'I'm trying to be so sexy.'

'He didn't sound like that.' I pull out onto the street.

'You're so blind.'

'And sometimes you see too much.'

I merge out onto the freeway and into the fast lane, but resist the urge to punch the pedal to the floor and get us there in half the time. Lila takes a nap with her head resting against the window and I bask in the peace of being on the road until we brink the edge of town, which glows against the night.

I nudge Lila's shoulder to wake her up. 'We're here.'

She blinks her weary eyes and sits up in the seat. 'What's up? Where are we?'

'We're in LA. Or on the outskirts of it anyway,' I say as her eyes sweep the towering buildings and the considerable amount of traffic in front of us. 'Can you look up the address on your phone?'

She cracks her window, letting the warm air blow in. 'Can't you just call him and tell him you're coming?'

'I want it to be a surprise.'

'Why? Are you trying to catch him doing something wrong, like, say, with Naomi?'

'No.' I flip on the blinker and check my mirror. 'I trust Micha.'

'But you don't trust *her*.' A large truck honks its horn and Lila glances out the window. 'I don't blame you. From the stories you've told me, she seems a little sketchy. In fact, maybe while we're here, we could have a little talk with her.' She pops her knuckles and I bust up laughing.

'Oh my God, what have you been watching?' Tapping the brakes, I slow down the car to match the traffic.

'How to beat the girl who's hitting on your best friend's boyfriend.' She grins at me and retrieves the phone out of her purse. 'What's

27

the name of the place?'

'The Slam,' I tell her and she arcs her eyebrows. 'What? That's what it's called?'

'Are you sure it's not called The Slam-er?' She laughs cleverly.

I roll my eyes. 'Ha-ha. You're so funny.'

She enters the location into the GPS and frowns at the long line of cars in front of us. 'It says it's like five miles into town . . . It's going to take forever.'

My eyes narrow on the road as the traffic crawls forward. 'No, it won't.'

'*Hey.*' Lila stabs a finger at me, reeling in her seat. 'You promised Blake you wouldn't race his car.'

I down shift and the engine purrs to life. 'I'm not going to race it. I'm just going to shoot the gaps.'

She secures her seatbelt over her shoulder. 'I don't even want to know what that means, but I swear to God, if we end up driving into the median, I'll never talk to you again.'

'O ye of little faith.' I rev up the RPMs and swerve over to the next lane, cutting off a red Camry. The driver honks the horn and Lila grips the edge of the leather seat. 'You know I've seen you drive this crazy before, right?'

She glares at me. 'And I'm okay when I'm the driver and know I have control of the situation.' I flinch at her words and she adds,

'It gives me a sense of safety.'

I loathe hearing the word 'control.' It reminds me of how much my mind craves it. It's sort of like an addiction, like alcohol or cigarettes.

I hit the brakes as the front of the car verges on the back end of a lifted truck. There's a tiny gap over to the next lane and I debate if it's doable.

'Don't you dare,' Lila warns with fear in her blue eyes. 'It's too narrow.'

The guy in the side lane slows down and I red-line the RPMs, crank the wheel at the last second, and squeeze us over easily.

Lila huffs out a breath as she slumps back in the seat. 'If I didn't love you so much, I'd totally hate you.' She fusses with her blonde hair and wipes some smeared eyeliner out from underneath her eyes.

I continue dodging in and out of traffic until we reach the exit. Driving like this makes me feel alive and by the time we reach the club Micha is playing at, adrenaline is coursing through my body.

'This place looks sketchy.' Lila crinkles her nose at the warehouse nestled between Larry's Biker Bar and The Adult Video Store. It's late, and the stars and moon light up the dry leaves and cigarette butts on the asphalt.

'You said that about Star Grove too.' I kick

open the door and step outside. 'And you survived that place.'

She rolls her eyes as she climbs out of the car. 'Star Grove doesn't look nearly as bad as this place.'

We head across the parking lot, walking close to each other when a group of guys smoking behind a truck make catcalls.

'I still can't believe Blake let me borrow his car.' I jump over a pothole. 'If I owned a Mustang, I sure as hell wouldn't lend it out to someone I barely knew, especially after I told him I like to race.'

'I told you it's because he likes you.' She elbows me as we turn down the alley that leads to the front entrance of the club. 'I have an eye for these things.'

'He has a girlfriend, Lila. And it seemed like they really love each other.' I sidestep a Dumpster and emerge onto the busy sidewalk. Cars drive up and down the road and bright graffiti decorates the metal exterior of the neighboring buildings.

Pausing in front of the entrance, I pull my hair out of the ponytail and it falls to my shoulders. Letting go of Lila's arm, I quickly tie the lace of my boot, then unfasten two of the top buttons on my plaid shirt and smooth out the wrinkles on my denim skirt.

'Wow, I've never seen you this fussy before,'

Lila comments as she refastens the ribbon lacing up the front of her maroon shirt. 'It's very entertaining.'

'I don't know why, but I suddenly feel really nervous,' I admit, tousling my hair with my fingers.

'It's because you *love* him.' Lila bats her eyelashes and I shove her gently. 'Relax. It's because you haven't seen him for, like, a month. Honestly, I'm a little afraid to be in the same room as you two. You'll probably have your clothes off and on the floor in a matter of seconds.'

Rolling my eyes, I enter the club where a bouncer with snake tattoos on his muscular arms and a scar on his lip blocks the path to the table area.

'IDs please.' His tone suggests we don't have them.

Lila and I take our fake IDs out of our pockets and hand them to him. He evaluates them carefully and gives them back to us, stepping aside to let us through.

We walk into an open room filled with tables and chairs. The air is musty, the bar is crammed with people, and the music is loud, but the sound of the singer's voice is more familiar than the beat of my heart.

'Aw, look at him up there all hot and sexy,' Lila says, but I barely hear her.

All of my concentration focuses on the stage near the far back wall. Beneath the low lighting, Micha sings one of his own songs, playing the guitar with his head tipped down and his hair hanging in his sparkling aqua eyes. My hands ache to touch him, tangle through his hair, feel the softness of his lips.

The band plays in the background and it takes my breath away as his lyrics flow over my body.

The silence in your eyes is more than I
*   can take.*
Look at me for once and see how my
*   heart aches.*
You keep me alive. You keep me
*   breathing.*
All I want, all I need is you.

The room blends away and it's just him and me. I hear Lila move away from me, probably heading to the bar to order a drink. It takes Micha only seconds to find me in the middle of the crowded room, like our hearts sense each other. He tries to maintain a straight face as he spills out the lyrics, but a trace of a smile reveals at his lips.

He finishes out the last set with a final chord, and then quickly turns to Naomi, who's wearing a tight black dress and knee-high boots. Micha says something to her as he hands her the guitar. She nods, tucking her black hair behind her ear, and he hops off stage, and his long legs stride for me as he shoves through the crowd. He doesn't slow down until he scoops me up in his arms, not caring that there are a ton of people watching us.

I fasten my legs around his waist and he kisses me intensely, stealing every ounce of oxygen from my lungs. Our bodies and tongues conform together, and the heat of him sears my skin. His lip ring scores into my bottom lip, but I want more. Begging him closer, I breathe him in, tasting him, wanting to feel him as much as possible before we part again.

When he leans back, a fire flares deep inside his aqua eyes and my stomach somersaults with excitement.

'God, I've missed you, pretty girl.' He kisses me again and his hands wander all over my body. Reluctantly, he pulls away, breathless. 'Don't take this the wrong way, but what are you doing here? Is something wrong?'

'No, nothing's wrong. Lila said I needed to come see you before you left.' I trace my fingers along the back of his neck and he shivers from my touch. 'She said that she was sick of my bad attitude and that I needed to get you out of my system, at least for a day or so.'

He bites at his lip, stifling a smile. 'You know you could never get me out of your system. It's not possible.'

'I know, but I can try,' I tease. 'In fact, I could try a lot.'

A naughty look dances in his eyes. 'I like the sound of that.'

He moves in for another kiss, deliberately this time, but with equally as much passion as all our kisses. 'I have two more songs to play and then you and I can leave.'

I blink dazedly. 'Where are we going?'

He lets out a breathy laugh as he presses up against me. 'First things first. We're going to go back to the hotel and take care of some much needed business.'

I try not to smile, but it's impossible. 'And then what are we going to do?'

'Then we'll go out and do something fun,' he promises, setting me back on the floor. He kisses my forehead, and then moves back through the crowd to the stage.

I find Lila at the bar and plop down in a barstool next to her. My gaze locks on Micha on stage as he starts to play a cover of his sad-turned-happy song — our song, as he tells me all the time.

'Oh thank God.' Lila stirs the red fruity

drink in her hand. 'You're happy again.'

Forcing my lips together, I suffocate my giddiness, but eventually it surfaces. It's terrifying, feeling this way. I didn't realize how down I was until now.

Micha

It's the first time I've ever been excited to be done performing. I can't wait to get out of the club and take her back to the room. The entire time I'm singing, my eyes are fixed on her. Deep down, I'm singing only to her.

When I finish, the band clears the stage. I hold up a finger at Ella, letting her know I'll be a second, and then go into the room where our instruments are.

'Someone got a nice surprise,' Naomi comments as she pulls her long, black hair up into a bun and glances at herself in the cracked mirror on the wall. 'Looks like you won't be going out with the band tonight.'

'I think we'll come out with you.' I put my guitar into the case and clip the locks. 'But I'm going back to the hotel room first and you guys might want to steer clear of it for a while.'

She rolls her eyes and Dylan, our drummer, lifts up his hand to give me a high-five. Dylan likes to call himself 'The Ladies Man' and spends a lot of time bragging about his hookups while we're on the road. It's annoying as shit and I dismiss his high-five.

'Take my guitar with you and I'll text you later.' I hand Naomi the case and walk backward for the door. 'Oh yeah, and would you mind if Ella's friend hung out with you guys for a while?'

She shrugs as she puts on some red lipstick. 'I guess . . . but is it that blonde one? Because she doesn't really look like she'll be too happy hanging with us lowlifes.'

I open the door. 'She just looks stuck-up, but she's cool.'

When I walk back out into the club, Ella and Lila are at the bar. Ella's drinking a beer, with her endless legs crossed, and Lila's sipping on some girlie fruit drink. They're talking about something and Ella's got a huge smile on her face.

Interrupting the conversation, I squeeze between them and press my lips to hers, giving her a deep kiss. When I draw back, her eyes are big and glassy and I love that I'm the one who put the look on her face.

'Oh great, now the clothes are coming off.' Lila crosses her legs and laughs, exchanging a look with Ella.

'What's up?' Dragging a finger across her collarbone, I step up behind Ella and circle my arms around her waist.

'It's nothing.' Ella rests her head against my chest. 'She's just making an inside joke.'

'Speaking of inside.' I take her hand and pull her to her feet. 'We need to go.'

She hauls me back toward the bar as I try to pull her through the crowd toward the exit. 'What about Lila? We can't just leave her here.'

Lila finishes her drink and slides the empty glass onto the counter. 'I can hang out in the car or something.'

I shake my head. 'That's not a good idea. Not in this kind of neighborhood. But Naomi said you can hang out with her and the band.'

Lila glances at Ella unsurely and when Ella nods, she sighs. 'All right, I'll hang out with her . . . I guess. But where are they going?'

'Just to dinner, I think,' I tell her as Naomi exits from backstage and makes her way across the room toward us.

'Ready to go?' Naomi asks Lila in a formal tone and gives Ella a tight smile. 'Hi, Ella, how are you?'

'Great,' Ella replies nonchalantly and her jaw spasms.

There's an awkward silence that only girls can create.

37

'Okay then, I guess we should get going.' Naomi raises her eyebrows and motions for Lila to come with her as she leaves for the back.

'*Please* hurry,' Lila says pressingly and trudges after Naomi toward the back area.

I tug Ella eagerly toward the front door, shoving people out of my way. When we step outside, I grab her arm, whirl her around, and pick her up.

'Where's your car?' I ask as she hitches her legs around my waist and my dick instantly gets hard.

She loops her arms around the back of my neck and her green eyes sparkle underneath the streetlights. 'It's parked out back.'

I stumble blindly down the dark alley as I kiss her fiercely and tangle my fingers in her long, auburn hair that smells sweetly of vanilla. I trip over the curb at the end, but regain my balance without breaking the kiss. My hand cups her ass and the other one explores the soft skin of her thigh.

'Did you wear this skirt just for me, so I'd have easy access?' I murmur against her lips as my fingers inch up her leg.

Laughing against my mouth, she pinches my ass. 'You at least have to get us in the car before you start doing stuff to me.'

'Yeah right.' I caress her tongue with mine,

savoring her, before moving away. 'I'm planning on throwing you down on the hood right here, right now.'

She restrains a smile. 'No way. There are people everywhere.'

My eyes skim the dark parking lot and a few perverts sitting on a dropped tailgate of a truck are watching us. 'Fine, point taken . . . Where's Lila's car?'

A guilty look crosses her face like she's done something wrong. 'I guess I forgot to tell you, but Lila's dad towed her car away a little while ago, so we had to borrow a car.'

I glance around again. 'Which one is it?'

She points over her shoulder at a car parked toward the back. 'The red Mustang right there.'

I eye her over suspiciously. 'Where did you two find someone who would let you borrow their Mustang?'

'Someone I know from school.' She shrugs coolly. 'It's not that big of a deal.'

'Was this person a guy?'

'Um . . . yeah . . . it's Blake's, but it doesn't mean anything. In fact, we dropped him off in Riverside at his girlfriend's house.'

My arms start to loosen around her as I decide whether to put her down on the ground or keep her close. 'So not only did he let you drive his car, but he drove with you?'

'Micha, stop it.' She constricts her legs around my waist, refusing to let me go. 'You're on the road all the time with Naomi and I let it be. Besides, you're always telling me to trust you, and you need to do the same.'

Fuck. She has a point, but I'm still jealous. It is a first for me and I'm not a fan of it.

Shaking it off, I walk for the car again, resolving to keep hold of her. Gripping onto my shoulder with one hand, she gets the keys from her skirt pocket and unlocks the car. Without putting her down, I maneuver the driver's-side door open and set her into the seat.

I rest my hand on the top of the door and stare down at her. 'And for the record, I do trust you. It's guys I don't trust. They think with their dicks.' She sighs and I slam the door, pretending like it's not annoying as shit that I'm climbing into some other guy's car.

★ ★ ★

She drives the car really slowly to the hotel. When I ask her why she's driving like an old lady, she blows out a frustrated breath and tells me she promised Blake she'd behave while she drove it. This makes me feel a little better.

40

'So he's a pussy,' I say, not even trying to hold my smile back.

She parks the car in front of the trashy two-story motel littered with beer bottles and cigarette butts, and some rough-looking people are hanging out on the stairway and balcony.

'Micha, what's your problem? Why is this bugging you so much?' She aims to sound upset, but a hint of laughter escapes in her voice.

I get out of the car and lower my head back into the cab. 'I don't like that this guy gets to hang out with you and lend you his car when it should be me.'

When she climbs out, she accidentally drops her keys on the ground. Bending over to pick them up, I get a glimpse of her black, lacy panties. 'I know it's hard, isn't it?'

I can't help myself. 'Oh yeah, it's very, very hard.' My tone insinuates my dirty thoughts and I slide over the hood of the car. Snagging her by the hips, I yank her against me. 'All right, I'm done talking about Blake for a while,' I say and kiss her.

Without another word, I slip my hand into hers and lead her up the stairs, past the vending machine and the two women who are yelling at each other on the balcony. By the time I have the door open to the room, I'm already unbuttoning her shirt. My lips seal

41

against hers as I kick the door shut, continuing to unfasten the buttons.

My knuckles graze across the soft skin of her stomach and I groan, drawing my lips away from her briefly so I can tug her shirt off. I toss it onto the floor and crash my mouth into hers again. Spreading my fingers along her lower back, I request more of her. I can't get enough.

Her hand runs down my chest until her fingers find the bottom of my shirt and then she pulls it over my head and chucks it onto the floor. With our tongues entwined, I back us toward the bed.

She fiddles with the button on my jeans and a groan escapes my throat as we collapse onto the mattress. 'God, I've fucking missed this,' I mutter.

She leans away, with a smile tugging at the corners of her lips. 'Is that the only reason you've missed me? Because you needed to get laid?'

I brush strands of her auburn hair out her face. 'No, I miss everything. Your laugh, your smile, the way you pretend to be mad at me when really you think I'm funny.' I kiss her cheek softly. 'I miss the way you taste.' I press my lips to her jawline and her neck arches. 'The way you smell.' I suck on her neck, rolling my tongue along her skin as my hand

42

glides up her thigh and to the edge of her panties. 'The way you feel.' I slip my fingers inside her and a moan falters her lips as her body bows up.

'Micha . . . ' Her eyes get lost as I feel her the way I've wanted to for the last month.

'Yeah, I miss that too,' I say and reconnect my lips with hers.

Ella

I didn't realize how much I missed him until now. His fingers continue to feel me as his tongue strokes the inside of my mouth. I breathe out his name, moaning as I lose control of my body and mind, with my fingertips digging into his shoulder blades.

After I regain myself, I peel off my skirt and lie back on the bed, ready for more. He gets out of his jeans and boxers and reaches for his wallet to get a condom.

I grasp his hand, halting him, and rub my finger along the infinity tattoo on his arm. 'You don't need one.'

He cocks an eyebrow, looking at me like I'm crazy. 'Yeah, Ella . . . I don't think — '

I cover his mouth with my hand. 'No. Not because of that. You don't need one because I'm on the Pill.'

When I lower my hand from his lips, he doesn't look happy, which I didn't expect.

'Why did you go on the Pill?' he wonders. 'We barely see each other.'

I pinch his nipple and he flinches, laughing. 'Thanks for the accusation, but I think it's pretty self-explanatory, since the last time we had sex, things got a little too heavy and you almost forgot to put one on.'

'Yeah, good point.' He conceals his body over mine, thinking about something that seems to entertain him.

'Why do you have that look on your face?' I sketch my fingers up and down his back.

He sucks his lip ring between his teeth and then a smile breaks through. 'It's nothing.'

'It's something. You have this goofy grin on your face, so just tell me.'

'Trust me. You don't want to know.'

'Fine.' I tighten my legs together, so he can't get any closer.

'So that's the way it's going to be?' He grins wickedly, then pins my arms above my head and dips his lips beside my ear. 'I was thinking about how nice it was going to feel inside you without a condom on.'

I shake my head, but let my legs fall open and I collide my lips into his. Keeping my arms trapped, he nips my bottom lip with his teeth as he thrusts inside me and my entire

44

body ignites with ecstasy.

He shuts his eyes and inhales deeply through his nose. 'Fuck, Ella . . . ' His eyes open and he rocks in me.

Sweat beads our skin as our bodies conform together. Cupping the back of his head, I pull his lips against mine, take his lip ring into my mouth, and explore it with the tip of my tongue. My legs squeeze around his hips as he keeps pumping inside me and I let out a blissful moan. My head tips back as I lose it again and Micha begins to slow down until he finally stills.

We're panting and heat radiates off our bodies. He brushes my hair away from my damp forehead and looks me in the eyes. It feels like there's something he wants to say, something meaningful, but instead he just kisses my forehead and grins. 'Ten more minutes and I'm back in the game.'

★　★　★

Two hours later, we are fully dressed again and driving to the club to catch up with Lila and the band. It's after midnight, but the town is alive. Cars line the road, people walk up the sidewalks, and lights shine against the night.

After Micha begged me for five minutes

straight to let him drive, I finally surrendered and handed over the keys, but only after he swore not to drive like a crazy person.

He throttles the gas anyway and rips the tires against the asphalt as he floors the car onto the main road.

'You promised.' I stab a finger at him. 'Behave.'

'This thing's weak,' he says, pleased. 'What's it got under the hood?'

'I don't know.' I shrug. 'I didn't look. I was too busy trying to get here to see you.'

He reaches over the console and places his hand on my thigh, bringing warmth between my legs. 'Come on. You know you want to let me see how fast it can go. And then afterward, we can pull over and you can take all that excitement out on me in the backseat.'

'You are ridiculously horny,' I tell him, smiling. 'But I'm sure you know that.'

'I do,' he says simply, halting at a stoplight. The red glow illuminates the cab. 'I'm on the fucking road, away from you all the time . . . it's becoming a real problem.'

Panic strangles me as I think of him being far away in New York surrounded by women who would probably happily take care of his problem. I exhale gradually, so he won't hear the unsteadiness of my breathing.

'Hey.' He strokes my inner thigh with his

thumb as the light turns green. 'I know what you're thinking and you need to relax. I would never do anything to hurt you.'

I smile, but it doesn't feel real. People never mean to do things that are hurtful, yet sometimes it just happens, through an intense moment, through brief rationalization, or by simply speaking words that only belong inside one's head.

Or simply by giving up for a second.

People hurt each other all the time.

Micha

Ella has a wandering mind by the time we pull up to the club, but so do I. I'm not sure if her surprise visit was a good thing or a bad thing because it'll make it harder to leave when morning comes around.

It turns out that only Naomi, Chase, and Lila are at the club. Dylan left with the hostess, but no one really seems to know where to — or they just don't care.

There's some really cheesy music playing in the background and a woman wearing red boots and a cowgirl hat is dancing in front of an old guy, trying to seduce him, but she's drunk and keeps falling down.

An instant tension builds at the table once

we sit down. Lila targets Ella with a heavy look and mouths *bitch* while nodding her head at Naomi.

I raise an eyebrow, glancing between Ella and Lila. While Naomi's distracted with Chase, Lila leans over the table and shields the side of her face with her hand. 'Remind me to tell you a lovely little story later.'

It's hard not to roll my eyes at the silliness. 'Should we order an appetizer or something?'

'We already did,' Naomi snaps, shooting me a dirty look. 'And we ordered drinks, but neither has been brought out yet.'

I hold my hands up in front of me and lift my eyebrows. 'Okay, sorry for asking.'

She practically snarls at me and I wonder if a cat-fight broke out between Lila and her. 'Well, I'm getting annoyed with the crappy service.'

I drape my arm around Ella's shoulder and whisper in her ear, 'What are you looking at?'

She jumps, startled, and turns her head toward me. 'It was nothing. I was just dazing off.'

I track the direction she was looking, to an old couple cuddled up together in a booth. They're a little bit rough around the edges, like they've had one too many road trips across the country on their Harleys.

'Why were you staring at the old couple?' I

play with her hair.

She shakes her head promptly. 'I wasn't.'

I stare at her lip as she nibbles on it nervously, but decide to let whatever she's been weird about go for now, not wanting to ruin the one night we get together for the next month.

Ella

For some reason, I find myself staring at an old couple and picturing what it would be like if Micha and I were still together at that age. The man feeds the woman a bite of his food and she leans over to give him a kiss. It's fascinating watching them because my parents were never that affectionate with each other.

The more I think about it, the more my nerves own me. I can't see Micha and me together, old and sitting at a table, feeding each other — I can't see anything.

Micha is concerned about me, like he always is when I'm acting like a weirdo. I focus on the conversation, nodding my head, even though I have no idea what's going on.

When we're leaving, Lila seizes my elbow and rips me away from Micha's grasp.

'What are you doing?' I say, stumbling to

49

keep up with her as she tows me around the corner of the brick restaurant and into the smoking area. It's dark and the air feels a little damp compared to Vegas' dry heat.

'That Naomi is a bitch.' She waves her finger as she talks.

My eyebrows furrow as I check to make sure no one is listening to us at the corner of the building. 'Why? What did she do to you?'

'She didn't do anything to me.' She crosses her arms and her face reddens with anger. 'She said stuff about you.'

'Like what?'

'That you mess with Micha's head. That you're no good for him.'

My jaw drops. 'She said that to you?'

'No, but I overheard her.' Her eyes wander to a group of guys standing by the corner observing us. 'She thought I was in the bathroom, but I was coming back and I heard her talking to that Chase dude, who by the way is so hot.'

'The one with a lot of tattoos and with a Mohawk thing going on?' I ask and she nods. 'He doesn't seem like your type.'

She shrugs and then quickly shakes her head. 'That's beside the point. I think Naomi wants Micha, and I don't trust her.'

'We've gone over this a thousand times.' I hold my breath as a guy with a cigarette walks by and blows smoke in our direction. 'I trust *him*.'

'I think you're making a mistake.' She picks some mascara off her eyelashes. 'I think you should ask him to quit the band.'

'No way, I would never do that to him,' I say, appalled.

'It's your call,' she replies. 'But I'm saying I smell trouble.'

'Yo, Ella May!' Micha hollers from the corner of the building and Lila and my gazes dart to him. 'What are you doing?'

I glance at Lila. 'Thanks for worrying about me, but it'll be okay.'

She sighs and we walk over to Micha, who's waiting for me with his hand extended. 'Is something wrong?'

I stare into his eyes, glimmering with happiness. 'No, everything's great.'

Micha

Usually, everyone in the band crashes in the same room. Naomi takes one of the beds and the rest of us flip a coin to see who gets the other. Tonight, I get an extra room so Ella and I can have more time together.

After some charming persuading on my part, I convince Lila to sleep in the same room as the band. She doesn't seem too thrilled about it though, since Dylan won't stop bothering her.

Once we're alone, Ella flops down on the bed and drapes her arm over her head. 'I'm exhausted. What time is it?'

I glance down at the leather-banded watch on my wrist. 'Almost three o'clock.'

'Really?' She props up on her elbows. 'Do you always stay up this late?'

'Usually.' I unfasten my watch and slip off my boots, prowling toward her. 'And I'm good for a few more hours at least.' I shuck off my shirt, climb onto the bed, and cover her body with mine. Her fingers trace my stomach muscles and the black cursive font of the tattoo on my ribs.

'I'll always be with you, inside and out,' she reads. 'Through hard times and helpless ones, through love, through doubt.'

I lean back a little, bring her hand to my mouth, and gently kiss her palm. 'You know I wrote that for you.'

'No, you didn't.' Her eyelids flutter as I breathe on the sensitive spot of her wrist. 'You wrote that when you were, like, sixteen.'

'Actually fifteen.' I release her hand and lie down on top of her, supporting my weight with my arms. 'I remember sitting down to write it and the only inspiration I had was your sad eyes — I couldn't get them out of my head.'

She pouts. 'I don't have sad eyes, do I?'

I brush my finger along her cheekbone and underneath one of her green eyes. 'You did. All the time. And sometimes you still do.'

'You look sad sometimes too,' she tells me with her auburn hair spread out across the pillow below her head. 'But right now you look happy.'

'That's because I am happy.' I start singing her the lyrics and it makes her grin broaden.

'There we go,' I say and kiss her deeply, nipping at her lip and tracing my tongue along the inside of her mouth.

She wraps her long legs around me and things turn heated. Threading my fingers through her hair, I caress her neck with my tongue until I know she's going to have a hickey. Her shoulder shudders upward from the touch of my breath and she giggles.

I put a small gap between us and look her in the eyes. 'Does that tickle?'

She shakes her head with a solemn expression on her face. 'No, not at all.'

I pinch her side playfully and she jerks sideways, attempting to roll out from under me.

'Please don't.' She laughs, struggling for air. 'Pretty please.'

I listen to her, because there's something else I'm dying to do. I begin to undress her, deliberately at first, but then my movements turn desperate and I end up ripping some of the buttons off her shirt.

Minutes later, our clothes are in a pile on the floor and I'm back inside her. As I stare into her eyes, I consider begging her to come with me on the road, but the moment is fleeting and I realize I just can't do that to her.

★   ★   ★

I wake up in a quiet room with Ella in my arms, and her naked body curled up against me. I wish it was possible to wake up every morning like this, but then someone would have to give up something important.

'God, what the fuck am I going to do?' I whisper aloud to myself.

Morning is peeking through the curtain and cars buzz down the main road in front of the hotel. I watch Ella sleep for a bit, while I run my fingers along her back, until finally her eyelids peek open.

'You're awake.' She blinks the tiredness away.

I twist a lock of her hair around my finger. 'I couldn't sleep.' She starts to sit up, but I tighten my arms around her and hold her to me. 'Just stay put for a few more minutes. I like holding you.'

Her eyes examine me, and she rests her head back on my shoulder. 'What's wrong? You seem upset.'

I smooth away the worry line between her brows with my thumb. 'Have you ever thought about what we're going to do with our lives? With each other?'

She bites at her bottom lip. 'Sometimes I think about it.'

'And where do you see us going?' I ask with caution, not wanting to scare her with what I'm thinking about asking her. I need to test the waters first.

Her eyes round and her breathing becomes frantic. 'Are you breaking up with me?'

I snort a laugh. 'Why the fuck would you ever think that?'

She props up on her elbow and gazes down at me, her hair a curtain around our faces. 'Because you have this look on your face like you're about to tell me some horrible news.'

'It's not bad news.' I guide her body on top of mine. 'But I'm not sure if you'll be happy about it either.'

She clutches onto my shoulders as she pushes herself up, so she's straddling me and I can feel her warmth on my cock. The blanket falls from her shoulders and her breasts are just above my face.

'Please hurry up and tell me, then,' she begs. 'Because you're scaring the shit out of me right now.'

'I think . . . ' I stop, remembering my mother and my father, and how things turned out for them. 'It's nothing. Honestly it wasn't really that important.'

Her face falls. 'No, that look on your face isn't nothing. Since when do you keep things from me?'

'I'm not keeping anything from you.' I'm just holding out for a while until I know we're both on the same page. 'Now come here.'

I sit up and put my mouth over her breast, sucking on her nipple and distracting her. When I move my mouth away, she's panting and the light reflects in her eyes. Wrapping my hand around the back of her head, I steer her lips toward mine and thrust my cock inside her. She breathes fervently against my lips, and moments later we've both forgotten about the conversation.

3

Ella

It's been a week since the LA trip and I feel like shit all the time. Micha's been really busy and I barely get to talk to him. Plus Lila started dating Preston and she's never around. My muscles ache just from walking, my head hurts all the time, and every task is tiring.

I'm waiting outside the therapist's office, with my bag on my lap, when I get a text from my brother.

DEAN: Call me asap.
ME: Can't. In a meeting.
DEAN: Don't be a brat. CALL ME.

My therapist walks out of the office and motions me to come in as the phone beeps again. I shut it off and sit down in a chair in front of the desk, decorated with a nameplate, a cup full of pens, and a tall stack of folders.

Her name is Anna and she's young, maybe in her late twenties, with blonde hair that's cropped short around her jawline. Every time I see her, she's in a pantsuit. Today, it's a black pinstriped one.

'Hello, Ella.' She takes a seat behind her desk and puts on her square-framed glasses as she takes out my file. 'How was your weekend?'

'Interesting,' I say. 'To say the least.'

Noting my tone, she looks up at me. 'And what was interesting about it?'

I scratch at my back along my infinity tattoo. 'I went to visit Micha in LA.'

She opens a notebook. 'And how did that go?'

I hesitate. 'Good, I think.'

She scratches something down on the paper. 'You seem like you're unsure.'

I slouch back in the seat and fold my arms. 'It's just that . . . well, every time I go to see him or he comes to see me, it gets harder to say good-bye.'

She sets the pen and notebook down on her desk and removes her glasses. 'Saying good-bye is always hard, but sometimes it's necessary to move on in life.'

'I don't want to move on from him.' Panic gusts through me like a tornado. 'I love Micha.'

'That's not what I'm saying,' she explains quickly. 'I'm saying that sometimes saying good-bye is the hardest part of life.'

I hate when she plays mind games. 'Are you referring to my mother? Because I told you last time that I was over that.'

'Ella, you're not over it,' she says. 'Otherwise you wouldn't have said that.'

I prop my elbow on the arm of the chair and rest my chin in my hand. 'Then what does this good-bye thing have to do with?'

'It has to do with you.' She takes a mint out of a tin and puts it in her mouth. 'And you struggle to say good-bye to things: your guilt over your mother and your father, your pain, your feelings. You have such a hard time letting go of your past.'

'I know that,' I admit. 'But I'm working on it.'

She pauses, tapping her fingers on the desk. 'Tell me this: Where do you see yourself in a year or two?'

'I don't know . . . I haven't really thought about it that much.'

'Try to think about it for a minute, if you can.'

I raise my chin from my hand and search my brain, but all I can see is Micha and me out on that damn bridge as he falls into the water.

'I don't know.' I grip the armrests of the chair as my pulse accelerates. 'I really don't . . . Holy shit.'

'Relax, Ella, everything's going to be fine.' She opens the desk drawer and takes out another folder. 'I think we might want to start

59

considering doing an evaluation for anxiety and depression.'

My eyes narrow at her. 'No way.'

'Ella, I think it's important that — '

I shove up from the chair and swing my bag over my shoulder. 'I'm not talking about this.'

She says something else, but I'm already out the door. I will not discuss having a mental illness. I'm not sick. I'm not.

Burying the conversation, I turn on my phone and read the text Dean sent me. 'Dad left rehab. Call me now . . . ' *What?* I punch in his speed-dial number as I walk outside into the sunlight and put the phone to my ear.

'Why the hell did you turn off your phone?' he snaps.

'I told you. I was in a meeting.' I head across the quad, zigzagging in between people and ducking under a Frisbee flying through the air.

'Well, you need to get back home,' he orders. 'Dad bailed and no one can find him.'

'I'll call Micha's mom and see if she can find out where he is. If he's at home.' I start to hang up.

'I already got ahold of her.' He sounds aggravated. 'And she's on a vacation with some guy she's dating.'

'Oh . . . ' I didn't even know his mom was

dating someone. 'Then what do we do?'

'*You* drive up there and check on him,' he says like it's my obligation.

'Why can't you do it?'

'Because I have work and a wedding to plan — a life.'

'I have a life,' I argue, reaching the border of the grass. 'And we can always call someone else. We can call Denny.'

'You call Denny then,' he says, and I hear Caroline's voice in the background. 'Look, I have to go, okay? Call Denny and let me know what's going on as soon as you do.' He hangs up on me.

Frustrated, I dial information and get the number for Denny's bar. By the time I call, I'm trotting up the stairs to Lila's and my two-bedroom apartment.

Someone picks up after four rings. 'Hello, Hub and Grub, this is Denny.'

'Umm . . . yeah, this is Ella. Ella Daniels. I was just wondering if my dad was there or if you'd seen him.'

'Yeah, he showed up here this morning.' He hesitates. 'I thought he was in rehab.'

'Apparently he checked himself out.' I take the house keys out of my bag and unlock the door. 'How bad is he?'

'I'm going to be honest with you, Ella. He's pretty bad,' he says bluntly. 'He showed up here this morning and he's been drinking ever since. Nonstop. I offered him a ride home, but he refused.'

I close the door and toss the keys on the counter. 'Can you keep an eye on him for a little bit until I can figure out what to do with him?'

'Yeah, I guess,' he says with reluctance. 'Look, Ella, I understand your situation, but I got a bar to run and . . . well, when he gets this way he causes a lot of problems. I don't mind helping, just as long as it's not bad for my business.'

'I'll get down there as soon as I can,' I promise. 'And I'm really sorry about this.'

He sighs. 'It's okay. I know it's hard for you. I mean, you're just a kid.'

I was never a kid. Not really. I was doing the dishes and cleaning the house at six, cooking my own food at eight, and making sure my mom took her medications by the age of ten.

I say good-bye and hang up, sinking down onto the suede couch. The apartment is small, with white walls and tan carpet and a TV in the corner. There is a narrow dining area between the kitchen and the living room. The place smells like cinnamon and the kitchen sink is overflowing with dishes.

I press my fingers to the sides of my nose. '*Shit* . . . Who am I supposed to call?' I let my hand fall to my lap and call Ethan.

He answers after three rings. 'Okay, so this is kind of weird. You never call me.'

'I have a favor to ask you.' I pause, working up the courage. 'Can you go pick up my dad from the Hub and Grub and stay with him until I can get there?'

He's silent for a second. 'Yeah, I can do that.'

'Thank you,' I say, grateful. 'I'll head up as soon as I can. I promise. Twelve hours at the max.'

'Don't kill yourself getting up here, Ella. I said it was fine, so come when you can.'

'Okay. I'll call you when I'm on the road.'

'Sounds good.'

I hang up and drop the phone onto the coffee table, wondering where the hell I'm going to find a car. I start to call Micha, but then stop myself. I haven't talked to him in over a day and the last thing I want to do is call him up and start bawling.

Besides, there's nothing he can do about it. He's clear across the country.

Micha

'If you keep hitting the wrong note,' I warn Naomi, 'I'm going to have to take the guitar away.'

63

We're sitting on the bed in the studio apartment with our guitars on our laps. There is dirty laundry all over the floor and garbage all over the counters. Dylan and Chase are at the bar trying to get laid. I'm wearing my pajama bottoms without a shirt on and Naomi's hair is balled up on her head, damp because she just got out of the shower.

'Don't be a dick,' she jokes, tugging the rubber band out so her damp hair can fall to her shoulders. 'The note I'm playing sounds a lot better than the one you think we should hit.'

I shake my head and strum the strings of my guitar. 'That all depends.'

She plays a chord and talks over the noise. 'On what?'

'Whether you're playing for a roomful of tone-deaf people.' I smirk ruthlessly.

She rolls her eyes and sets her guitar down on the bed. 'You're such an asshole sometimes.'

She's right, but it's for a reason. About two days ago, I was walking around sightseeing and searching for a building that I'd heard my father worked at. I'd just gotten off the phone with my mom, who not only told me she was going on vacation with some dude half her age but that my father was now living in New York City.

I just wanted to see where he worked, for

no other reason than out of curiosity. As I stood out in front of the building, a man crossed paths with me chasing down a taxi. It was my father and I started to turn away, but he saw me and waved. I wanted to return it by showing him my middle finger, but couldn't do anything except stand there gaping like a little kid.

He strolled over to me with an uncomfortable look on his face. He was in a black suit with a trench coat over it and stared at me with eyes exactly like mine. 'Micha, what are you doing here?'

'I'm living here for a little bit.' My tone was sharp. 'What are you doing here?'

He pointed at the lofty building with a metallic exterior. 'I just got transferred here for work about two weeks ago. I called your mom and told her about it.'

I pretended like I didn't know it already. 'Well, you really need to stop calling her. She doesn't need to talk to you.'

He eyed me over and his expression turned cold. 'So why are you living here?'

I fiddled with the chain hooked to my jeans, inching in my shoulders as a mob of people push past me. 'My band and I have a gig at a club for the next month.'

A condescending look concealed his face. 'Why am I not surprised? I should have known you'd turn out doing something like that.'

I clench my hand into a fist, fighting not to hit him. 'What the fuck does that mean?'

He looked around at the people passing by us, like he was worried someone overheard me. 'Look, Micha, I didn't mean anything by it. I'm going to go.'

I turned my back on him and walked away. On the way back to the apartment, I realized that my dad was always a douche bag. Even when he was still my father, he would nitpick every little thing I did and tell me I was wrong a lot.

'Hello.' Naomi claps her hands in front of my face and I flinch. 'You're totally spacing out.'

I carefully set my guitar down on the floor and lean back against the headboard. 'I thought you were going out tonight.'

She shrugs and stretches out on the bed on her stomach, crossing her arms and resting her chin on them. 'I didn't feel like it. Besides, you've seemed a little down lately and I didn't want to leave you alone to drown in your sorrows.'

'I'm not drowning in my sorrows.' I take a gulp of my soda. 'I'm just confused.'

'About what?'

'About stuff.'

She sits down beside me so we're both staring at the foot of the bed. 'It's Ella stuff again, isn't it?'

'I don't want to talk about it.' I set the soda down on the nightstand and give it a little spin. 'I don't feel comfortable talking to you about her.'

She rubs her lips together, thinking heavily about something. 'Why not? You have before.'

'Only because I was wasted and I tend to get a little chatty when I'm like that.' I can't talk to Naomi about what's going on in my head because I owe it to Ella to tell her first. 'I basically talk to anyone when I'm drunk.'

'Don't pretend like you hate talking to me, Micha,' she says. 'I know you like to. You're just too blinded by your own feelings.'

I'm lost. 'What the hell are you talking about?'

Suddenly, she is leaning toward me with her eyes closed and her lips out, throwing me off guard as she tries to kiss me. Pieces of her hair fall in front of her face, and for a second, I'm motionless as I think about letting her kiss me — letting her take my mind off shit.

Then all my feelings for Ella catch up with me and I shift away, practically crawling onto the nightstand to get out of her reach. 'What the fuck are you doing?'

Her eyes snap open and her pupils are

large. 'Come on, Micha. Don't try to tell me you haven't thought about it.'

I shake my head slowly. 'Nope, I haven't. Not even once.' Her cheeks turn pink and I feel like a douche bag. 'Look, I'm sorry, but you know how I feel about Ella, so I don't know why you'd even try it.'

She slides her legs over the edge of the bed and turns her back to me. 'It doesn't seem like you love her as much anymore. You don't even talk to her on the phone all the time like you used to.'

'That's because I'm trying to sort through some stuff.' I give her a pat on the back because I can tell she's about to cry. The whole situation is awkward. 'Are you going to be okay?'

She jerks her shoulder upward and shrugs off my hand before running into the bathroom. The door bangs shut and rattles the thin walls.

I collect my guitar from the floor and flop down on the bed, playing my favorite song. Eight months ago, I would have been all over her invitation, but not anymore. It was more of a turnoff than anything.

That's when I realize the thing I've been wondering about for the last week.

Ella is it for me. The way I feel about her is never going to change. I will love her forever, but I need her closer to me, not thousands of miles away.

How am I supposed to tell her, though, that I'm ready to begin her future, when I know she has no clue what her future is yet?

4

Ella

I'm starting to wonder if this is going to be my life forever, if I'll always end up back in Star Grove at the house that clutches my childhood.

The house looks the same: a broken rain gutter, garbage bags piling up on the side of the house, and the Cutlass still balanced on the cinderblocks in front of the garage. The house's siding is peeling and some of the branches have fallen from the tree beside the window.

Ethan's truck is parked in the driveway and he's sitting on the back steps playing around on his phone. I get out of the rental car that looks like the kind of vehicle clowns stuff themselves into.

Ethan looks up and he arches his eyebrows at the car. 'What the fuck is that thing?'

'It was the cheapest one at the rental place.' I sit down on the steps next to him and stretch out my legs in front of me. 'Is he inside?'

'Yeah, he passed out on the couch as soon as I got him home.' He puts his phone away and rolls up the sleeves of his gray Henley, revealing his extensive tattoos.

'You got a new one.' I point to a tattoo of a quote written in Latin.

Nodding, he touches the lines with his finger. 'A couple weeks ago.'

Staring at Micha's house next door, I ask, 'How bad was he to get out of the bar?'

He tips his head forward, looking down at the ground, and his black hair falls into his face. 'He was kind of a pain in the ass to get here. He took a swing at Denny when we were taking him out to the car.'

I slump back, resting my elbows on the step behind me. 'I'm sorry you had to go get him. I just couldn't think of anyone else to call.'

'I'm not mad that I had to. I'm mad that you had to come all the way here to take care of him.' He sounds uncomfortable.

'What?' Confusion swarms my brain.

He fiddles with a frayed area on the knee of his jeans. 'I think it's bullshit when the kids have to act like the parents.'

'Are we talking about me still?' I ask, eyeing him over. 'Or is there something else you'd like to share . . . like something that's going on with you.'

'I'm good.' He nudges me with his shoulder. 'It's a story for another time.'

'But you never share your stories,' I remind him.

'Neither do you,' he retorts. 'Except for with Micha.'

'Yeah, I guess,' I unintentionally say aloud and he shoots me a funny look. 'Never mind. I'm going to go check on my dad and then maybe we could go get something to eat. My treat for having to come deal with this crap.'

'Is that really a treat?' he jokes with a sarcastic smirk. 'Eating dinner with you?'

I make a face and walk into the kitchen, and the screen door slams shut behind me. Particles of dust float in the air and I fan my hand in front of my face. 'God, it smells like a dead animal in here.'

'That's because no one ever cleaned up before I left.' My dad appears in the doorway, wearing a baggie green T-shirt and jeans with grease spots on them. His skin has gotten a little color since the last time I saw him and he looks somewhat younger, but his eyes are bloodshot just like they used to be. He's not wasted, but hungover, which can be equally as explosive.

'I thought I did clean up.' I glance around at the brown countertops, still stacked with vodka and tequila bottles and the table piled with overdue bills. 'Dad, why did you leave rehab?'

He slumps down into a chair at the kitchen table with his shoulders hunched over and his head falls into his hands. 'They tried to get me to talk about your mother.'

I grow uneasy with the situation. 'I'm sure

that was hard for you, but running away won't solve the problem. It'll only make it worse. Trust me, I know.'

'Trust you?' He raises his head and rubs his scruffy jawline. 'Trust you like I trusted you to watch your mother that night?' He repeats the words he said to me when we tried to get him to go to rehab.

It's like I've been punched in the gut and I press my hand to my stomach, forcing my lungs to work. 'I'm sorry.'

His eyes widen and he quickly gets to his feet, toppling the chair to the ground. 'Ella, I didn't mean that. Sometimes I just say things . . . and I don't know why I do.'

'It's okay.' Just like my therapist told me to do, I breathe through the internal pain as I back for the door. 'I'm going to go get some dinner. Do you want anything?'

He shakes his head and his eyes water over. 'Ella, I really didn't mean it.'

'I know you didn't.' I burst out the back door and suck in a deep breath of fresh air.

Ethan glances up at me and then stands to his feet. 'I was thinking the Drive-Inn and we can take my truck because there's no way in hell I'm climbing into that clown car.'

I could hug him right now, but I don't. 'Sounds good to me.'

We sit in his truck eating French fries and hamburgers with the neon lights flashing into the cab. Ethan is checking out one of the waitresses who is bending over to take the order of the car next to us. It's been quiet between the two of us.

'You heard what he said to me, didn't you?' I finally ask, stirring the ranch dressing with a fry.

He picks a pickle off his hamburger, pulling a face as he tosses it out onto the tray secured to the window. 'I didn't hear much. Besides, it's not something I haven't heard before.'

'I don't understand what you mean.' I chew my fry, scanning his eyes for an explanation.

'I'm saying parents suck.'

'Care to elaborate?'

'Not really.'

When it grows quiet again, he puffs out an irritated breath. 'You remember back in, like, second grade how I used to come to school all the time with bruises on me?'

I take a sip of my soda and put it back in the holder. 'Wasn't that the year you broke your arm?'

'That among other things.' His forehead creases as he spaces off, staring out the windshield. 'That year my dad got addicted to painkillers and he was always pissed off about something . . . anything. And he liked to take it out on my brothers, me, my mom — basically whoever he could.'

It clicks what he's saying. 'I didn't know that . . . I'm sorry.'

'No one does. Not even Micha.' He balls up the wrapper of his burger and tosses it out onto the tray. 'So yeah, I get that parents can be douche bags to their kids, but in our cases, it was — is more because of the addiction than their actual feelings.'

I'm not sure what to say other than thanks.

He tosses an empty cup of fry sauce onto the tray and the heaviness in the cab clears. 'You owe me big time, not only for picking up your father but for sharing. I hate doing that.'

'Ha-ha.' I hand him my garbage and his smile expands across his face.

To the side of us, a blue Camaro rolls up, revving the engine. Mikey is in the driver's seat, bumping his head to the music that's blaring out from the stereo. All the feelings of when he made Micha crash his Chevelle into the tree rush through me.

'Fucking asshole,' Ethan mutters under his breath as he starts up the engine and lets it roar, pumping the gas.

I roll my eyes at him. 'What are you doing? You're in a truck.'

'It's got a Hemi in it,' he says in a fake Southern accent. 'And do you know he goes around bragging about winning that race?'

'Why the heck is Grantford Davis in there with Mikey?' I ask with shock, staring at the back window of the Camaro. 'I thought they hated each other.'

Ethan starts to laugh. 'Grantford is Mikey's little bitch now due to a lost race. He basically has to do whatever Mikey says. It was part of the bet.'

Micha would be thrilled if he knew that. He always blamed Grantford for the night on the bridge, even though I don't. However, it still makes me smile seeing Grantford in the back with his cowboy hat on and a miserable look on his face.

I tap my fingers on the console while Mikey yells something foul at us from over his music.

'You have a look on your face like you're about to get us into trouble.' He slurps the rest of his drink and drops it out onto the tray.

'I feel like starting a little bit of trouble. In fact, I need to.' Eyeing Mikey through the tinted window, I pick up my half-full shake. 'Do you remember that time we were driving down Main Street and I threw that shake on the windshield of that parked car because Micha dared me to?'

'You want to relive that?' The yellow lights on the marquee illuminate in his brown eyes. 'Because if I remember right, we got into some deep shit for that — Micha and I got our asses kicked.'

'We won't for this,' I assure him. 'And anyway, I'm not going to throw it on his car. I'm going to throw it in his open window and right on his lap.' He stays quiet, rubbing his hand across his jawline and I add, 'Are you in or out?'

'Of course I'm in. I'm always in.' He lowers his hand onto the steering wheel. 'I'm just thinking of the best way to ditch him when he tries to chase us down.'

I glance over at Mikey, hollering at one of the waitresses on roller skates. 'You think he will?'

Ethan grasps the shifter. 'Maybe . . . he's got his friends with him.'

I start to roll my window down. 'Does it really matter if he does? I know for a fact you can kick his ass.'

He nods. 'True, but he's got Danny Farren in the car and that guy's fucking huge.'

I withdraw my hand from the window. 'Do you not want me to do it?'

'No, do it,' he says as the waitress comes up to collect the tray from the window and Ethan drops down a few dollars for a tip.

'We'll just have to drive until we ditch him . . . Oh yes, I fucking got it. I'll ramp the truck over the turnout hill. His Camaro will never be able to get over it unless he wants to bottom out his car.'

'Just try not to kill us.' I roll down the window and wave my fingers at Mikey.

His eyebrows dip together. 'What the hell are you doing here? I thought you ran away or some shit.'

Gripping the cup in my hand, I stick my head out the window. 'I went to school. You know a place where you learn . . . Oh wait, you probably don't.'

'Just do it,' Ethan coughs in his hand. 'And let's bail.'

'You better watch it,' he sneers, running his hand through his black hair. 'Or one of these days someone's gonna shut that mouth of yours permanently.'

I bat my eyelashes at him and flip him the finger as I chuck the shake straight through the rolled-down window.

He curses as it lands on his lap and he jumps up, bumping his head onto the ceiling. 'You bitch.'

'Go,' I command, rolling up the window quickly.

The tires squeal as Ethan backs out, nearly running over an old lady. Cranking the wheel,

78

he burns rubber out of the parking lot. The sound of Mikey's Camaro chases after us as we drive fast toward the turnout. I feel like a kid again and wish I could grasp onto the freeness, but once it's time to go home, it'll be over.

Mikey inches up to the bumper of the truck and starts flashing the headlights at us. Ethan accelerates as houses and trees blur by until the turnout comes into view on the side of the road. The turnout used to be an entrance to a road that led back to a spot underage people liked to party at, but when a few people — Micha included — got busted, the town blocked it off with a fence and a dirt hill.

'You're going too fast,' I warn, grabbing the handle above my head. 'You're going to nosedive it.'

'Relax, I got this.' He downshifts. 'And since when do you worry about shit like that?'

'I'm just worried about your truck.' I prop my foot up on the dash to keep myself in the seat. 'But if you don't care, then by all means ramp away.'

He laughs and floors the pedal. The engine flares and the tires squeal as the truck flies straight up the hill. There's a brief moment where we are airborne and then we hit the ground hard. I'm thrown forward by the impact and bash my head on the dashboard as the car bounces to a stop.

'Ah, I think I just cracked my skull,' Ethan complains, grasping his head.

'That makes two of us.' I touch the tender spot on my head and rotate in my seat to look behind us. Headlights shine over the side of the hill and a shadow of Mikey appears at the top of it, along with three others.

'You better go.' I wave my hand for Ethan to move forward. 'He can walk over the hill.'

He composes himself and drives down the rocky field, leaving them in the distance. Once we're on the dirt road and tucked far away into the trees, we both relax.

'Wait a minute.' It dawns on me. 'What are you going to do when he comes after you?'

'I've been thinking about taking a vacation from this place.' He makes a sharp veer to the left, directing the truck toward the side road that will take us back to our houses. 'Guess now is as good a time as any to do it.'

'You're going to just up and leave?' I turn sideways in my seat to look at him. 'And go where?'

'I'm thinking of a solo road trip, like *Into the Wild* only on wheels, not foot.'

'Oddly enough, I can actually picture you doing this.'

There's a trace of a smile on his face as he

turns the car onto the road. We don't talk for the rest of the drive, but it's a nice silence. When he drops me off, I thank him again and tell him he should come with Lila and me to the wedding, since it's kind of a road trip. He says he'll think about it.

I walk inside, leaving the carefree night behind in order to grow up again and face my demons head-on.

5

Micha

Things are awkward between Naomi and me. It's the next morning and we're supposed to be practicing at a club, but she's over flirting with the bartender, who is twice her age and has a really long goatee.

It's fairly quiet, since it's barely past noon. There are a few people eating in the booths and chatting at the bar and one of the waitresses keeps coming up to Dylan, Chase, and me to see if we need anything.

I'm in the middle of a chord when my phone rings. I set the guitar down by my feet and see Ella's name on the screen.

'Hey,' I answer in a light tone. 'I was just thinking about calling you.'

'I must have read your mind then I guess.' She's trying to sound happy, but the pitch of her voice is off.

I turn in the chair so my back is to Dylan and Chase. 'What's wrong? You sound upset.'

'I'm fine.' She breathes into the phone loudly. 'My dad just ran out of rehab and I had to drive up to Star Grove and take him back.'

'Why didn't you call me?' My voice echoes through the room so I lower it. 'I would have come over and helped you.'

'That's why I didn't call you.' Her tone is strained. 'You didn't need to come out. Ethan helped me and it's all good. I'm taking my dad back to the rehab right now and then I'm heading back to school.'

'Do you need me to fly out there?' I stand up and pick up my guitar, ready to go.

'No, I'm fine, Micha,' she assures me. 'I need to start taking care of myself a little bit more, but I promise I'm not having a meltdown.'

I should be happy, but I'm not. 'When are you heading out to the wedding?'

She pauses and the phone statics. 'In, like, a week, but you don't need to come. I know you're busy with stuff.'

'What the fuck is going on?' I'm getting pissed. 'Why are you blowing me off?'

She sighs heavily. 'I'm not blowing you off. I'm trying to let you live your life without my burdens . . . Look, I have to go. I just pulled up to the rehab center.' She hangs up before I can say anything else.

I rake my hands through my hair and then kick the brick wall behind the stage. 'Goddammit.'

Everyone in the club looks at me with

terror in their eyes and I jump off the platform, storming for the door.

'Where are you going?' Naomi calls out, turning away from the bartender, ready to head after me. I ignore her and walk outside to the busy street.

Things aren't going the way I planned. I haven't even told Ella how I'm feeling — what I want from her — and she's already pushing me away. Maybe I need to figure something else out.

Or maybe it might be time to move on.

Ella

'Do you want me to walk you in?' I say to my dad, putting the car into park. We're out in front of the rehab center, a small tan brick building with a narrow bench area in front of it where people are smoking. The sky is cloudy and leaves fall from the trees onto the hood of the car.

He shakes his head as he unbuckles his seatbelt. 'I'll be fine, Ella. And you should probably be getting on the road before it gets too late.'

'Are you sure?' I check. 'Because like I said back at the house, you can talk to me if you need to.'

He gazes at the entrance door. 'I didn't mean what I said . . . I don't blame you. I know it wasn't your fault.' My gaze meets his eyes, which have cleared of alcohol but still carry so much pain and hatred. 'I know it's probably hard for you to remember, but I didn't used to be like this. Things used to be good, and then your mother started taking a turn for the worse and everything went downhill. It was hard to deal with, and I handled it wrong.'

I'm stunned. He's never talked to me like this before, but he also hasn't been sober for more than five minutes.

'Dad, do you regret things . . . ' I swallow the lump in my throat. 'Do you wish that sometimes you would have just left and had a normal life?'

He lets out a shaky breath. 'Honestly, yes, sometimes I look back and wish I would have run out. I probably would have been a lot happier. I'll always hate myself for feeling that way, but it's the truth.' He opens the door and climbs out, ducking his head back into the cab. 'Thanks for bringing me back.'

He shuts the door and walks up the sidewalk, putting a cigarette into his mouth as he joins the people in the smoking area. A woman with red hair hands him a Zippo and he lights up, taking a drag. I sit in the car for a while and let his words replay in my mind with a heavy feeling weighing on my shoulders. Is this Micha's and my future? The therapist already wants to check me for depression, which was how my mother started. What if it ends up that I am depressed? What if Micha and I stay together and I start to go downhill? What if I ruin his life?

By the time I leave the parking space, all I want to do is go home, climb into bed, and shut down my mind.

★　★　★

'Ella, get your butt out of bed,' Lila demands, jerking the blankets off me. 'Or I swear to God, I'm going to dump a cup of ice water on you.'

The sunlight trickling through the window stings my eyes. I curl up in a ball, cradle my knees to my chest, and cover my head with my arms. 'Leave me alone and close the curtain. The light is giving me a headache.'

She turns down the song playing on the stereo, 'The Tide' by Spill Canvas, and sits down on the edge of the bed. She's wearing a white shirt, jeans, and a pair of high-heeled boots. Her hair is curled up and her lips are stained pink, along with her cheeks.

'Are you going out?' I bury my face to the

pillow and my voice muffles. 'If you are, can you pick up some milk? I drank it all last night.'

She tugs on my shoulder, kind of roughly, and forces me to look at her. 'You have to stop this. You've been in bed for almost three days . . . What the heck happened back in Star Grove?'

'Nothing,' I mutter. 'I dropped my dad off at rehab and then drove back here.'

'What did your dad say to you?' She says it with accusation.

'Nothing.' I roll onto my stomach and smash my face into the pillow. 'Look, Lila, you can sit here and dig into this all you want, but there's nothing there. I just feel like shit and want to be alone.'

She dithers and then gets up from the bed. 'I'll be back later tonight with some milk.'

'Thank you.' I shut my eyes. 'And can you turn the music back up?'

A few seconds later, Spill Canvas fills the room again and I drift off to sleep, happy to let my mind enter sleep mode.

★   ★   ★

'How long has she been like this?' Fingers lightly trace up and down my back.

'Since she came back from dealing with her dad,' Lila says with worry in her tone. 'So,

87

like, four days. She barely gets out bed and she won't eat anything.'

'What the hell happened?' Micha sounds equally as concerned.

I rotate onto my side, blinking my exhausted eyes against the sunlight spilling through the window. Micha is sitting on the edge of my bed with his hand on my back and his hair has a little wave to it, which means he's recently been sleeping.

'Nothing happened,' I say and they both jump.

'That's a lie.' Lila paces the floor with her hands on her hips. Her blonde hair is twisted up and she's got on a purple lacy dress. 'We know something happened.'

Micha is wearing all black, with his chain hooked to the belt loops. His eyes search mine and my insides quiver. 'What did your dad say to you?'

I sit up and his hand falls off my back to the bed. 'He didn't say anything.'

'Ella May' — he reaches for my face — 'don't feed me bullshit.'

'I'm not feeding you bullshit, Micha Scott.' I climb out of the bed and drag my feet toward the bathroom. 'Did you ever consider that this is who I am? That maybe you can't save me because you'd have to save me from my own head?' I lock the door and collapse onto the floor, hugging my knees to my chest as thoughts race through my head.

I wish he wasn't here.

I wish he would just let me go.

I wish I didn't have to wake up anymore and deal with life, because it hurts. It all hurts.

Seconds later, someone knocks on the door. 'Ella, open the God damn door before I break it down.'

'I want to be left alone,' I snap. 'I never asked you to come here, Micha.'

'I know you didn't,' he says softly through the door. 'Lila called me because she was worried about you. And so am I. You act like you might be going back to that dark place again.'

'I'm not. I promise.' I feel too drained to deal with anything else, so I crawl over to the shower and turn it on, letting the sound of the running water drown out his voice. It feels like I should be crying, but my eyes are dry.

I lie on my back on top of the fuzzy purple rug on the floor and stare up at the small crack in the ceiling. I never expected him to come here. I wanted more preparation, but it's time to face the inevitable.

I'm letting him go. Cutting the strings. Because I love him that much.

I made the decision on my way home, as my dad's words continually haunted me. I want something better for Micha than a dark, murky future.

Suddenly, the doorknob lock pops up. The door swings open and Micha stands in the doorway with a bent hanger in his hand.

'What are you doing, pretty girl?' he asks, taking in the sight of me. 'One minute we're good and suddenly you're shutting me out again.'

Closing my eyes, I inhale, and then open them again, breathing out. 'We need to talk.'

He shakes his head, looking like he understands what's coming. 'No, we don't, unless it's about something happy.' He tosses the hanger into the sink and drops to his knees in front of me. 'You can have your mood swings, but I'm not going to let you shut me out. It'll blow over.'

I prop myself up on my elbows. 'No, it won't. It's part of me.' I muster a shaky breath. 'I think we should break up.'

Quickly shaking his head, he lies on top of me. 'Stop it. I'm not going to let you do this. Just tell me what's going on and I'll try to fix it.'

My whole body aches. 'Nothing's going on. I just don't want to do this anymore. It's getting tiring.'

His eyes blaze with anger and he crashes his lips to mine, suffocating my thoughts momentarily as his tongue slips deep into my mouth. I kiss him back as his thumb runs along each one of my ribs, but when his hand heads down south, I snap back into reality and start to panic. I have to do something — anything — to make him hate me; otherwise he'll never let me go and he has to let me go.

Placing a hand on his chest, I gently push him away and look directly into his aqua eyes. 'Micha, I cheated on you.'

He rolls his eyes. 'You're so full of shit.'

'I'm being serious.' I let my hand fall from his chest. 'I've been wanting to tell you for a while, but I didn't know how to.'

He leans back. 'No, you didn't.'

I sit up and tuck my legs under me, plucking at a thread on the rug. 'Please don't make this any harder than it is. I did it and I'm sorry . . . I didn't plan it or anything. I was just drunk and it happened.'

He's starting to believe me and I feel like the world's biggest asshole, but one day, when he's married and has kids and he's happy, this moment won't matter to him.

'Who was it with?' His voice is quiet, but quakes with rage.

I force down the massive lump in my throat. 'That doesn't matter.'

His gaze bores into me. 'Yeah, it does.'

My legs tremble as I stand up and turn off the shower. 'I'm not going to tell you so that you can go beat the shit out of him.' I start to walk around him, but he sidesteps me, blocking my path as he puts a hand on each side of the doorway.

'Look me in the eye and tell me you did it,' he growls. 'Tell me that you fucking ripped out my heart and stomped on it.'

My tongue feels like lead, but I manage to keep my voice steady. 'I'm sorry, Micha. I really am. I'd take it back if I could, but no one can change the past.'

Turning away from me, he punches a hole in the wall just below the light switch. He storms off and, moments later, the front door slams shut. Silence is all that follows, which is what I want.

I want him to hate me, just as much as I hate myself.

That way I can't bring him down with me.

★　★　★

Days feel like weeks as I plummet into a deeper hole of darkness and exhaustion. Thoughts of giving up drift through my mind and all I want is to shut my eyes and never see the light of day again.

The idea starts to seem better and better

and I head to the bathroom to do . . . something. When I pass the mirror, though, I pause
in front of it. My eyes are big and bloodshot
and my skin is pallid. My thoughts drift back
to when Micha made me look in the mirror at
myself and he told me he loved me. I gently
sketch the infinity tattoo on my back as a
cloudy haze lifts from my mind.

There are people in this world who love
me.

I wonder if my mom thought about this
before she took her life.

I grab my phone, slip on my shoes, and run
out of the house. It's midafternoon and the
sun is shining as I sprint across the parking
lot toward the school's main entrance. I haven't
showered in days and still have on a pair of
shorts and a T-shirt I've been sleeping in. My
hair is tangled in a ball behind my head and I
have no makeup on, but it doesn't matter.

I burst into the therapist's office and luckily
she's eating a sandwich instead of talking to a
patient.

She springs up from her chair. 'Ella, what's
wrong?'

Breathing profusely, I lower myself into the
chair in front of her. 'I think I need help.'

6

Micha

It's been over a couple of weeks since Ella sliced open my heart. My life's turned into a shithole, full of booze and meaningless women, although I can never get anywhere with any of them. Just when things are about to go somewhere, Ella's sad eyes flash through my mind and I bail out. It's like I'm back in high school again, searching for something to fill the void in my heart. Only the hole is twice as wide and the person who made it bigger is the only person who can fix it.

I'm sitting in the small apartment the band is renting for a month, writing some really messed-up lyrics that are too painfully insightful for an audience. I'm getting more riled up the further into the song I get when there's a knock at the door.

I toss the pen onto the bed and drag my butt over to the door to open it.

'Dude, you look like crap.' Ethan pushes past me and makes a circle around the room. It's a studio apartment with a bed in the corner and a set of old-school sofas in the center that face a television. 'So this is where you've been staying?'

There are clothes all over the floor and I kick some out of the way as I trudge back to the bed. 'It's not any worse than where we grew up.'

He points over his shoulder at the door. 'I beg to differ on that one. Do you know some guy just tried to sell me a hooker on my way up here?'

'That would be Danny,' I say, picking up the pen. 'He's always trying to sell something.'

Ethan turns to me with this wary look on his face. 'So I'm on the road totally enjoying being by myself when I get this call from the lovely Miss Lila saying that you and Ella broke up.'

I rub the back of my neck tensely. 'I don't want to talk about it.'

Ethan sits down on the couch and crosses his arms. 'What happened?'

'Do you really want to talk about our feelings again?' I toss the notebook and pen aside. 'Or do you want to go out and do something fun? How long are you here for? I don't have to play tonight so we can go out. There's this really awesome club I've been wanting to check out and Dylan assures me

95

there's a lot of slutty women there.'

'As much as I love slutty women, I didn't come here to party.' Shaking his head disappointedly, he continues. 'I came to tell you something Lila told me. I would have just called you, but I was down in Virginia and I thought, what the hell, I'd come tell you myself.'

I pull on a T-shirt and shove my wallet into my back pocket, ready to leave him and go out by myself. 'Make it quick.'

He rests his arms on the top of the sofa and his boots on the coffee table in front of it. 'She didn't cheat on you.'

I'm in the middle of reaching for my keys when I freeze. 'What are you talking about?'

'That's why Lila called me,' he explains. 'She said that as much as she hates to stab her best friend in the back, she thought it was too important not to tell me what Ella told her, after a lot of shots of tequila. She made the whole thing up. Said she did it because she wants you to be happy and in her eyes you can't be happy with her. Whatever the fuck that means. I never really understood half of the things she did — or does.'

My arms fall to my side, unsure whether to be pissed off or relieved. 'Let me get this straight. She lied, told me she cheated on me, just so she could break up with me.'

Ethan surrenders his hands up in front of himself. 'Don't get pissed off at the messenger.'

'I'm not pissed off.' I sit down on the edge of the bed and drape my arms on my knees. 'I'm confused as hell.'

Ethan picks up a photo of the band from off the table and examines it. 'That would make two of us.'

I flex my hands and pop my neck. 'What the hell am I supposed to do?'

Setting the photo down, he deliberates it. 'You feel like taking a road trip?'

'Is the wedding this weekend?' I sink back against the wall and fiddle with my lip ring. 'Do you feel like driving my sorry ass to Chicago and back?'

He shrugs. 'I got nothing better to do.'

'All right then.' I grab my empty bag off the floor and start stuffing it with clothes. 'Let's go on a road trip.'

Ella

Lila and I are getting ready to head out to the wedding. We rented a car for the trip, a midsize one this time, but it still takes forever to hit sixty.

Before we head out though, I make one last

visit with my therapist. Anna felt it was important, considering I just had a nervous breakdown only a week ago.

My head is clear now, or at least partially, but it makes no sense to me what happened or why I said those terrible things to Micha. It made sense at the time, but it was like I was in a dream and when I woke up, the consequences punched me in the stomach. I considered calling him and apologizing, but I can't work up enough courage.

'You've been doing better then?' she asks, jotting in a notebook. 'There hasn't been any exhaustion or headaches, sensitivity to light?'

I shake my head. 'I've been feeling okay and the medication seems to be helping.'

'Good, I'm glad.' She puts her pen back in the black ceramic cup with the other pens. 'And remember what I said: act out, yell, scream, cry, whatever you need to do to get it out. Repressing it is where a lot of your problems come from.'

I nod. 'I'll remember that, I promise.'

'If you need anything at all while you're on your vacation, call me.' She hands me her card with her phone number on it and I put it in my purse. 'And I mean that, Ella. Call me, even if it's just to talk about the chicken you ate.'

I get up from the chair. 'Chicken?'

'They always have chicken at weddings.' She smiles, but then she grows serious. 'Remember, just breathe and take things one step at a time. Don't rush life. You need to take it easy for a while and focus on yourself.'

'I will,' I promise her and walk out the door, carrying her words of wisdom with me.

★   ★   ★

'I have to say that this is seriously the prettiest wedding I've been to.' I take in the black and purple candles on the table and the flower petals scattered on the white tablecloths that cover each of the eight tables.

The wedding is taking place outside, underneath a white canopy in the backyard of Caroline's parents' house, who live in a two-story mansion with columns and a wraparound porch. I dreamed of living in one of these houses when I was a little girl, but then I turned six and painfully realized that it wasn't possible.

'What's the plan for tonight?' Lila glances down at the Rolex on her wrist. 'I mean the wedding's tomorrow, but still, I don't just want to sit around and watch them set everything up. I want to have some fun.'

'I don't think we're obligated to do anything.' I twist the cap off my soda and take a swig. 'I already got fitted for my bridesmaid's dress, which is *so* weird.'

Her face contorts with confusion. 'Why's that weird?'

I screw the cap back on the bottle. 'Because Caroline hardly knows me, so I don't understand why she wants me as one of her bridesmaids.'

'You're going to be her sister-in-law, Ella.' Lila scoops up a handful of petals and sprinkles them back onto the tablecloth. 'And she seems really nice.'

I glance over at Caroline talking to the wedding planner. Her black hair grew out a little since the last time I saw her and she's wearing a long black dress with a jean jacket over it. Dean's at work and I've barely seen him since we showed up yesterday morning.

'We could go back to the hotel and order room service,' I suggest, returning my attention back to her. 'And charge everything to the room so Dean has to pay for it.'

She giggles, winding a strand of her blonde hair around her finger. 'As fun as that sounds — since I'm not really a fan of your brother — I think we should go out and have some fun.'

I rotate the bottle of soda between the palms of my hands. 'Lila, I can't drink while I'm on this medication.'

'We don't have to drink. We can go out and have some sober fun.' Her eyes suddenly light up and she claps her hands animatedly. 'Oh, we can go find a really fancy restaurant and charge it to the credit card my dad hasn't canceled yet.'

A small smile curves at my lips. 'I think we're both feeling a little scandalous tonight.'

She laughs, throwing her head back dramatically. 'Or maybe we both have family members who are total douche bags.'

I laugh too and it feels weightless, like breathing in the fresh air. 'All right, let's do it. But no sushi. I hate that crap.'

We hike across the grass toward the paved driveway where the car is parked. It's chilly in Chicago compared to Vegas and when we get in the car, I crank up the heat. 'You want to look something up on the GPS?'

She scrolls through her phone. 'We have to go back to the hotel first.'

I back out of the driveway, maneuvering between the cars blocking the way. 'Why? You look fine.'

She looks down at her pink skinny jeans and her floral shirt. 'I know I do, but I left the credit card on the nightstand last night when we ordered pizza.'

'Okay then, to the hotel it is.' I drive like a lunatic out onto the main road, skidding the tires in a pile of gravel, and Lila shoots me a dirty look.

I shrug innocently. 'I'm hungry.'

She rolls her eyes and plays with her phone during the five-minute drive to the hotel. I park out front underneath the canopy and leave the engine running. 'Do you want to just run in?'

She shakes her head and drops the phone into the middle console. 'Come in with me, please. That front desk guy is such a creeper. He kept looking down my shirt the entire time we were checking in.'

'Wasn't he, like, really old?'

'He had to be at least in his forties.'

'Ew,' we both say and cringe.

I roll the car forward into a spot, shut it off, and get out, meeting her around the back of the car. When we reach the sliding-glass doors, Lila catches my arm and stops me before I step foot over the threshold.

'Okay, so whatever happens, I just want you to know that I did this for your own good,' she says and frees my arm.

My eyebrows furrow. 'Lila, what did you do . . . '

She struts into the lobby toward two guys standing near the seating area across from the front desk. It takes my mind a second to process that it's Ethan and Micha.

'Damn it, Lila.' I'm not ready for this. What I said to Micha . . . it's unforgivable, even if it wasn't true. I'll never be able to forget the look on his face, like he was child who just learned that his dog died.

Like always, his aqua eyes immediately magnetize to mine and I force my legs to move toward them. He has on a really nice pair of jeans and a red plaid shirt. Leather bands cover his wrists and his blond hair is tousled. It makes my hands ache to touch him, draw him, be with him forever.

When I reach them, Lila gives me a guilty smile and shrugs. *I'm sorry*, she mouths.

I slant my chin up to look Micha in the eyes. 'Hi,' I manage to say stupidly.

Amusement gleams in his eyes. 'Hi.'

We stare at each other and a wave of intense emotions rolls over me. I love him more than anything.

God, why does my head have to be broken?

Ethan clears his throat and offers his hand to Lila. 'Maybe we should go check out the pool? It looked pretty big.'

'Why, that's a wonderful idea,' she says like she rehearsed it. She takes his hand and they walk to the elevator area in the corner of the lobby.

My eyes remain on them until they are out of view, then with difficulty, I redirect my attention to Micha and my heart leaps into my throat. 'So . . . '

He laughs at me, surprisingly happy. 'Are we going to keep the conversation to one-word sentences?'

My shoulders unstiffen and my lips loosen to a tiny smile. 'I'm sorry . . . about everything.'

'You don't have to be sorry.' His intense gaze penetrates me as he sucks his lip ring between his teeth. 'Stuff happens, right?'

He's different — happier. What has he been up to for the last couple weeks?

Edging around him, I drop down into a chair in the seating area near the computer station.

I start with a simple question. 'How are things going with the band?'

He sits down in the chair across from mine, so we're facing each other, our knees barely inches away. 'They're doing well I guess, but don't know . . . I think I might try to do some stuff on my own.'

'But I thought you were happy with being on the road,' I say. 'And I thought you liked your band.'

'Not really.' He inclines forward and relaxes his arms on his knees. 'Honestly, I'm not sure if I was ever happy with the situation. Dylan's freaking annoying and Chase barely talks.

And Naomi, well she's getting on my nerves.'

My thoughts drift to his lip ring and my mouth salivates to taste it. 'Then why were you on the road with them for so long?'

His gaze flicks to my lips and hunger flashes in his aqua eyes. 'Because I love to play and they were my ticket in, but I hate being on the road all the time.'

I tuck my hands underneath my legs to keep from reaching over and running my fingers along his lips. 'Where will you go? Back to Star Grove?'

He shakes his head. 'No way. I have a couple ideas, but I have to run it past a few people first.'

The way he says 'people' makes me wonder if they're important to him. My mind races with the idea that he's met someone else. It's been only a couple weeks since I crushed his heart, but Micha is amazing and most girls see that.

'You'll have to let me know where you end up.' I gently bump my knee into his and fake a smile. 'I just might come visit you.'

He lets out a quiet laugh, but his gaze is relentless. 'Is there anything you want to tell me?'

He seems so happy and I don't want to ruin it for him.

'No, not really, other than I'm starving.' I

get to my feet, tugging down the bottom of my shirt. 'Lila said she was buying dinner.'

He offers me his elbow. 'Then to dinner it is.'

I loop my arm through his and we head toward the door, side by side, just like we used to do when we were friends.

7

Micha

I'm not sure I'll ever fully understand what goes on in that head of hers. I gave her the perfect opportunity to tell me she never cheated and she totally dodged it. But in her eyes, she probably thinks that I'll move on.

Maybe it's time, but how am I supposed to move on from the one person I know I'm supposed to be with?

'Dude, I can't pronounce a single thing on this menu.' Ethan runs his fingers along the list of appetizers, blinking his eyes. 'Are these prices in US dollars? *Fuck*.'

A stuck-up-looking couple point their noses up in our direction. The restaurant seems overdone, with the trimming in gold, small chandeliers hanging over the top of each table, and silverware more shiny than the sun. It kind of reminds me of my dad's house. And I haven't seen or heard from him since our awkward meeting in New York.

Ella shuts her menu and tosses it into the center of the table, looking at Lila with an entertained expression as she bats her long eyelashes. 'Oh Lila Dila, I think you might have to order for us common folks, who can't read French.'

Ethan and I shut our menus and toss them into the middle of the table, agreeing with her.

Lila sighs and tosses the menu on top of the stack. 'Do you guys want to bail and walk to the Applebees I saw on the corner?'

'Yes,' Ethan, Ella, and I all say at the same time.

We leave the table in a hurry, before the waiter can come back and try to bill us for the rolls and drinks. We cause a scene as we dash out of the stuffy restaurant laughing our asses off. It's Friday and the sidewalk is as crowded as the traffic on the street. Lights dance across our faces and there's excitement buzzing in the air.

Ella raises her hands above her head as she squeezes through a group of guys and my protective instincts kick in. I put my hand on her back, keeping her close as one of the guys tries to check out her ass. I can't really blame him, since I'm doing the same thing.

She has a tight pair of jeans on and a black shirt short enough that there is a sliver of space between the top of her jeans and the bottom of her shirt. Her pale skin looks soft and I let my finger run along it gently, as if it's accidental.

She peers over her shoulder and the lights reflect in her eyes as she shouts over the noise, 'This reminds me of senior year when we took that road trip to New Orleans!'

'The one where you took your shirt off and flashed everyone.' I wink at her and she swats my arm.

'That didn't happen and you know it,' she says, forcing back a smile.

'I know!' I yell over the loud music from a band playing in front of a gift shop. 'But that night was much more intense than this!'

The noise fades out as we walk into the restaurant. There's a row of people waiting for a table, but it's still much better than the other place. Lila heads up to the hostess standing at the front to put our names down on the waiting list.

'That night was intense, but only because of you.' Ethan smirks maliciously. 'If you could have just kept it in your pants, then we wouldn't have had to run away from the club.'

Lila returns and her eyes scan the three of us. 'I'm so lost. Who couldn't keep it in their pants?'

'It's a good thing that you're lost, trust me.' I pat her arm as Ella and Ethan start to laugh. 'These two are just trying to embarrass me with a drunken mistake of my past.'

"But she looked so hot when we were dancing," Ella says mocking me in a deep voice. "'And I swear she looked younger.'"

Ethan busts up laughing, leaning in toward Ella, who's laughing just as hard. Ethan told me about their little shake thing with Mikey and it seems like it kind of broke down a barrier between the two of them.

I shove Ethan and he staggers into a tall blonde with a big rack and his hand ends up touching her boob. Ella whirls toward the wall laughing her ass off.

'I'm sorry,' Ethan apologizes to the blonde with an amused grin. 'I didn't see you there, sweetheart.'

She's probably around the same age as us, maybe a little older. She narrows her eyes and stomps off toward the seating area with her arms crossed as she sinks down at the end of the bench.

'Thanks for making me look like a perv.' Ethan scowls at me and then glances discretely at Lila.

'You don't need my help with that, man.' I notice that Ella is still facing the wall and her shoulders are shaking. 'Oh pretty girl, are you alive over there?'

Shaking her head, she turns around with her hand covering her mouth and tears streaming out of her eyes. 'I'm sorry,' she says between laughs. 'I just can't stop picturing that lady in New Orleans and how you almost did her in the bathroom. And then we had to drag you out of the club as she chased after us.'

'That's what happened?' Lila starts to giggle and her legs almost buckle from under her as she hunches over, clutching at her stomach.

'She wasn't that old, like maybe thirty-five or forty,' I argue, moving aside as some people walk in through the door and let in a cool breeze. 'And I was *drunk.*'

Ethan pats my shoulder and gives me a sympathetic look. 'It's okay. We all love our cougars.'

I punch him in the arm and Ella laughs so hard she can barely stand. I decide she needs to be punished too so I fix my gaze on her. She stops laughing and her lips shift to a frown.

'You don't scare me, Micha Scott.' She backs toward the corner. 'I know you won't hurt me.'

'You're right. I won't ever hurt you.' I spread my hands out to the side, so she's got no place to run. 'But I did see a water fountain down the block.'

'Please don't,' she pleads with her hands out protectively in front of her. 'It's like fifty degrees outside.'

'You deserve it.' I easily pick her up and throw her over my shoulder.

'Micha.' She squirms as I push out the doors and onto the sidewalk. We turn heads as I march toward the fountain at the end of the street just in front of a park. When I reach the marble edge of it, I pause, deciding what to do. Jump in and toss her under the spraying water? Or just set her down in it?

'What is it with you and water?' She elevates her head and brushes her hair out of her face to look me in the eyes. 'Whether it's sprinklers or showers — you're always getting me wet.'

Unable to help myself, I spread my fingers along the back of her thigh and give her ass a squeeze. 'Am I making you wet right now?'

She looks like she's going to cry, which was not the reaction I was expecting. 'How can you joke around with me? After what I did?'

I shrug, tug my pants higher up onto my waist, and step into water, which fills up my boots instantly. 'Fuck, that's cold.' I wade out to one of the various streams of water that surround two angel statues slanted together with harps in their hands. Water soaks my jeans as I set her down in the middle of it, letting her get drenched.

She squeals, panting from the cold. 'You are the meanest guy I've ever known.'

Water rivers from the fountain and down her rock-hard body. It takes me back to the time in the shower when I touched her all over for the first time. God, I fucking miss touching her like that.

'You know that's not true.' I step forward, to the edge of the stream, and take in her wet clothes. 'In fact, I think you know I'm the nicest guy you'll ever meet.'

She doesn't argue, just moves out from the water, and wrings out her hair. 'I think we need to talk.'

A weight falls from my shoulders and I open my mouth to tell her we should go somewhere to talk, when someone screams. Our eyes dart to the edge of the fountain where Lila is sitting in the water, her clothes and hair soaked, and Ethan is standing on the marble step, laughing hysterically.

Ella busts up laughing as Ethan steps into the pool of water that surrounds the fountain and we end up having a full-on water fight. We stop only when security shows up and we run into the nearby park in our wet clothes. I'm not much of an artist, only with lyrics, but if someone were to snap a picture of us in the fountain, I'm sure they would see a rare moment of perfection.

Ella

I haven't had a night like this since I was fifteen and Micha and I spent the entire day out at the lake on a small raft we 'borrowed' from the neighbors. It was one of those days of simplicity, but it meant everything because there was no darkness, only light.

We get a lot of glares as we walk through the lobby of the hotel in our sopping clothes, leaving a trail of water along the tile floor. The guys didn't get their own room and apparently they're too broke, so Lila and I decide to let them stay, even though it makes me uneasy.

When we get up to the room, Micha peels off his shirt and chucks himself onto the bed, while Ethan kicks his boots off by the door.

Ethan rubs his hands together. 'Who's up for a community shower?'

'Are you including Micha in your request too?' I joke maliciously as I shut the bedroom door.

He scowls at me, pulling a disgusted face. 'Shut up.'

I stick out my tongue as Micha shakes his head disappointedly. 'Pretty girl, you took it one step too far.'

I laugh, grabbing some pajamas out of my bag, and run into the bathroom. 'Since you're the one who threw me in, you can take the shower last.'

He starts to run for me and I close the door, laughing. Once I'm alone, I assess the night. I don't understand. Why is he being so nice to me? Does he . . . did he figure out I was lying?

I strip off my clothes and toss them in the corner, then turn on the shower, waiting until it warms up before I step in. I'm washing my hair with the hotel shampoo when the lock on the door clicks.

I know who it is because he taught me how to pick a lock. 'Seriously, Micha, no more for the night.'

'It's me,' Lila says and something lands on the counter with a clank. 'I just needed to brush my teeth. I think I got fountain water in my mouth.'

Soap stings in my eyes. 'Did you pick the lock?'

'No, Micha did it for me.' She turns the water on briefly, but it's enough to make the temperature change.

I shiver as I rinse the rest of the shampoo out of my hair. The sink turns off and then it turns quiet. 'Lila?' I wonder if she left.

'Are you ever planning on telling him the truth?' Lila finally asks. 'That you didn't cheat on him, but that you had a . . . '

'Nervous breakdown — you can say it.' My hands remain in my hair and soap drips down my face. 'And I don't know if I'm going to tell him.'

I hear her sit down on top of the toilet. 'Can I ask why not?'

Swallowing hard, I peek out from the curtain. 'Because he seems happy, and if he is, then I don't want to ruin it for him. That's all I've ever wanted for him.'

She sighs heavy-heartedly. 'Ella, when are you going to realize that you two belong together? Everyone who lays eyes on you can see it and is envious of it because that kind of love isn't supposed to exist.'

I wipe some water from my face. 'What kind of love are you talking about?'

'The kind of love that owns you.' She gets up, gives a quick look in the mirror, and combs her fingers through her damp hair. 'The kind where you know the other person inside and out. Where you can go through hell and back and still make it out okay.' She leaves me alone with her heavy words echoing in my head.

I shut off the water and climb out of the shower. After I'm dressed, I exit the bathroom with my hands crossed over my chest, because I forgot to grab a clean bra.

Micha is leaning against the headboard

with his shirt and shoes off, and the remote pointed at the television. His eyes connect with mine and a smile curls at his lips.

'Why are you crossing your arms like that, pretty girl,' he says with a mischievous sparkle in his eyes.

I lie flat on my stomach on the bed next to his. 'Where're Lila and Ethan?'

'They went to raid the vending machine.' His eyes roam across my body and my skin tingles as my breath catches. 'So it's just you and me.'

I press my lips together to hide the sound of my erratic breathing. 'So it is.'

He slides his legs off the bed and he studies me momentarily. 'I should probably take a shower.' He has a look on his face like he's enjoying himself. Without saying another word, he gets some clothes out of his bag on the floor and struts off to the bathroom, doing that sexy walk he does when he knows someone is watching him.

I end up passing out and when I wake up, the room is dark and soundless. The blankets are pulled over me and someone's warm breath is dusting my cheeks. I was under the impression that I'd be sharing a bed with Lila, but I hope the warm body sleeping very close to me isn't hers.

'Are you awake?' Micha whispers and his

breath tickles my cheek.

I let my eyes adjust to the dark and make out the outline of his face. 'Kind of.'

I hear him sucking on his lip ring. 'I can't sleep. I have too much pent-up energy.'

'Over what?' I utter quietly.

'Over you,' he says in a low voice. 'And the fact that you're sleeping only inches away without a bra on and all I want to do is touch you. It's driving me crazy.'

'How can you want to touch me after what I did?'

'How can I ever not want to touch you?'

His words confuse me in the strangest way, but I crave his touch, so slowly, I hitch my leg over his hip. His breathing hitches and then the palm of his hand slides up my bare leg, leaving a trail of heat along my skin. He doesn't say a word as his hand sneaks up the side of my shorts, scoots my panties to the side, and seconds later his fingers are inside me.

My teeth clamp down on my lip as he starts to feel me thoroughly. It's like we're doing something forbidden in the dark room with Ethan and Lila only a few feet away. His mouth fumbles against my lips as his warm tongue urges them apart. He keeps moving his fingers inside me as he nips at my lip and feels my breasts with his free hand, rubbing his thumb along my nipple, driving my body crazy.

'Micha . . . ' I groan.

'Shh . . . ' he murmurs against my lips.

He continues to suffocate me with his kisses until he pushes me over the edge. Clutching onto him, my head tips back and I try to breathe through it quietly.

When I recompose myself, he kisses my forehead and slips his finger out of me. 'Now I can sleep,' he whispers, and within minutes, his breathing becomes calm.

I'm left wide-awake and I have a feeling he did it on purpose.

8

Micha

I wake up feeling good. The sun is shining through the window and my mind is calm and relaxed. I know it was a dirty move to get back at her, but it wasn't like it was a punishment for her either. I just left her wide awake, hot and bothered, a feeling I'm becoming very familiar with.

I sit up, rub my eyes, and realize Ella and Lila are missing from the room.

'Well, good morning, princess,' Ethan says from the table. He's eating a doughnut and has an energy drink in his hand. 'Did you have a good night's rest?'

'Where is everyone?' I climb out of bed and slip on a black T-shirt.

He stuffs the rest of the doughnut into his mouth and dusts the crumbs off his hands on the front of his jeans. 'The alarm didn't go off so they ran out of here about ten minutes ago, freaking out about not having enough time to get their hair done. Or at least that's what Lila was saying . . . *Ella* seemed a little *distracted.*'

I eye him over as I search through my bag for my watch. 'Are you insinuating something? Because you have this stupid look on your face and it's getting on my nerves.'

He sips his drink and pushes up from the chair. 'Only that the next time you two fool around in the dark with other people in the room, you might want to try being a little bit quieter.'

'Do me a favor,' I say, 'don't say anything to Ella. You're gonna make things weird.'

'Weirder than you two already made them?' He crushes the can and shoots it into the trashcan in the corner. 'Because those noises from last night are going to haunt my nightmares for a long time.'

I change the subject, clipping my watch onto my wrist. 'What the heck are we supposed to wear to a wedding?'

'How the hell should I know?' He glances down at his long-sleeve black shirt pulled over a gray T-shirt and his dark jeans. 'I was going to go like this.'

Grabbing a black pinstriped shirt and a pair of my nicest jeans, I head off to the bathroom.

'Has she admitted she was lying?' Ethan flips on the television and flops down on one of the beds, crossing his feet.

I halt in the doorway and glance over my

shoulder at him. 'No . . . As usual, she's being stubborn.'

'Here's a thought.' He drops the remote on the nightstand. 'You could always tell her you know and save yourself all the drama.'

'It's not that simple,' I explain. 'I don't like to push her into doing things . . . because . . . ' I trail off, knowing I can't tell him about the bridge or how she looked on that bathroom floor when she told me.

When she's ready, she'll tell . . . at least I hope. But what if she doesn't? What if I've spent my life chasing a ghost?

★   ★   ★

'Okay, so I'm severely disappointed in the bridesmaid lineup,' Ethan comments, eye-balling the bridesmaids standing just outside the canopy entrance.

We are sitting in the back row waiting for this little shindig to start while people scurry back and forth through the tent. The front of the area is decorated with purple flowers and the main aisle is lined with black and purple ribbons.

'I think they're all married,' I tell him, resting my foot up on my knee. 'And about ten years older than you.'

He sighs and leans back into the fold-up

chair. 'What am I supposed to do then? This thing doesn't start for another hour and I'm getting bored.'

'I'm sure you'll survive . . . ' My attention drifts to Ella as she walks beneath the canopy and up to Caroline, who's talking to a short guy in a gray suit, waving her hands animatedly. Ella has on a short, black velvet dress that shows off her long legs and bare shoulders. There's a purple ribbon around the middle and a purple flower in her hair.

She's fucking beautiful. That's all there is to it.

'Dude, wipe the drool off your chin.' Ethan slaps the back of my head.

I shove him and he pushes me back. Letting out a deep breath, my eyes reconnect to Ella. She says something to Caroline and hands the glass of champagne to her. Caroline downs it and gives the glass back to Ella before rushing away, holding the front of her dress.

Ella sets the glass on a chair and presses her fingers to the bridge of her nose as her gaze finds me. Her eyes silently plead for me to follow her as she ducks out of the tent.

'I'll be right back,' I say, rising to my feet. 'And try not to get into any trouble while I'm gone.'

I weave through the aisles and duck outside into the sunshine and cool air. A forest encloses the house and Ella strolls down the grassy hill until she vanishes into the trees crisped with autumn.

'What is she doing?' I mutter as I follow her.

When I step into the forest, she's leaning against a tree and the thick forest obscures every aspect of the wedding, except for the muffled noise of voices. It's like we're in our own private little world.

I walk slowly toward her. 'What are you doing out here?'

Her hands are tucked behind her back and she's chewing on her bottom lip anxiously. 'I didn't cheat on you. I lied about it.'

I reduce the gap between us so we're within reaching distance. 'I know you didn't.'

Her eyebrows dip together. 'How did you know?'

'Lila told Ethan.' I inch closer to her, and my gaze skims down to the cleavage popping out of the dress. 'And Ethan told me.'

Her shoulders slump as she exhales, relieved. 'Why didn't you say anything?'

'Because I figure you had some reason why you weren't telling me.' My fingers itch to touch her, long to run along her body and feel inside her.

'I'm sorry. It was the only thing I could think of that would make you let me go. You deserve better than what I can give you.'

'I don't understand why you don't think you're good enough for me.'

'Because I'm not.' She shrugs nonchalantly. 'Because eventually you'll hate me . . . It's inevitable.'

'I could never hate you.' I tuck a strand of her hair behind her ear and let my fingers stroke the side of her neck before I pull away. 'I couldn't even hate you when I thought you cheated. Yeah, I was furious, but I still loved you.'

'That day I said that — those days I couldn't get out of bed, I was having a nervous breakdown. My therapist put me on some stuff for anxiety and depression.' Her eyes turn watery like she might cry. 'Micha, you don't want this, trust me. I watched my mother's problems eat away at my dad . . . I'll drag you into that dark hole with me. You just need to go. Walk away. *Please* walk away.'

With the pad of my thumb, I wipe a tear that escapes her eye. 'I hate to say this Ella, but your father is fucking weak. He can't blame what he does on anyone but himself. And I'm not him and you're not your mom. Just because their story ended badly doesn't mean ours will.'

She turns her head away to avoid my gaze. 'I don't want this for you.'

I hook my finger under her chin and force her to look at me as I brace a hand on the tree beside her. 'I'm sorry, pretty girl, but you really don't get to choose what I want, what I do, or who I get to be with. So unless you want me to leave you because you don't love me anymore, I'm not going anywhere.'

When she doesn't say anything, I crash my lips into hers and she gasps as her fingers knot into my hair. Crushing my body against hers, my hand wanders down her side, along the curve of her breast, each rib, and to the bottom of her dress. I reach up it, grab hold of her panties, and slide them down her legs. When they're to her knees, she draws back slightly and kicks them off, and then she flips the button of my jeans open. I lift her up and press her against the tree as I thrust inside her.

When I reunite my mouth with hers, she bites down on my lip. It drives me crazy as she gently pulls my lip ring into her mouth while running her tongue along it. Holding her by the hip, my other hand travels up her body to the top of her dress, and I yank it down to cup her breast.

Her eyes glaze over as her head falls back. 'Micha, I do love you but I . . . '

I kiss her fervently, drawing away only for a second to say, 'I love you too.'

Ella

I don't know how it's possible for it to feel this good, just because he's inside me, but it does. God, it does. My intentions weren't meant to lead to sex when I came down here. I just wanted to tell him the truth away from everyone — he deserved the truth.

I think Lila was right, though. Micha's love owns me and I'll probably always end up giving into him as long as he keeps trying. But I still fear I'll break him, and that boy is too damn sweet and beautiful to ruin.

He's thrusting inside me as he pins my arms above my head and the bark of the tree scrapes my back. But it's worth the pain as I scream out in bliss and my worries fleetingly vanish.

His movements begin to slow, and then he pushes deep inside me one last time, before stilling. We pant, fervently clinging onto each other, our skin damp, our hearts racing.

'I really love that dress,' he whispers in my ear and the heat of his breath makes me shiver. 'You look beautiful in it.'

A smile touches my lips and I slant back to look him in the eyes. 'You tell me that too much. It's making me cocky.'

'No, I'm the cocky one.' His smile is almost blinding.

My face turns serious as I lightly brush my swollen lips to his. 'We still need to talk — '

'Ella!' Lila's voice echoes through the forest. 'Caroline needs you!'

I jump out of Micha's arms and adjust my dress back over my breasts as I search the ground. 'Where's my underwear?'

Micha laughs as he watches me search through an area of tall grass. 'I guess you're going to have to make it through the day without them.'

I put my hands on my hips. 'You want me to stand up in front of a bunch of people, at a wedding, without anything on underneath my dress?'

He shrugs, doing up the button of his jeans. 'It'd be kind of nice. You could have a cool breeze and if you bent over just right — '

'Ella!' Lila's voice is getting closer. 'Where the heck are you? I know you came out here! I saw you!'

'Micha, please, if you know where they are, just tell me.' I peek behind the tree and when I turn around, he has a smile on his face and my black thong is dangling off his finger.

I snatch them away and slip them back on, smoothing out my dress. Then I hurry back through the trees, pulling bits of leaves and twigs out of my hair with Micha at my heels, chuckling under his breath.

Lila is waiting at the border of the forest and her eyebrows arc when she sees Micha is with me. 'Umm . . . Caroline needs you to get ready.' Laughter hints her voice.

'Okay.' I hurry up the hill, leaving the two of them to walk back to the canopy together.

I don't know what to do. I still believe that I'm not good for him, even though he insists the opposite, but I can't seem to stay away from him.

Around the corner of the canopy, there is a line of bridesmaids dressed in the same black velvet dresses and the groomsmen wearing matching tuxes. Caroline is at the front next to her father, an older man with salt-and-pepper hair. Her wedding dress is beautiful, not quite white but close, with a black ribbon tied around the center and the bottom flowing out at the waist.

Caroline's expression relaxes as she presses her hand against her heart, crushing some of the flowers in her bouquet. 'Thank God, Ella.' She bunches her dress up and rushes toward me. 'Why do you have leaves in your hair?'

My hand shoots up to my hair and bits and pieces of twigs fall out. 'I went for a walk in the woods.'

'Hurry up and get in line.' She gives me a small bouquet and shoos me toward the back of the line. 'It's about to start.'

I hurry beside the groomsman, who's shorter than me with black hair that curls up at his ears. He's probably my age and I feel his eyes on me, checking me out, but my attention remains ahead at the front of the line. Inside, Dean is standing next to the minister in his tux and his brown hair is styled to the side. He looks happy and I envy him with every ounce of my heart.

I've never thought about marriage like most girls do. When I was younger, I didn't play dress up and make the boy next door be my groom. I never looked that far forward into the future, because I feared what lay ahead.

But watching Dean about to get married, I wonder if marriage is in my future. I struggle to breathe as panic strangles me, wanting to see it, but all there is is a black hole with no images.

The music starts and my thoughts snap back to reality. The line moves forward gradually and the groomsman links arms with me.

'My name is Luke, by the way,' he whispers in my ear.

I jolt away from him. 'Mine's Ella.'

He smiles at me as we enter into the canopy where purple and black ribbons hang from the ceiling, lights sparkle along the walls, and rows and rows of violets decorate the front area. Everyone is staring and I grow more anxious, but I breathe through it. When we reach the end of the aisle, I happily release Luke's arm and walk to the back of the row of bridesmaids.

Clutching onto the bouquet, I focus on Caroline and Dean, but there is a heightened sense of awareness that Micha is watching me from the back row.

The minister starts his speech and my mind automatically drifts to my future again. I want to see it desperately. I want to know how my life goes.

Adrenaline consumes my body and I fidget with the petals on the violet flowers, mentally telling myself to stay calm as Dean and Caroline read their vows. Listening to their words of love and commitment, my body stills. I want this. So much. I want someone to be mine forever — I want Micha.

But I need to become a person we can both love; otherwise we'll never make it.

9

Micha

I can't take my eyes off her the entire ceremony. She's never been much of a crier in public so it's startling to watch her try to choke back the tears and all I want to do is comfort her.

Dean looks really happy, which kind of annoys me. Ella might have dusted what he did under the rug, but it doesn't mean anything to me. He's part of what broke her — part of why Ella will never be the same girl.

The minister declares, 'You may kiss the bride.'

Dean and Caroline lean into one another and kiss, and everyone stands up and claps. As they walk down the aisle, people throw rose petals at them from the baskets placed in front of each chair. Lila collects a handful and joins in, throwing petals in the air.

Ethan rolls his eyes. 'I suddenly remembered why I never go to weddings,' he utters under his breath. 'They're too cheesy for me.'

'Yeah, I guess,' I reply, not completely

agreeing with him. 'But the cheesiness does have a point.'

Once Caroline and Dean leave the canopy, the groomsmen and bridesmaids follow in a line. The guy Ella's been paired up with annoyingly keeps checking her out and he whispers something to her as they walk outside.

The crowd moves across the yard to the back deck of the house, where another canopy is set up over tables decorated with rose petals and candles. There are lights strung across the ceiling and a massive chocolate fountain against the back wall.

Ella waits at the front where a cameraman is getting set up to take pictures. As she waits, her gaze collides with mine. She rolls her eyes, like she thinks this whole thing is silly and I wink at her.

Ethan, Lila, and I steal a few glasses of champagne and plates of cake and pick a table near the bar, drinking in silence as the music turns on.

'So how long are we obligated to stay here, do you think?' Ethan gags on the glass of champagne. 'God, rich people have bad taste in drinks.'

'Hey,' Lila protests, setting her glass on the table. 'I think it's good.'

'That's because you're rich,' Ethan jokes,

shoving up the sleeves of his shirt, and then he takes a bite of his cake. 'And you were brought up to think that expensive stuff tastes good.'

Lila sticks out her tongue and there's purple frosting on it. 'I think you might be the one with bad taste.'

Ethan scrunches his eyebrows, like he's overthinking. 'Nah, I have excellent taste.'

Ethan used to give me crap about Ella and me needing to screw and get it over with. I'm considering telling him the same thing about Lila and him.

Ella drops the bouquet before slumping into the chair next to me. 'God, weddings are exhausting.'

I pluck a piece of grass out of her hair and flick it on the ground. 'You want to get out of here? We could go get some dinner or something.'

'I can't leave yet.' She frowns, rests her head back on the chair, and stares up at the ceiling. 'There are more pictures to come.'

She straightens up in the chair and steals a bite of my cake, leaving a little bit of purple frosting on her bottom lip. I want to lean over so badly and lick it off.

'What?' she asks when she notices me staring.

I reach toward her and she freezes as my

thumb grazes her bottom lip. 'We should dance.'

She arches her eyebrows. 'Since when do either of us dance?'

'We always dance.' Extending my hand to her, I get to my feet.

'But our dancing is a lot different than their dancing.' She points a finger at the area where people are slow dancing. 'We'd probably scar their innocent little minds.'

'Come on, Ella May, dance with me.' Dazzling her with my most alluring smile, I keep my hand out, hoping she'll take it.

Sighing, she laces her fingers with mine, and I pull her to her feet. When we reach the center of the dance floor, I twirl her around and collide her into me. A smile tugs at her lips as I put my hands on her hips. Guiding her closer, she hooks her arms around the back of my neck.

As we dance to the music, I put my lips beside her ear and sing along with the lyrics.

She leans back to look me in the eyes. 'How do you know the lyrics to 'The Story'? Most guys don't listen to Brandi Carlile.'

'Shh . . . don't tell anyone.' I wink at her and hug her closer. 'And you used to listen to this song all the time. How could I not know the lyrics?'

She clutches onto me as I continue to sing.

Her head rests on my shoulder and I'm no longer scared of telling her how I feel. I want her to know — need her to understand, because holding it inside is no longer an option.

'I love you, Ella May,' I whisper, kissing her cheek. 'And one day I want to be doing this exact same thing at our wedding.'

Ella

'The Story' by Brandi Carlile plays through the room, soft lyrics that tell a story that hits straight at my heart. Micha is looking into my eyes deeply and winning my heart more than he already has.

Then he tells me that he wants to do this exact thing at our wedding and my lungs compress. I want to run away and hide, but I fight to hold onto my sanity.

'Micha, I — '

He puts a finger over my lips. 'Don't say anything, okay? Just think about it for a while. I'm not talking about right this second. I just want you to know how I feel.'

I lift his finger away. 'I have to say this because it's important that you know how I feel. I can't do this right now.' His face falls as I continue. 'But someday, yes. I need to get myself together first. I need to be okay with myself before I give you my whole heart.'

He studies my face. 'I'm not sure what you're saying.'

'I'm saying I think we should be friends until I can figure out how to get myself together again,' I explain. 'I don't want to do anything to hurt you, and right now I just don't know if I can do that.'

He cocks an eyebrow. 'You want us to be friends? Because I'm not sure that's possible.'

'We have to, and then maybe one day down the road, after I've put my shit together, we can be more, but only if you still want to.' I summon a deep breath, my insides hurting as I add, 'If someone better comes along, I don't want you to hesitate because of me.'

'No one else could ever be better than you,' he says, and I start to open my mouth to protest, but he talks over me. 'But if that's what you need, then I'll do it. We can be friends . . . for a while.'

He's not completely committed, but I didn't expect him to be. He's the most determined person I know.

I kiss his cheek and then place my head on his shoulder, breathing in the comforting smell of him as we sway in sync to the music, holding on, yet letting go.

10

Micha

It's been a few days since Ella and I parted from the wedding, but it feels like months. We talk on the phone several times a day, but it's not the same between us and I miss being with her.

'Man, I'm so bored,' Ethan complains as he surfs the channels with his boots kicked up on the coffee table. 'Can't we just go do something?'

I'm lying on my bed reading the message over and over again. A text showed up on my phone yesterday from my dad. It said he needed to see me — that he had something he wanted to ask. I've been staring at it, deciding if walking down that road with him again is a good idea. We've met two times and each one was uncomfortable and painful, but my mind won't be able to settle until I know what he wants.

'I don't know . . . I guess we could go get something to eat.' Sitting up, I swing my legs off the edge of the bed, and text my dad, asking him where he wants to meet up.

He texts me back quicker than I anticipated, asking me if I can meet him at the
bakery up on Ninth Street in about an hour.
Wavering, I finally text back that I will.

'Never mind. I can't go out.' I put on a
black hoodie and zip it up. 'I have to go meet
someone.'

He targets me with a condemning look. 'A
girl someone?'

I scoop up the house keys from off the top
of the dresser. 'No, it's just someone I used to
know.'

His face twists with confusion. 'It's not
Naomi, is it? Because I'd like to advise that
you stay away from that — she's crazy. She
basically tried to rape me last night.'

'Like you didn't like it.'

'Hey, I like my women and everything, but
she's a little too much. She went from the
bartender to some dude handing out flyers on
the street to me. Besides, she has a thing for
you.'

'I know that.' I put my wallet into the back
pocket of my jeans. 'You weren't the only one
she hit on last night.'

'Wow.' His eyes widen. 'And I thought I
was bad.'

I stuff my phone into the pocket of my
hoodie. 'Can you do me a favor? Can you tell
Dylan or Chase when — if — they show up,

that I might not make it to practice?'

He rummages through the very slim selection of food in the fridge. 'Do you think they'll show up? I mean, you haven't seen anyone but Naomi since you got back and neither of them showed up to practice yesterday.'

'I know that.' I open the front door and notice it's raining. 'But just in case they show, will you tell them?'

He shrugs as he selects a carton of juice out of the fridge. 'Yeah, I'll tell them . . . but doesn't it seem like your band's falling apart?'

'Kind of,' I mutter and shut the door. Pulling my hood over my head, I trot downstairs and out into the rain, splashing through puddles as I march toward the street.

Ever since the little incident with Naomi, things in the band have gotten rocky. It started with her not wanting to be around me, and then Dylan and Chase lost interest when they discovered they could make a lot of money bartending at this club exclusively for women.

Right now, though, I'm more concerned about what I'm about to walk into with my father.

★   ★   ★

When I arrive at the bakery and see my dad sitting at a table, I almost pussy out. I tap my hand anxiously on my leg, staring at him through the window as rain drips down on me. He's reading the paper and drinking a cup of coffee. Dressed in a gray suit and a red tie with a briefcase next to his feet, he looks like a lawyer. Suddenly, I realize I have no idea what he does or who he is. He's nothing more than a stranger, like the people passing by me on the sidewalk.

I man up and walk into the bakery. It smells like vanilla and kind of reminds me of Ella. Two of the eight tables are occupied and the cashier girl behind the display, filled with cupcakes and cookies, undresses me with her eyes.

My dad looks up from his coffee and his aqua eyes widen. 'Oh, Micha, you showed up.'

I slide out a chair and sit down across from him. 'Of course I showed up. When I say I'm going to be somewhere, I always show up. That's the kind of person I am and you'd know that if you knew me.'

He clears his throat multiple times while smoothing out invisible wrinkles on his tie. 'Look, Micha, I'm really sorry for what I've done. For being a shitty father and for just not being there.'

141

My forehead creases as I cross my arms and slump back in the chair. 'I don't get why you're saying that, because the last two times I saw you, you made it pretty clear that you didn't really care about me and you wanted nothing to do with me.'

Tearing some packets open, he adds sugar to his coffee with unsteady hands. 'Things change . . . some stuff happened, and . . . well, I need your help.'

I stare at him expressionlessly. 'Is that why you said you were sorry to me? Because you want something from me?'

He discards the empty packets onto the table. 'Do you want me to get you something? Do you want some coffee?'

'I want you to continue on with what you want,' I say coldly. 'Because I'm really fucking curious where this conversation is going.'

He stirs the coffee and wipes the spoon on the lip of the cup. 'I'm not really sure how to start this conversation . . . ' He drops the spoon onto the table. 'I was recently diagnosed with aplastic anemia . . . Do you know what that is?'

'Do I look like a doctor?' I shake my head, annoyed.

'Well, I'll skip the boring medical terms and get straight to the point. It's a rare disease and I've got a severe case of it.' He stares down at the cracks in the table, with his eyebrows knit, and wrinkles form around his eyes. 'I need a blood and marrow transplant and the best thing for that is to get a relative to be the donor.'

'Are you dying?' I eye him over. 'You look healthy.'

'No, I'm not dying.' His voice is as cold as ice. 'But I'm not healthy either, and this could help me.'

'What about your other kids? Why can't you ask them?'

'I don't want to do that to them. They're too young and . . . I don't even want them to know I'm sick.'

I hover over the table, putting my palms flat on the table, burning with anger, and the chair legs grind loudly against the floor. 'So let me get this straight. You want me to do it, even though you haven't talked to me in years? You bailed on me when I was a child and I still don't even know why you didn't at least stay in touch with me.'

'Micha, I said I was sorry.' He reaches across the table like he's going to pat my hand, but retreats, which is a good thing because I probably would have punched him. 'And this is bigger than that — I'm sick.'

I shove away from the table. 'I'll have to think about it.'

He picks up his briefcase and stands up too. 'Can you at least go get checked to see if you'll make a good donor? These things take time.'

Sometimes I wish I could be a douche bag and walk away. 'Fine, I'll go get checked, but it's not for you. It's so I don't have to feel guilty.'

Ella

It's been almost two weeks since the wedding and I talk to Micha every day on the phone. The conversations are light, except for the occasional dirty comment from him, but that was always normal, even when we were friends before.

I miss him like crazy and think about him an unhealthy amount of hours during the day. He consumes my thoughts, my body, my dreams — he's what drives me to be better.

It's midday, the sun is glistening from the blue sky, and the air smells like fresh-cut grass and autumn. I'm walking across the quiet campus yard toward my therapist's office with the phone up to my ear.

'You did not do that,' I say to Micha with a smile on my face. 'You are such a liar.'

'I did,' he argues with humor in his voice. 'I

threw down my guitar and told them I was out — that I didn't want any more drama.'

I swing the main entrance door open and step inside the vacant hallway. 'So you quit the band — you're just done, after months on the road with them?'

'It actually happens more than you think,' he replies and I hear Ethan's voice in the background. 'And I quit like a week ago, but I didn't want to tell you until now.'

My mouth sinks into a frown as I lower myself into a chair outside the therapist's office. 'Why? I wouldn't have talked you out of it. As long as you're happy, you can do whatever you want. That's all I've ever wanted for you.'

'I am happy. Very, very happy,' he promises me enthusiastically. 'But that's not the reason I didn't tell you.'

'Okay . . . what's the reason?' I hear Ethan's voice again. 'And why is Ethan there? Isn't he supposed to be on his big, adventurous trip, mountain-man style or whatever the hell he calls it?'

'My Mountain Man Journey!' Ethan shouts. 'Get the wording right, woman.'

'Am I on speakerphone?' I ask. 'Micha, if I am, take me off of it. Please.'

'I can't. You'll take this better if you're on speakerphone.' He blows out a breath. 'This way you'll contain your anger a little bit better, because you know Ethan will be listening and use everything you say against you.'

I glance from left to right, noting no one's around in the office. 'What's the news?'

He clears his throat, like he's preparing to make a big speech. 'After the whole band breakup went down, I decided I needed a change. And so did Ethan, since he realized he wasn't as much of a mountain man as he thought.'

'That's not the real reason,' Ethan objects. 'I just felt sorry for your dumb ass because your band broke up.'

'Anyway,' Micha talks over him. 'We both decided that it was time for a change and so I started looking around for a permanent thing that wouldn't require a lot of traveling.'

'I thought you didn't want to do that kind of stuff.' I drop my bag on the floor and hunch back in the chair. 'I thought you wanted to be part of a band and be on the road.'

'Nah, I'm better by myself,' he tells me. 'Maybe I'll keep my eyes open for a new band, but the one I was with was turning into a lost cause. And for now, I've found a place to play. Plus I got a side job. The pay is shit, but it works for now and it's better than going back home.'

'What's your side job?'

'It's for this male escort service. I figured

it'd be great. I get to dazzle women all day — which we both know I'm awesome at — and I'll get paid to do it.'

I roll my eyes, but play along. 'Wow, that sounds like a job you'll be really good at and I'm sure it'll be a lot of fun. The more I think about it, it's like your dream job.'

'Yeah, I know, right?' he says cleverly. 'Although, I have heard stories about some fetishes guys run into and it sounds like things can get a little awkward, but I'll do what I gotta do to survive.'

'You're such a dork.' I shift in my seat, tucking my legs under the chair as the secretary walks by with a stack of papers in her hands. 'What are you really doing? Better yet, where are you?'

'Ethan and I got a part-time job in construction, but it's just an in-between thing.' He pauses and there's a loud bang. 'At night I'll be playing at The Hook Up.'

'Hey. There's one of those in Vegas,' I say over the sound of the paper shredder. 'I didn't know it was a national thing, though.'

He hesitates. 'It's not a national thing.'

'You're in *Vegas*?' My voice comes out high-pitched and the secretary glares at me through her thick glasses as she feeds papers through the shredder. Turning in the seat, I lower my voice and put my finger to my ear to hear better. 'You and Ethan moved to Vegas?'

'Yeah, we're in Vegas right now as we speak, setting up our stuff in this teeny tiny apartment,' he clarifies. 'But it works and I'm happy with it.'

Unsure how to respond I stay quiet, drumming my fingers anxiously on my knee. The front desk's phone rings and the secretary answers it.

'Tell me what you're thinking, pretty girl,' he urges and there's a beep as he switches it off speakerphone. 'Ethan can't hear you anymore.'

'I'm thinking . . . I don't know what I'm thinking . . . ' I drift off as the therapist's door swings open and she sticks her head out.

'Ella, I'm ready for you.' Widening the doorway, she motions me in.

'I have to call you back,' I tell him. 'I'm headed into the therapist's office right now.' I hang up before he can say anything, collect my bag from off the floor, and take a seat in front of the desk.

Anna sits down in her chair, selects a pen from the cup, and takes her notebook out of the desk drawer. Today, her pantsuit is this bland shade of brown and her hair is pinned back. She puts on her glasses and reads over last visit's notes.

'That was Micha on the phone,' I explain before she can ask, because she's going to. 'And I just found out he moved here.'

'Oh, I see.' She drops the pen and notebook down on the desk, and scoots her chair forward. 'By the way you sound, you're not happy about this.'

'I'm not sure what I am.' I mull over my feelings. 'On the one hand, it's nice to have him close in case I need him, but I'm trying not to need him, so it could be bad that he's close. Does that make sense?'

'It makes a lot of sense.' She fans the pages of the notebook. 'How long did you say you've known Micha?'

'Since forever. I mean, I can remember being four years old and being fascinated with how he sat out in the garage with his dad and worked on cars. Although, I was always too afraid to go over there and talk to him — he actually talked to me first.' A laugh tickles in my throat. 'Actually, he bribed me to climb over the fence first, with a juice box and a toy car.'

'Why were you too afraid to talk to him?' she probes.

'I don't know. I guess maybe I always felt like I was living in some alternate world that no one understood, not even him.' I shrug, picking at my fingernails. 'I still feel that way sometimes, like maybe I see things differently than most people.'

She thrums her French-manicured nails on the desk. 'I think you worry too much about how you think.'

'But that's kind of a given,' I say. 'I've known this for a while, but what I still don't understand is how to stop worrying.'

'That's because I don't think you understand the original cause,' she states. 'From what you've told me, Ella, your childhood was full of worry.'

'I didn't worry all the time,' I protest. 'There were relaxing . . . moments and I lived my life the way I needed to in order to survive. If I didn't worry, then no one would have paid the bills, made sure everyone ate, or had clean clothes.'

'That's not quite what I mean, but that is part of it.' She removes a photo from the folder and lays it flat on the desk in front of me. 'What do you see when you look at this?'

It's a stock photo of a man, a woman, and a little girl, all with the same blue eyes and platinum blond hair. 'Umm . . . that you like to take the inserts from picture frames and keep them in your office.'

'Ella, it's not good to make jokes to hide your feelings,' she insists. 'Just tell me what you see.'

'I see a family, I guess.'

'Do they look happy?'

I study the smiles on their faces. 'They seem as happy as anyone else.'

She edges it toward me and taps it with her finger. 'Describe the picture to me.'

It's a strange request, but I do it anyway. 'Well, the man's got his arm wrapped around the woman's shoulder and he looks like he loves her, although his smile's a little bit too shiny, if you ask me. The woman's carrying the little girl and they both look happy too. Although, I don't get why they're so damn happy. They're just getting their damn picture taken.'

She accidentally creases the corners of the photo when she puts it into her folder. 'Did your mother or father ever hug you like that? Or do you remember being that happy when you were a kid?'

It's like she's asked me a pre-calculus question and my mind muddles at the complexity. 'No, but that stuff's not real. It's fake, for show purposes to make people feel good when they look at the picture frame.'

'No, Ella, it's real. Happiness does exist,' she answers sadly. 'Now, things aren't always that way, but families should have their happy moments and children should get hugged and feel loved.'

'I did — do — feel loved.' I massage the sides of my temples, feeling as though a concrete block has been dropped onto my chest. 'I've been hugged . . . a few times.'

'A few times in the last twenty years?' she asks, stressing her point. 'Because that doesn't seem like a lot.'

'I've been hugged plenty of times,' I say, offended. 'Micha hugs me all the time.'

'Again, we go back to Micha. Let's exclude him from this conversation for a minute and focus on your family.' She scribbles a few notes down in the notebook. 'Did your parents ever hug you? Laugh with you? Take family trips?'

'We went to the zoo once when I was six, but my mom was bipolar and couldn't do a lot with us. And my dad . . . well, he loved his Jack Daniels.' I pause as anger simmers at the tip of my tongue. 'What are you getting at?'

'I'm not trying to get at anything,' she responds kindly, clicking the cap back onto the pen. 'I'm just trying to let you see your life.'

'That it's crazy — that I'm crazy? Because I already knew that, without the recap of my shitty life.' My hands tremble and my palms sweat at harsh memories that make up my life. I begin to hyperventilate and my vision spots.

'Take a deep breath,' she instructs, waving her hand in front of her chest in a cleansing gesture and I obey. 'Now, you're not crazy, Ella. You've just had a rough life.'

My brain pounds inside my skull. 'Then what does this have to do with anxiety or depression or whatever it is you think's wrong with me?'

'I think that sometimes you don't think you deserve to have a good life — that you're not a good person. That you don't deserve to be loved.' She shuts a folder, stacks it with a small pile, and overlaps her hands on top of the desk. 'And I think that's why you push people away and what's causing a lot of the depression and anxiety.'

I flop my head back against the wall. 'I'm this way because my mom died and it was my fault. I'm this way because I know my head's screwed up and I don't want to drag anyone down with me.'

'All those things you said aren't true,' she says and I lift my head back up. 'And our goal here is to get you to believe that.'

We talk a little bit more about lighter stuff, like how my classes are going and what my plans are for Christmas. When my time's up I go back to the apartment.

Lila's not home from class yet and it's quiet. I grab a Dr. Pepper from the fridge and take the phone out of my pocket, staring at the picture on the screensaver of Micha, Lila, Ethan, and me at the wedding.

'I look happy there,' I say determinedly and then I dial Micha's number.

'You called back,' he answers after two rings. 'Ethan owes me twenty bucks.'

I chew on my thumbnail. 'He bet I wasn't going to call you back?'

'He bet you'd blow me off.' He lets out his fake evil laugh. 'That the Stepford Wife Ella had returned.'

'Nope, no Stepford Wife Ella here.' I tap the top of my soda and flip the tab open. 'Only a confused one.'

He stops laughing. 'Do you want to talk about it?'

'No, not really.' I sigh exhaustedly and swallow a sip of the soda.

He gives a lengthened pause. 'Ella, friends can talk to each other about stuff they're going through.'

'I know that.' I set the soda on the counter and plop down into a barstool. 'But I just spent the last hour talking to my therapist about it and I'd rather take a break from my own head, if that makes any sense.'

'It makes perfect sense.' He hesitates momentarily, like he's deciding if he dares say something. 'You should come over and see our new place. It's just a bunch of boxes right now, but we could go out to dinner or something.'

'I don't think — ' I start.

He cuts me off hastily. 'You can bring Lila too.'

I swear the boy has too much insight into my head. 'All right, I'll see if Lila's up for it when she gets back from class.'

'Don't blow me off, Ella May.' He pretends to be stern. 'I mean it. I know where you live and I will hunt you down and punish you in the dirtiest ways.'

'I'm not blowing you off. Jeez, relax, you weirdo,' I tease him back. 'I'm sure Lila will want to, but I have to check.'

'Good, I'll see you in a bit.' His voice portrays confidence. 'Oh, you know what we should do?'

I spin the can of soda around on the counter, wary to answer. 'What?'

'We should have a naked party.' Hilarity laces his voice. 'And you can only come in the house if you take off all your clothes. It'll be like the entry fee. Give me your pants and shirt and you're allowed to come.'

I frown, even though it sounds interesting. 'No naked parties.'

'Hey, I had to try,' he remarks in a tempting tone. 'I'll see you in a bit.'

We hang up and I change into a pair of red corduroy shorts and a black tank top with a heart in the middle. I pull my hair up in a ponytail and put on some eyeliner and lip gloss, then wait on the couch for Lila to show up.

She walks in, waving at Parker, who is backing away from the door. 'See you later, maybe.' She shuts the door and sighs, leaning back against it. 'God, he's getting on my nerves. He won't give it up.'

'Maybe you should stop giving it up to him then.' I hide my smile with the soda can.

'Hey, I have needs too.' She ambles to the kitchen and searches the fridge shelves for a snack. 'Not everyone can be committed to that no-sex thing like you.'

'I'm trying to fix myself before I make my life more complicated,' I say, picking the tab off the can. 'And so that when . . . if Micha and I end up together, I can be a person that he won't resent.'

She grabs an apple and a bottle of water and joins me on the couch, tucking her skirt underneath her legs as she sits down. 'You know it's never going to work, right? There's no way you two are going to be able to keep your hands off each other for more than, like, a week. Actually I'm betting five days. Ethan went with seven.'

'You made bets on it?' I gape at her. 'Wait a minute, did you know they were moving here?'

She shrugs and bites into the apple. 'Ethan might have mentioned it a time or two on the phone.'

I tip my head back and suck out the last drop of the soda. 'We're supposed to go over to their new place, if you're up for it.'

She removes the cap of the bottle of water. 'Sure. I don't have plans, but how are we going to get there? Because I'm still on my bus strike.'

'We can either call Ethan to come get us' — I frown — 'or borrow a car. I prefer borrowing so I can leave when I'm ready to. If Ethan comes and gets us, they'll hold us hostage, trust me.'

'That doesn't sound that bad.' A piece of apple falls out of her mouth and lands on her lap. 'But if you want to borrow a car, then we can. You can ask Blake.'

Remembering how annoyed Micha got over the Mustang, I hesitate.

'Yeah, that's probably not a good idea, huh?' She retrieves her phone from the pocket of her jeans. 'Who else could we call?'

Smashing the middle of the can, I put it on the coffee table. 'Parker?'

She shakes her head and one of her curls slips out from underneath the headband in her hair. 'No way, then it'll be even harder to get him to go away. Besides, he's a weirdo about letting people drive his car.'

'Then I have no idea.' After a few minutes of consideration, I unlock the screen of my phone and send Blake a text.

ME: Hey, I have a huge favor to ask you.
BLAKE: What's up?
ME: I need to borrow your car for a few hours.
BLAKE: Sure, but you'll have to drop me off at work and pick me up.
ME: That works for me.
BLAKE: I'll be out of class in a few minutes. You wanna meet up in the parking lot?
ME: Yeah, be there in 5.

* * *

Tucking my phone into my back pocket, I collect my purse off the back of the chair. 'I got us a car, but we have to go down to the parking lot right now.'

Her phone rings and she silences it without looking at the screen. 'Who did you call?'

I slip my sandals on and check my bag to make sure the house keys are in it. 'Blake.'

She springs up and tosses the apple core into the garbage next to the sofa. 'You know

Micha's going to be pissed at you for showing up in Blake's car.'

'He won't be mad,' I point out, opening the door, and sunlight filters in. 'Just a little annoyed and you're the one who suggested it first.'

'I know I did, but then I realized it's probably not a good idea.' She sighs as we head down the staircase. 'You have a tendency to see things so distorted sometimes. He's going to be pissed, because you told him you needed to be friends for a while, and then you show up in some other guy's car.'

I sidestep a tree and then dodge swiftly to my right as a guy playing football comes running in my direction to make a catch. 'You drive and we can say that you borrowed it, and then it'll be all good.'

'All good?' She takes a pack of gum out of her pocket and pops a piece into her mouth. 'Yeah, we'll see how good it is with all that sexual tension you two are going to have.'

She offers me a piece and I take one, knowing she's right.

Micha

'It smells like a locker room in here.' Ethan wrinkles his nose as he opens the fridge. 'Oh

God, there's leftover spaghetti in here.' He picks up a Tupperware bowl filled with red crap and examines it closely. 'Nope, I'm not sure what this is.'

'Throw it out, man.' I pick up a heavy box marked 'dishes' and carry it into the small kitchen that's in desperate need of a paint job. There are chips in the green countertops and one of the walls has been spackled in multiple places. 'It looks like it's moving.'

He tosses me the bowl, dry heaving at the horrible smell coming from it. 'Your turn. I took the last run of garbage out.'

I shake my head and head downstairs with the bowl out in front of me. The apartment complex is in a noisy area, especially by the playground. Children are on swings, running around, laughing, yelling, crying. It reminds me of everything Ella, Ethan, and I never had.

When I reach the Dumpster, a red Mustang flies into the apartment complex parking lot. It pulls up beside Ethan's truck underneath the carport and I stroll over, a little annoyed when Ella climbs out of it.

By the look on her face, she knows she's in trouble. She gives me a tentative wave. 'Hi.'

My gaze skims across the shiny hood of the car. 'So the Mustang makes a grand return into our lives.'

She gathers some of her auburn hair

behind her ear. 'Lila borrowed it.'

I press her with an unrelenting look. 'I can tell when you're lying.' When I advance to the passenger side, Lila hops out of the car. 'You could have had Ethan or me pick you up.'

'I know I could have.' Ella lollygags toward the curb. 'But I wanted to be able to go home when I wanted to.'

'I'm going to go inside,' Lila interrupts, glancing up at the two-story apartment. 'Which one is it?'

Without taking my eyes off Ella, I point my finger to the second floor. 'Top floor, first door on the right.'

She nods and hurries up the stairs, which creak with the clicks of her high heels.

'The car really doesn't mean anything, Micha.' Ella scuffs her sandals across the asphalt, avoiding eye contact with me. 'And I mean that. It was just a car to borrow.'

'I understand that it might not mean anything to you, but it probably does to Blake,' I assure her, stuffing my hands into my pockets to resist the temptation to run my hands all over her body and try to take claim of her again. 'Guys don't lend cars like this to a girl they have no interest in.'

She sighs and peeks up at me through her eyelashes. 'I probably shouldn't have come over. It's too weird.'

'It's weird only if you make it weird.' I start for the staircase and she follows me. 'Stop worrying so much, pretty girl.'

'Easier said than done,' she mutters with a frown forming at her lips.

When we reach the bottom of the stairs, I move to the side and signal for her to go ahead. 'Ladies first.'

She gives me a tentative smile and trots up the stairs, trailing her hand along the railing. Smiling to myself, I walk behind her with my eyes focused on her backside. She has these little red shorts on that are tight enough that a small sliver of her ass peeks out. I've missed that ass a lot.

At the top of the stairway, she glances over her shoulder and catches me eyeballing her. She puts her hands behind her and whirls her back toward the wall. 'Did you have me walk up first to check out my butt? I thought we were going to be friends.'

I shrug, not giving a shit that she caught me. 'I used to check out your ass all the time before when we were just friends. You just never noticed.'

She combs her fingers through her auburn hair. 'You're going to make this hard, aren't you?'

'Probably,' I admit to her honestly and her face falls. Quickly, so she can't stop me, I sweep some of her hair out of her eyes and lightly kiss her cheek, winking at her when I step back. 'Relax, though. I won't rip your clothes off until you ask me to.'

'You're relentless.' She restrains a grin. 'And it's not going to help me if you keep touching me and looking at me like that. I want to get better for you, but I have to take it easy with complex situations until I learn how to deal with them. Think of it as like when an alcoholic is recovering and they're told not to get into a relationship until they can handle stuff rationally.'

'Did your therapist say that to you?'

'Yeah.'

Sighing, I shove open the door and hold up a couple of my fingers. 'All right, I'll be on my best behavior. Scout's honor.'

She bends my fingers back playfully as she rolls her eyes and then steps into the house. She observes the old leather sofa Ethan stole from his mom's house, the television on a crate, and the table in the dining room, which is between the kitchen and the living room.

'This is so a guy's apartment.' She sniffs the air and then flinches, fanning her hand in front of her face. 'It even smells like a guy.'

I pinch her ass and she lets out a squeal. 'It smells manly.' I strut off to the kitchen before she can get mad at me for my little stunt.

She starts chatting with Lila and Ethan while I peel the tape off the dishes box on the kitchen table and take out a stack of plates. From the counter, my phone rings. It's the hospital from New York where I took the blood test.

Reluctantly, I answer it. 'Hello.'

'Hi,' a woman with a squeaky voice says. 'Is this Micha Scott?'

I slant my back against the counter and stare at the wall. 'It is.'

'This is Amy, from the NYU Medical Center,' she says. 'I called to tell you that your test results confirmed you're a candidate for the transplant.'

'Okay, thanks for letting me know.' I hang up on her, clutching the phone in my hand. '*Fuck*.'

Ethan pops his head into the kitchen. 'We're going to go get something to eat. You down . . . Are you okay? You look weird.'

'I'm fine.' I chuck my phone onto the table and the back pops off. 'And yeah, dinner sounds good to me.'

He nods his head at the front door where Ella and Lila are waiting. 'Let's roll then.'

Once he walks out, I sneak quite a few large swigs of vodka from a bottle I dig out of one of the boxes, then stuff a couple of mini bottles into my pocket. The hospital calling is a painful reminder that my father only came to me when he needed something from me. But that's not the real problem. I've accepted that he won't ever see me as anything more than a person he used to know. What's getting me riled up is that deep down, I don't want to do it for him. I want to make him suffer and that feeling is eating away at me.

I don't want to feel like that, but I can't turn off the resentment.

Ethan steps back into the kitchen with an irritated expression on his face. 'What are you doing? Let's go. I'm freaking hungry.'

'I'm coming. Jeez, keep your panties on.' I storm for the door. 'And we're not driving in that damn Mustang.'

Ella

Micha's pissed off about the Mustang and makes a big dramatic speech about how he's not riding in it. No way in hell. Uh-huh. The more the night goes on, it becomes clear that his anger is from something deeper, and the car is just a cover-up.

When Ethan turns into the parking lot, I decide that karma hates me, because it's the restaurant we dropped Blake off at earlier — the one he works at.

I scoot forward in the backseat of the truck and fold my arms on top of the console. 'I don't want to eat here.'

'Why not?' Micha glances at the restaurant's neon signs and flashy decorations hanging from the sloped trimming of the roof. His eyes are bloodshot and he's pronouncing his words slowly, which usually means he's either tired or drunk. 'It looks good to me.'

'Because the food's really gross,' Lila chimes in, unlocking her seatbelt. 'There's a place in the middle of town that has really good ribs. It'll only take us, like, fifteen minutes to get there.'

Micha shakes his head dramatically and I swear he's being a pain in the butt on purpose. 'Nah, I really think this place looks good.'

Lila and I trade a worried look as Micha and Ethan hop out of the car and slam the doors, leaving us alone in the dark cab.

'This is not good,' I mumble, eyeing Micha as he walks around to the back of the truck. He tips his head back and takes a swig from a bottle. 'Especially since he's in such a bad mood.'

'I think he's drunk,' Lila whispers as I crack the door open. 'I thought I smelled booze on his breath.'

I exhale loudly. 'Yeah, I'm pretty sure he is, which means we're probably walking into a drama pit.'

'Are you sure Blake's working still?' Lila slides over in the seat so she can climb out on my side.

I nod. 'We have to pick him up, remember?'

The four of us walk across the parking lot toward the entryway. It's dark enough that the stars are speckling the sky, and in the distance, the strip's lights glimmer in florescent colors. There's a sway to Micha's walk and he trips over his own feet when he jumps up to touch the top of the doorway, rolling his ankle when he lands.

'Yep, we're definitely walking into a drama pit,' I utter under my breath as Ethan swings the door open.

Inside the restaurant the lights are dim and the air is musty. It's crowded and noisy, but there are a few vacant booths. Little lanterns hang above each table and soft country music flows from the speakers.

Blake is serving shots from behind the bar to a group of rowdy-looking guys. I clear my throat and make eye contact with Lila, nodding my head discretely in Blake's direction. She tracks my gaze and her expression drops.

'Hold on, I got an idea.' She waltzes up to the hostess, a brunette in a white shirt and black slacks. Lila sneaks her a tip from over the counter and then she comes back with a cheery smile on her face.

'It's all taken care of,' she says in a quiet voice. 'And yes, I know I'm the bestest friend ever.'

'What did you do?' I ask, but she just keeps smiling.

When the hostess leads us to our table, I realize Lila bribed her to take us to a corner booth that is secluded away and out of sight of the bar. I want to hug her, but it would be weird, so I sit down and Lila slides in beside me.

Ethan pauses at the end of the other side of the booth. 'No way, I'm not buddying it up with Micha. Lila can sit on my side.'

Lila glances at me. 'Is that okay with you?'

My nerves jumble and it shows in the unsteadiness of my voice. 'I think I — '

'I don't give a shit where I sit.' Micha's eyes stray to the end of the aisle. 'In fact, I think I'm going to go hang out at the bar.'

Lila jumps up and scurries to the other side to sit with Ethan, inserting strands of her hair underneath the headband. Micha falls into the booth beside me and drapes an arm behind me. He has a short-sleeved gray shirt on and his warm skin grazes the back of my neck. His face looks flushed and his breath reeks of vodka.

Shielding my face with the menu, I lean toward him and whisper, 'You're drunk.'

He blinks his eyes at me innocently. 'Why would you ever think that?'

I state the obvious. 'Because you smell like vodka.'

'I threw back a few shots before we headed out and a few in the parking lot.' He places the palm of his hand on top of my thigh. 'Relax, I just want to have some fun.'

'That's not why you did it.' I lower the menu back onto the table. 'You only drink randomly when you're upset.'

He rolls his eyes and withdraws his hand from my leg. 'How do you know? Maybe I changed while I was on the road.'

'Oh, so douche bag Micha's going to come out,' I hiss through my teeth. 'There's another reason I know you're upset. He makes his grand appearance only when you're angry.'

With his eyes on me, he flips open his menu. 'I'm upset because my dick hasn't gotten any attention for a couple of weeks.'

Ethan snorts a laugh and Lila's blue eyes widen. I drop my head onto the table, sigh, and stay that way until the waiter comes to take our orders. Raising my head from the table, I discover Blake standing at the end of our table.

He's wearing a nice pair of jeans, a button-down black shirt, and wisps of his dark hair are sticking up a little on the sides.

'Ella, what are you doing here?'

'Getting something to eat.' I keep my tone light, hoping we can skip the introductions.

He has a pen poised against a notebook. 'What? You just couldn't wait to pick me up tonight?' he jokes. 'You had to come see me early?'

'Aw, damn it.' I don't mean to say it aloud, but it slips out, and I quickly slap a hand over my mouth. 'I'm sorry.'

'Who the fuck are you?' Micha asks, glaring at Blake.

'I'm Blake,' he replies, adjusting his weight uneasily. 'Who are you?'

'I'm Micha.' A malicious look masks his face. 'And by that look on your face, I think you know Ella and I are dating.'

'Micha, I think — ' I start.

'Ella, just leave it alone,' Ethan interrupts, shooting me a warning look as he nudges my shin with his foot from under the table. 'You know it's not even worth it to try.'

I zip my lips together and focus on the menu. 'I think I'll have a chicken sandwich. What about everyone else?'

'I'll have you,' Micha says and my cheeks heat as his hand inches up my thigh.

I conceal my hand over his and stop it from going any farther, then look at Ethan for help. 'What should we do with him?'

Micha buries his face in my hair. 'Anything you want, baby.'

Ethan shrugs and tosses his menu into the center of the table. 'You know as well as I do that he's only going to get more intense before he passes out.'

'I think I'll come back in a minute,' Blake says and hurries down the aisle back toward the bar.

'Smart move on his part.' Micha sticks his hand into his pocket and reveals a mini bottle of vodka stashed inside it.

I snatch it from his hand and his glazed eyes snap cold. 'Give me that back, pretty girl, or else.'

'Or else what?' I chuck the bottle to Ethan and he catches it. 'You're going to say really mean things? I'd rather you use me as your punching bag than someone else.'

Micha narrows his eyes at me and I wait for what's coming, but Ethan stands up before he can say anything else.

'Let's take him home.' Ethan steps back and lets Lila out of the booth. 'Before he does something stupid.'

I've seen Micha like this a couple times and there's always an underlying reason, but getting to the bottom of it can be tricky. Even for his best friend.

*   ★   ★

It's dark and no one has the porch lights on in this section of the complex. I can barely see anything as Ethan fights to get Micha up the stairs.

'Just quit dragging your feet,' Ethan snaps as they trip to the side and Micha bangs into the railing and the whole stairway vibrates.

'If you'd just get out of my way.' Micha shoves Ethan to the side and attempts to take a step on his own, but misses. 'Then I'd be okay.'

'What should we do?' Lila asks from a few steps below, uncomfortable with the situation.

Sighing, I intervene, positioning myself in between Micha and Ethan. 'Put your arm around me.'

Micha gladly swings his arm around my shoulder and leans on me. I struggle to get him up the stairs and his weight nearly sinks me to the floor. Ethan dashes up in front of us to unlock the door, flipping the porch light on.

Micha buries his face into my hair and his teeth nick the top of my ear. 'You smell so fucking good. I swear to God, I want to eat you up.'

I contain the laughter tickling at the back of my throat. 'What you need to do is sleep.'

Ethan holds the door open and Micha and

I stumble over the threshold, nearly falling to the floor. We regain our balance, and as soon as the door's shut, Micha wrestles his shirt off and chucks it onto the floor.

Even though he's drunk and we're not supposed to be on that path, my gaze moves across his lean muscles, his smooth skin, and the tattoo tracing his rib cage, and something coils deep inside me.

He slips off his boots and belt and I'm worried his pants are coming off next. Lila promptly faces the corner, pretending to be engrossed in the blank screen of the television. Micha keeps his pants on, though, and staggers into the kitchen, reaching for the half-empty bottle of vodka on the counter.

'Oh no you don't.' I rush into the kitchen, steal the bottle away from him, and screw the cap back on. 'No more drinks for you, unless it's water.'

'I'll do whatever the hell I want, Ella May,' he says sharply as he moves back and his head bumps against the counter. 'That's what you do. Whatever you want. Push me away.'

I hold out my hands for him to take. 'Come with me and we'll get you into bed.'

He stares at me forcefully. 'Are you coming too?'

I nod, keeping our gazes connected. 'But only to get you there, and then I have to go home.'

He places his hands in mine, gripping them tightly, and I walk backward, guiding him down the hall. His bloodshot eyes are fastened on me and it's hard to keep my heart steady.

I tell myself repeatedly that the friendship line between us needs to stay and that he's drunk anyway. When I get him into his room, he collapses onto the bed, yanking me down with him intentionally. He vice-grips his legs around mine and hugs his arms around my chest, pinning me close to him as he burrows his face into my neck and he nips at my skin before stilling.

I squirm my arms and wiggle my legs, but he only constricts his grip. Panic rushes inside me the longer he keeps me trapped and I loathe my messed-up head.

'No way,' he breathes, nuzzling closer. 'I'm not letting you go.'

'Ethan,' I call out quietly, working to keep my voice composed. 'Can you come in here?'

Moments later, Ethan appears in the doorway and braces his hands on the door frame. The sleeves of his black hoodie are rolled up, showing the colorful tattoos on his arms. 'Did you need something?' He grins, entertained at the sight of us.

I jerk my shoulder upward. 'Can you help me get him to let me go?'

Rubbing his scruffy jawline, he considers

my request. 'I think it's better if you stay there. That way if he wakes up still drunk you'll have to deal with him.'

'Ethan,' I hiss, but he walks away, laughing to himself.

I call out for Lila a few times, but she never responds, and I wonder if Ethan told her she could go home. After a lot of squirming, I manage to get one arm free. I rub my tired eyes, watching Micha and listening to him breathe in and out as he falls asleep. I run my fingers through his hair and then trace a finger down his temple to his lips. *God, he's beautiful.*

'What's going on in that head of yours?' I whisper, returning my hand to my side.

He breathes softly, his breath caressing my cheek. I surrender the idea of getting away and kiss his forehead before snuggling up to him with a small smile. Next time I visit my therapist, I can tell her I was hugged for ten hours straight.

11

Micha

I open my eyes to Ella sleeping soundly in my arms, with one of my hands on her hip and the other just below her breast. I'd be extremely happy, but my head is pounding, my stomach burns, and I have no idea what the hell happened last night — what I did or said.

Carefully, so not to wake her up, I climb out of bed and go into the bathroom. The room spins and my brain feels like it's going to explode inside my skull.

After I puke my guts out, I brush my teeth and return to the room. Ella's awake, sitting up in the bed and leaning against the headboard.

'How are you feeling?' A tiny bit of amusement glistens in her eyes.

'You think my pain is funny?' I crawl onto the bed and lie down on my stomach with the taste of vomit burning at the back of my throat. 'What the hell happened last night?'

Her fingertips travel up and down my bare back in circular motions. 'Well, it started with you drinking half a bottle of vodka and it ended with you trapping me in your bed.'

I raise my head up and cock an eyebrow at her. 'Did we . . . '

She shakes her head and lowers her body down so she's lying on her side next to me. 'You just wouldn't let me go. You're kind of evil when you get that drunk.'

'Did I say mean things to you?'

'No, but you tried to start a few fights.'

'I'm sorry,' I say, frowning. 'For whatever I did.'

Her big green eyes blink at me. 'I don't want you to be sorry. I want you to tell me what's up.'

'Nothing's up,' I lie, looking away. 'I just went a little overboard.'

'You know, this isn't fair.' She tugs on my arm and I look at her. 'You make me tell you everything and when I won't, you chase me down, pin me down, or tease me until I give in to you.'

'You could always try that,' I tell her in a low, husky voice. 'It might be interesting to see how it goes. In fact, I dare you to try.'

Her body goes rigid. 'Micha, just talk to me.'

I shake my head stubbornly. 'I told you to try to make me first and then maybe I will.'

She bites down on her bottom lip,

contemplating, and then pushes on my shoulder, forcing me to roll onto my back. I could easily win this battle, but that's not the point. She sits up and swings a leg over me. Her messy auburn hair curtains our faces and her eyeliner is smeared, but she's still gorgeous.

She works to keep a straight face. 'Now tell me why you were so upset last night.'

'Nah, I'm good,' I say. 'I think I'll keep it to myself.'

Her hands come down on my shoulders roughly and she tightens her legs around my waist, accidentally rubbing against me and making my cock go hard. 'Please just tell me.' She bats her eyelashes and it's ridiculously adorable.

'All right, I'll tell you.' I sneak my hands onto her hips and knead my fingers into her skin. 'But for the record, I never bat my eyelashes at you.'

She smiles proudly. 'I know. That was my secret trick. You were always a sucker for it.'

My hands move around and grope her backside. 'Are you telling me you played me?'

'Don't change the subject,' she says, allowing me to leave my hands where they are. 'Tell me what got you so upset last night.'

'My father has some kind of weird disease.' I let out a breath, feeling the heaviness crumble. 'And he needs me for some blood and marrow transplant thing.'

Her face drains to a ghostly white. 'Is he . . . is he going to be okay?'

I nod. 'Yeah, it's not life threatening or anything, but I . . . '

'But you what?' she urges me to continue, massaging my shoulders with her thumbs.

I look away from her and stare at the crack in the wall. 'I don't want to do it for him. I want him to suffer and I feel like shit because of it. I mean, am I that big of a dick that I'd let him be sick, just because I'm pissed off?'

She relaxes her weight on me as her lips twitch to turn upward. 'That's why you're upset? Because you feel guilty for being angry with him?'

'Why does it sound like you think that's funny?' My gaze settles back on her. 'It's not funny.'

'It's not.' She struggles to maintain a stoic face. 'It's just that . . . you're adorable. You're upset because you feel bad for thinking badly.'

'Don't ever call me adorable.' I squeeze her ass and her body tenses closer to me, making me even harder. 'No guy ever wants to be called that.'

Laughter flees her lips as she unintention-ally wiggles against my hard-on. 'I don't care.

You are. You are so adorable, Micha Scott. I don't think there's another guy in the whole world who's as sweet as you.'

I give her a cold, hard stare. 'You want to see how nice I am?' With one rapid movement, I flip us over, so her warm body is underneath me. My stomach burns, but I choke the nauseated feeling down. 'If you keep calling me adorable, I'm going to flip you over and show you how manly I really am.' Her lips part in shock and her cheeks turn pink. I place my hand on her cheek and let my thumb drag below her eye. 'Now that's adorable.'

Her body quivers beneath me, but her voice is composed. 'So what are you going to do? About your dad?'

I lean back, but still keep her hips trapped between my legs. 'I always knew what I was going to do. I was just having an inner conflict with the crappy thoughts filling up my head.'

'So you're going to help him.'

'Yeah, I'm going to help him.'

Her chest heaves up and down as her vast eyes gaze up at me. 'It's really hard just being friends with you.'

Her bluntness stuns me and I consider ripping her clothes off and making love to her right now. 'What do you want me to do with that statement because I have thousands of ideas.'

She offers me a tight smile. 'I don't want you to do anything yet. I just wanted you to know that that's how I feel — that you make me feel that way. I'm supposed to be working on sharing my feelings.'

I gently kiss her cheek and then move off her, but not before rubbing up against her once. She gasps at the feel of me and I grin.

'You're a better person than you think you are, Ella May.' I point to my mouth. 'See, you got me smiling.'

She rolls her eyes as she climbs off the bed and straightens out her shirt. 'All I have to do is take my clothes off and you would smile.'

I stare at her, picturing her sweaty and naked and underneath me.

'Stop looking at me like that.' Her breathing is erratic. 'You're making it hard to breathe.'

With my eyes still on her, I pick up my phone off the top of one of the many boxes stacked around my tiny bedroom. 'You want to take a trip to New York?'

She arches her eyebrows. 'As friends?'

I nod, dialing my father's number. 'If that's what you want.'

'It's what I want for now,' she says. 'And yes, I'll go with you, because I love you.'

Ella

It dawns on me the morning after Micha got wasted that he might have a problem. He's doing what my dad did by using alcohol to deal with his issues. Even though it might be difficult to confront him about it, it seems like I should.

I bring it up to my therapist during my last visit before my trip to New York, but she disagrees.

'I don't think that's a very good idea at the moment, Ella,' she says loudly over the rain beating against the window. The sidewalks outside are flooded, the sky is a dark gray, and the wind is howling. 'You're still dealing with your own problems and bringing that kind of stuff up to people can bring out some ugly emotions.'

'Micha's not like that,' I disagree, raising the volume of my voice over the boom of thunder. 'He would never intentionally hurt me.'

'Confronting problems can be hard for anyone.' She puts her glasses on and reads through last session's notes. 'How have you been doing with everything lately? Has it been good?'

I tell the truth, even though my initial reaction is to sugarcoat it. 'I've been fine except for after I got off the phone with Dean. But things are always crappy when I talk to him.'

'What did he call you for?' she wonders.

A huge lump swells in my chest as I say softly, 'Because today is my mom's birthday.'

She doesn't look at me with sympathy, which is why I like her. 'Was he rude to you during this conversation?'

I struggle to breathe. 'A little, but that's because he still blames me for our mom's death, I think.'

Her pencil is poised above her paper, ready to take notes. 'Do you ever talk to him about how you feel when he hurts you?'

I shake my head. 'No, and I don't want to.'

Her hand moves quickly across the paper as she writes something down. 'What did you do after you got off the phone with Dean and you were upset?'

'I wasn't upset,' I correct her. 'Just sad, so I went back to my room and curled up in a ball for a little while. I pulled myself out of it, though.'

'That's good.' She takes off her glasses and there are red lines where the frames pressed against her nose. 'What time are you leaving for New York?'

Tipping my head back, I glance at the clock on the wall above my head. 'In, like, four or five hours.'

'Are you going to be okay?' she inquires. 'You'll be alone on the trip with Micha.'

'I'll be fine,' I assure her. 'I know you don't

want me to date him — and I'm not — but he's still my friend and he needs me.'

'I never told you not to date him, Ella.' The rain picks up, veiling the window with water, and she raises her voice. 'I just told you that until you can build a steady life you should try to take things easy, and relationships generally are not easy.'

I curl a strand of my hair around my finger. 'How will I know when I'm ready to be with him again?'

She offers me an encouraging smile. 'Only you know that, but can I advise you to take baby steps with any relationship you get into, so your thoughts have time to slow down and you can see what's real?'

My thoughts are racing as I rise to my feet and swing my bag over my shoulder. 'I guess I'll see you when I get back.'

She escorts me to the door. 'Take care, Ella, and remember, if you need anything just call me.'

I wave good-bye and step out into the rain, taking off toward the apartment. My boots splash through the puddles, and even running the entire way, my clothes and hair end up sopping.

Ethan and Micha are sitting on the living room couch when I rush inside and slam the door, locking out the rain. Their eyes dart to me and amplify.

Micha takes in my jeans and T-shirt clinging to my body and the beads of water running down my face. 'Didn't you have a jacket you could put on?'

I wring out my hair, making a mess on the entryway tile. 'No, I didn't think it would rain.'

'What? The dark clouds weren't a dead giveaway?' Ethan asks mockingly and grabs a handful of chips from a bag on the coffee table.

'It usually doesn't rain here.' I head toward my room while my boots leave a trail of water on the carpet. 'Do I have time to take a shower before we leave?'

'Yeah, you're good,' Micha calls out. 'Just make it a quick one.'

I close my bedroom door, slip off my wet clothes, and go into the bathroom attached to the bedroom, leaving the door cracked. The warm water of the shower eases my stiff muscles and I let it run along my body longer than I'd planned.

'Ella, are you alive in here?' Micha's voice increases over the sound of the running water.

I rub the water from eyes. 'Yeah, I was just about to get out.'

I wait a minute for him to leave, and then shut off the water and draw the curtain back to step out, but he's still there, leaning against the counter.

'Shit.' I grab the curtain and cover myself. 'I thought you left.'

He crosses his arms and his feral eyes bore into me. 'I wanted to make sure you got out. We need to go.'

I reach for the towel on the hanger and wrap it around myself before releasing the curtain and stepping out. His gaze tracks me all the way as I walk into my room.

I dig through my dresser drawer for some clothes and select a gray-and-black-striped hooded T-shirt and a pair of jeans. 'All right, give me a minute to get dressed and I'm good to go.'

He picks up a drawing of the girl with cracks in her face and studies it. 'When did you draw this?'

Sighing, I pull on my panties without taking off the towel. 'Right before I came to visit you in LA.'

He drops it back onto the dresser and his fiery gaze shifts to me. 'It looks like you were sad when you drew it.'

I pull my pants on, stumbling around the room as my foot gets caught in the middle of the pant leg. 'I was sad about not being able to see you.'

A ghost smile touches his lips as I stare at

my bra in my hand, racking my brain for a way to get it on without flashing him. 'Did you run into some trouble?' he asks.

I blink at him impassively. 'Would you mind stepping out for a minute?'

He gives an overexaggerated nod. 'I would mind very much.'

Shaking my head, I turn around and let the towel fall to the floor. Hooking an arm through each strap, I put the bra on and reach around to clasp it together, but fingers brush my back.

'I know I'm not supposed to say this, since we're supposed to be friends.' Micha breathes in a husky tone as he clips the clamps together. 'But you are ridiculously beautiful.'

My lungs constrict as I peek over my shoulder and his luscious lips are only inches away. 'You're right,' I say, breathless as my heart hammers inside my chest. 'You really shouldn't say things like that.'

His gaze moves to my lips, full of desire like he might kiss me, and a needy moan trembles from my mouth. Nibbling on his lip ring, he backs away, his eyes never wavering from me until he shuts the door and disappears into the hall.

Blowing out a quivering breath, I quickly put my shirt on and comb my hair, wishing he had kissed me.

Ethan drops us off at the airport with barely
enough time to get checked in and make it to
the gate before the plane starts to board.
Everyone keeps thinking we're newlyweds
and Micha is amused by it; however, it makes
me uneasy. Newlyweds equal marriage,
something I'm not ready for.

As we're getting ready to get onto the
plane, Micha tells me to go ahead without
him. He's got something to do and he'll meet
me on the plane. Collecting my bags, I line
up with my boarding pass in my hand as he
saunters off toward the gift shop area with his
bag over his shoulder.

On the plane, I find our row and put my
smaller bag under the seat, then stuff the
larger one into the overhead compartment. I
sit down by the window and gaze out at the
blue sky and the wing of the airplane,
wondering how bad flying is, since I've never
been on a plane before.

'You look nervous,' Micha remarks when
he reaches the end of the row.

'I'm fine,' I assure him. 'I was just lost in
my thoughts.'

He shoves his bag into the compartment
above our heads and his green plaid hooded
shirt rises up just enough to show a thin

space of his lean stomach muscles and smooth porcelain skin. My thoughts fill with images of running my fingers up his chest, along his stomach, savoring his soft skin.

'Are you enjoying the view?' He cocks an eyebrow as he adjusts his shirt back over my view.

Hiding my smile, I turn toward the window. 'I guess so.'

He sits down in the middle seat and when I look back at him, there's a paper bag on his lap.

I point at it. 'What's in there? Is it anything good?'

He opens the bag and moves it toward me. Inside is a chocolate cupcake, with pink and red sprinkles. My heart instantly surges with my love for him.

'Now, I know it's not the same.' He removes the cupcake from the bag and balances it in the palm of my hand. 'But I think it's close.'

Tears sting at my eyes as images of my mother flash through my mind. It was her thirty-fifth birthday and I was twelve. When I asked her what she would like for a present, she told me she wanted to bake cupcakes all day. It was a good moment in my life, although most people would probably view it as strange. But she was happy. I was happy.

Micha was happy. And the happiness brought a rare serenity to our lives.

'You remembered.' A tear escapes from my eye and rolls down my cheek.

'Of course I remembered.' He wipes away the stray tear. 'How could I not remember the day I had to make dozens and dozens of cupcakes?'

Through my tears, I manage to smile at the memory. 'I couldn't tell her no. It was her birthday and she seemed so happy.'

'And I was perfectly happy to do it,' he says, wiping another tear away with his finger. 'Although I did end up puking my guts out because I ate too much batter.'

'It's a good memory of my mom.' I shut my eyes, force back the tears, and release a shaky breath. 'Rare, but good.'

When I open my eyes again, he's watching me closely, like he's afraid I might break. I dip my finger into the frosting and lick it off.

He restrains a grin. 'How is it?'

I lick some frosting off my lip. 'Really, really good.'

A woman of about twenty-five or so, with curly blonde hair and sharp cheekbones, sits down in the seat next to Micha. She ogles him as she tucks her bag underneath her seat and shuts her phone off.

I lean forward and Micha winces, startled.

'You have an admirer.'

He glances over his shoulder and when he looks back at me, his face is lit with entertainment. 'Just one of my many.'

I lick a mouthful of frosting off the top of the cupcake, laughing, and he watches me intently, dragging his lip ring between his teeth.

'You know what I love?' he asks and I expect something dirty to come out of his mouth. 'How big your eyes are.' He puts a finger to the corner of my eye, touching it delicately. 'They're beautiful.'

The woman rolls her eyes as she buckles her seat-belt and grabs a magazine from the pocket on the back of the seat in front of her.

'You know what I love?' I ask, and he shakes his head. 'When you're lying naked in my bed.'

She pulls a disgusted face as she flips through the pages and Micha's forehead furrows.

Cupping my hand around my mouth, I put my lips near his ear. 'She's listening to our conversation and getting annoyed, so I thought I'd have fun with her.'

An evil smile expands across his face. 'You know what I love? Your naked body underneath mine, all hot and sweaty.'

She huffs exasperatedly and turns her back

toward us to face the aisle.

Grinning, I bite into the cupcake. 'That was fun.'

'That *was* fun,' he agrees and turns off his phone.

The plane begins to roll backward and it takes forever, but finally we're rushing into the sky. I breathe in and out, tapping my fingers on my legs, not really sure why I'm all wound up, other than it seems like I'm putting a lot of trust in the pilot.

Micha's fingers wrap around my wrist and he kisses my racing pulse. 'Relax, everything's fine.'

I snuggle up to him and rest my head on his shoulder. He brings out his iPod and puts one earbud in his ear. Sweeping my hair to the side, he puts the other one in mine.

He scrolls through the playlists and seconds later 'Chalk Line' by Strike Anywhere flips on, the acoustic version, so it's softer. Leaning into me, he sings along with the lyrics and the sound of his angelic voice lulls me to sleep.

12

Micha

After the plane lands and we check into the absurdly fancy hotel my father booked, we decide to go sight-seeing. The sidewalks are packed and the traffic is practically at a standstill. It's midafternoon, but chilly and the buildings are so tall, hardly any sunlight hits their lower sections or the sidewalks.

Ella has on a hooded jacket and fingerless gloves, but she shivers from the cold as she sips on her coffee.

'Are you cold, baby?' I ask, pulling my hood over my head.

She nods with the coffee close to her lips. 'I think I might have gotten a little too used to the Vegas weather.'

I step up behind her and rub my hands up and down her arms a few times, building warmth from the friction. 'Imagine how bad it's going to be when we go back home for Christmas. Star Grove is like twice as cold as here.'

She drinks her coffee as I encircle my arms around her, maneuvering us through the crowd. 'I don't think I'm going anywhere for Christmas.'

I return to her side and capture her gaze. 'What do you mean you aren't going? You can't stay at the campus by yourself for three weeks.'

'I don't want to go back to an empty house, Micha,' she says. 'And I won't be by myself. Lila's not going home either.'

We stop at the crosswalk and wait with the crowd for the light to change as traffic zooms by.

'You can stay with me,' I offer. 'I would even give you my bed.'

She looks at me crossly. 'Just like how you got us two beds in the hotel room?'

'Hey, my dad booked that room,' I say as she picks some pieces of her hair out of her mouth. 'It's not my fault.'

'Yeah right?' She rolls her eyes. 'How convenient for you.'

'It'll be very convenient for me.' I am treading on thin ice. 'That way if I'm feeling really hot and bothered I can just get you to put your leg over me and you'll let me feel you again. You know, you're kind of naughty when you're in a dark room.'

She glances at an older guy with thin hair and glasses who is listening to our conversation with a big grin on his face. 'That's not what happened,' she says.

I target an intimidating gaze at the pervert and he quickly turns around. 'That's exactly what happened, pretty girl, and you know it.'

She gulps her coffee to obscure her mortified expression. 'I have no idea what you're talking about.'

Threading my fingers through hers, we walk across the street with the mob of people and stop on the other side to take a look around.

'Did you want to go anywhere special while we're here?' I ask. 'Central Park? We could go ice skating?'

Her head tips back as she shields her eyes and stares up at the Empire State Building stretching toward the sky. 'I want to go up there.'

My chest constricts as the memories of her on the bridge rush through me: her standing on the beam over the water, ready to throw away her precious life.

'Are you sure?' I check, releasing a slow breath. 'Because there's a ton of stuff we could do.'

Smiling, she yanks on my arm. 'Yes, now come on.'

I shove the memory out of my head the best I can and reluctantly allow her to lead me across the street, because I'd go anywhere with her, even if I don't want to.

Ella

We have to wait in line to get on the elevators, but it takes us up to the top fast and gives me a little bit of a head rush. When the doors open, we step out and my stomach rolls with my nerves. Tossing my empty coffee cup into the trashcan, I head for the lookout area, which is blocked off by bars.

Micha tags along with me, even though he doesn't want to be up here. It makes him edgy, so I entwine my fingers with his as I peer through the bars and down at the lively city below. It's getting dark and colorful lights sparkle for miles. That's when it crashes into me, like the wind has been knocked out of me, the same helplessness I felt on the plane.

Micha senses my uneasiness and his arms enclose around my waist. 'Take a slow breath and just relax and enjoy the scenery.' He smothers my neck with kisses until I settle back down.

'It's beautiful,' I whisper. 'Like really amazing.'

He sucks on the sensitive spot below my ear, before moving his mouth away. 'It is, isn't it?'

Shivering from the cold and his touch, I lean back against him and he rests his chin on top of my head. 'And it's real.'

Not many people would get what I mean, but he does and his arms constrict around me. People wander around us, but I remain still, discovering what it feels like to have a peaceful moment where my thoughts aren't bunched up in my head.

Somewhere along the line, I begin to cry, but do it noiselessly, hoping he won't notice.

His fingers seek my cheeks and wipe away the tears. 'Why are you crying, pretty girl?'

'It's nothing . . . It's just that this is so normal,' I admit, dabbing the tears with my fingertips. 'I'm sorry. I don't know why I'm being such a baby.'

He kisses my head and guides me closer. 'You're not being a baby. You're being real.'

Feeling some of the burden fall off my chest, I pull his arms around me even more, never wanting him to let me go.

★　★　★

He gives me a piggyback ride back to the hotel because my feet hurt from all the walking we did. I can't stop laughing the entire time, because people keep looking at us strangely, although some are envious.

When we enter the lobby of the hotel, the bellman, who is wearing a funny hat and a buttoned uniform, approaches us with a stern look on his narrow face. 'No roughhousing in the lobby.'

Micha's boots scuff against the white marble flooring. 'Absolutely. We'll save that for the bedroom,' he replies as he backs into the elevator with me on his back.

The bellman scowls as the doors glide shut with Micha giving him a little wave. I move to climb off his back, but he links his arms underneath my legs as he punches in the button to our floor and the elevator jerks upward.

When it reaches our floor, he holds me in place as he walks through the doors and down the long hallway to our room.

A middle-age couple walks by and the woman presses her hand to her heart. 'Oh look, Harold, newlyweds.'

It kills my mood, but Micha laughs as he slides the keycard into the slot and opens the door. He gently sets me down, but scoops me right back up into his arms. 'Gotta carry her over the threshold, right?' He winks at the woman and she smiles, smitten.

He carries me into the room and kicks the door closed. 'Welcome to the honeymoon suite, where only dirty things are allowed to happen.'

I swat his arm as he heads toward the bed. 'We are not newlyweds, so stop pretending.'

His eyes glint wickedly and then he tosses me onto the massive bed decorated with a white comforter and mints on the pillows. My body bounces when I hit the mattress and I flip onto my stomach, narrowing my eyes at him as he laughs hysterically.

'I'm going to make you pay for that,' I warn with a dark look. 'Really, really bad.'

He backs toward his bag that's on the sofa. 'I'm looking forward to that.'

I roll onto my back and drape my arm over my forehead as I stare up at the ceiling, feeling happy, and I desperately want to hold onto it. 'I bet you are.'

Seconds later, he bounds on top of me, bracing himself with his hands just in time so he doesn't quite smash my body. 'I know what we should do.'

'No way. Whatever's about to come out of your mouth, I don't want to hear it,' I say and he traps my arms above my head. 'You're in one of your moods.'

'What mood?'

'Where everything you say is going to include being naughty. You know, I've often wondered if you just saved it for me, or if you did this kind of stuff with the girls you hooked up with.'

His jaw tenses and he slants away from me, still gripping my wrists. 'You know I was never with anyone long enough to do anything with them really.'

Our happy mood is dying because of me

and I don't want it to end. 'Tell me what you wanted to do and don't hold back.'

His aqua eyes sparkle like the ocean in the sunlight. 'We should wrestle.'

I shake my head from side to side. 'No way. The last time I wrestled you you sat on me for, like, ten minutes, laughing your ass off because I couldn't get up.'

'First off, get your story straight. I was straddling you, not sitting on you,' he says. 'And second off, I only stayed on you for that long because every time you tried to get away your body would rub against me and I was getting turned on.'

'We were, like, fifteen,' I contend. 'You didn't see me like that yet.'

'I was *fifteen*,' he retorts. 'And you were a girl.'

I giggle at his goofy smile. 'All right, let's wrestle, but I'm not holding back.'

Sucking on his lip ring, he backs off the bed, slips off his shirt, and tosses it onto the floor. 'Neither am I.'

I drop my face into my hands, shaking my head, aware I'm about to walk into a mess, but Anna told me to be my own judge of situations. Right now, I'm having fun and don't want it to end, so I get to my feet and stand up on the mattress.

'Just don't break anything,' I warn,

pointing at the glass lamps all around the room and the portraits on the wall. 'And don't break me.'

He smiles darkly. 'Oh trust me, I've got big plans for you when I win.'

I start to head for the side of the bed, but he matches my move and blocks my path with his arms out to my side.

To throw him off, I skitter to the other side but then whirl and backtrack, shooting for the open gap as I leap onto the floor and hurry toward the sofa.

'This isn't supposed to be a game of tag.' He winds around the couch toward me and I dash to the other side. 'You have to at least try to pin me to the ground.'

I back toward the bathroom, debating whether or not to lock myself in there. 'As soon as I'm within arm's reach, I know I've lost.'

He stalks toward me, his lean arms flexing as he pops his knuckles. 'Come on, challenge me. You know you want to. That is unless you're too scared.'

He's intentionally trying to get under my skin and it's working. I search for a solution and smile when I find one. With trembling fingers, I grab the bottom of my shirt, raise it over my head, and shake my hair out.

He leisurely takes in my bare skin and black bra. 'Nice move.'

I inch toward him and he matches my steps so we meet in the center of the room. I extend my hand for him, with no other plan than to graze my fingers along his stomach muscles, but he seizes my wrist and crashes our bodies together.

He lifts me up and my legs secure around his hips as his long legs stride toward the bed.

'This isn't wrestling,' I say, throwing my head back, laughing.

His lips upturn to a conspiratorial grin as he brushes my hair out of my eyes. 'I'm not going to throw you down on the floor to do this.'

'Do what?' I ask as he falls down on the bed, landing on top of me.

'This.' With a sinister look in his eyes, he gathers my wrists in one hand, rendering me captive, while putting a leg on either side of me.

My body writhes. 'How do I tap out?'

He leans in closely and strands of his blond hair tickle my cheeks. 'You don't.' He grazes his finger along my rib cage and I jerk upward.

'Don't you dare,' I advise, squirming to get away 'I mean it. It's not funny and this time I'll get you back.'

His fingers move along my stomach, dithering, before he squeezes my side. My muscles tense as I squeal. 'Micha, please don't,' I beg, forcing back the laughter. 'I'll do anything you want, just don't tickle me.'

He moves his hand away, looking pleased. 'And that's how you win wrestling.'

I stare up at him with anger in my eyes, but my body is ecstatic with being concealed beneath his. 'That was a dirty move.'

'What can I say, I like to play dirty.' He pauses, with his eyes piercing into mine as his breathing speeds up. 'Ella . . . I'm not sure how far to push you. I know you said you needed time to get better, but you're lying under me and it feels so fucking good — all I want to do is touch you right now.'

My chest heaves as I imagine his hands all over me and my therapist's words echo in my head: *baby steps.* 'You can touch me if you want . . . But just take it slow.'

He waits for me to retract my statement, but I clench my lips shut with nervousness and anticipation. Purposely, his hand tracks up my side and toward my breast as he gazes into my eyes. When his hand arrives at the bottom of my bra, he stops to test my reaction. I lay motionless, craving for him to go further, and bow into him.

His aqua eyes blaze as his fingers slide underneath my bra while his mouth dips toward my neck. Sucking on my skin just below my ear, his hand massages my breast and his thumb brushes across my nipple. He doesn't try to take my bra off and instead of his hand going into my pants, he keeps it on the outside as he rubs me between my legs.

He's keeping a boundary, so he won't take it too far. I love him so much there are no words to describe it. I'm extremely lucky to have him. I make a promise to myself that I will work on giving him what he wants and try to make him happy.

Seconds later, a blissful moan escapes my lips as he momentarily takes my anxiety away.

13

Micha

The next day is the transplant thing and we meet up with my dad at the hospital. The room they put us in is small, with a curtain, a couple of chairs, and this odd-looking machine with a lot of wires. It smells like Lysol and the loudness of the hallway flows in from the open door.

I read up on the procedure before I came out to New York and it's not too complicated. The doctor will put a needle in my arm and run some of my blood through a machine before it returns to my veins.

My dad is doing something on his phone as the three of us sit there in silence. Ella is scraping her fingernail polish off, and I can't stop tapping my foot against the floor. Ella's got a hickey on her neck from where I sucked on her skin last night. She tried to cover it up with makeup, but it's still visible and I love that it is.

'Micha, could you knock that off?' my dad asks rudely as he eyes my foot. 'I have a headache.'

I stop jiggling my leg and Ella slides me a sidelong glance before staring coldly at my father.

'Would you mind getting off your phone?' she asks him, pulling at the ends of her sleeves. 'It's kind of rude since *he's* here to help *you*.'

God, I love when she gets this way. Even though it's rare, her spitfire attitude is beautiful. At least to me, but probably not so much for the people she's directing it at.

My dad scowls at her harshly as he pushes a button on his phone. 'Excuse me?'

'Yes, excuse you,' she counters. 'Instead of doing that, you should be sitting here thanking him, don't you think?'

I cover my mouth with my hand to hold back a smile and place my other hand over hers, sketching my finger along her wrist, thinking about what it felt like to touch her last night.

My father looks at me, hoping I'll intervene, but I shrug. 'You're on your own.'

The nurse enters before anyone can say anything else. She has a clipboard in her hand and her eyes skim the papers. Her hair is the same shade as Ella's but she is at least ten years older, with brown eyes and freckles. 'All right, is it Micha?'

I flash her a charismatic smile. 'Yeah, you

even pronounced it right, which doesn't happen very often.'

She smiles at me, a little frazzled as she sets the clipboard down on the counter. 'It's probably better if you two wait outside. It'll take a little while.'

Ella looks at me and I nod my head while my dad hurries out of the room like it's on fire.

Before she leaves, Ella kisses me on the cheek. 'I'll be right outside if you need me.'

She's been acting weird since last night, more affectionate, which I don't mind, but it's puzzling.

Once the room is cleared out, the nurse prepares the machine and puts a needle in my arm. I barely notice the sting. My thoughts are with Ella and what she's saying to my dad.

Ella

As soon as I lay eyes on Micha's dad, it's clear he's an arrogant asshole. He's wearing a suit and carrying a brief-case, like he needs to prove he has somewhere important to be. Micha hasn't really talked to me much about what goes on between them, but it's obvious that it's been bad.

After the nurse asks us to leave, I sit in the waiting area and Micha's dad seats himself across from me. It's loud, with screaming children and people coughing.

'You're that little girl who lived next door, aren't you?' Micha's dad asks with a disdainful tone. He looks like Micha, with aqua eyes and attractive facial features, only older. 'The one who had the family with all the problems.'

He hits me in my weak spot and it takes a lot of mental preparation before I retaliate. 'Aren't you the asshole who walked out on his family?'

The old lady beside me turns her head in our direction, shunning me with a look for my foul language.

Micha's dad leans forward in his seat, buttoning up the cuff of one of his sleeves. 'I'd like to know why you think you can talk to me this way. You don't know me.'

'But I do know you.' I cross my legs and rest my arms on my lap. 'You're the man who walked out on the greatest person you'll never know. And you know what, I'm kind of glad you did, otherwise Micha might have turned into a dick like you.'

Micha's dad looks at me like he wants to slap me and the old lady narrows her eyes at me, about to say something, but I leave the room before she gets an opportunity.

I wander around the hospital halls and pass the nurse's desk, deciding to steal a lollipop from out of the bin to give to Micha as a joke. The hospital is a sad place, full of crying and screaming people and beeping machines. It's like everyone is waiting around for someone to die and it puts an unnerving feeling in the air. It brings me back to the day my mother died and we went to the hospital with her, even though she was pronounced dead on arrival. I didn't cry, but my dad and Dean did, hugging each other while I stood near the end of the hall, watching the nurses and doctors walk by.

I felt out of place, like I shouldn't have been there. Finally I ended up leaving and walked all the way home, curled up in my bed, and stared at the ceiling until the sun rose, knowing my life would never be the same.

When I reach the psychiatry services area, it feels like an invisible hand winds around my neck and strangles me. I back away from it quickly, bumping into a nurse wearing blue scrubs.

'What are you doing?' She glances over my shoulder at the shut door. 'You shouldn't be back here.'

I inch away from her. 'Nothing. I was just

looking for the restroom.'

I collect my thoughts about how I might end up in a place like this and I return to the front desk area. Micha is waiting for me in one of the chairs, flipping through a magazine. His skin is pale and his blond hair sticks to his forehead. He has on a Rise Against T-shirt and black jeans and the leather bands that were on his wrist are replaced by a bandage.

Hiding the lollipop in my hand behind my back, I approach him. 'You made it out alive.'

He looks up at me and smiles tiredly. 'Of course I did, but where did you wander off to?'

'Nowhere really.' I sit down in the chair beside him and he tosses the magazine onto the table. 'I wanted to get away from your father.'

He searches my face. 'What did you say to him? Because he came back to the room all pissed off.'

I give a one-shouldered shrug. 'Nothing but the truth.'

Grinning, he stretches his legs out in front of himself and raises his arms above his head. 'If it's okay with you I'd like to go back to the hotel room and sleep. That took a lot out of me.'

'Don't you want to wait for your dad to get out?'

'Nah, not really.' He drops his hands to his lap. 'What are you hiding behind your back?'

My mouth curves into a grin as I extend my hand out to him with the red lollipop in my palm. 'This is for being a very brave boy.'

He laughs softly and takes the lollipop. 'God, I love you.'

I get to my feet and help him to his. His movements are lethargic as we head toward the sliding-glass doors. He peels the wrapper off the lollipop and puts it in his mouth. 'As much as I love your gift, there are a ton more ways you could make me feel better when we get back to the room.'

I laugh under my breath, not protesting, because at that moment I'd do anything for him.

14

Micha

The leaves have fallen from the trees and the air has cooled, but it's nothing compared to Star Grove. It's almost time to go home for Christmas break, and Christmas seems to be everywhere. Ella is still being stubborn about it. I try multiple times to convince her to go with me, but every time she declines politely.

Two nights before Ethan and I are supposed to leave just happens to be my first gig at The Hook Up. It's Friday night and every table and booth is full. People crowd the bar, yelling out orders to the bartender, a midtwenties woman with bright tattoos on her arms and dreadlocks and a piercing in her nose. There are red and green lights strung up along the ceiling and a Christmas tree centerpiece on each table.

It's been a while since I played by myself and there's unnatural nervous energy pouring through my blood. From the back doorway, my eyes scan the room, taking in the noisy people.

Someone pinches my ass from behind and

I spin around. 'What the fuck?'

Ella smiles brightly at me. 'You're nervous.'

My eyes stroll lazily down her body. Her hair is done up in this messy twist with bits and pieces framing her face, her full lips shine in the light, and she's got this short, green, thin-strapped shirt on and a pair of skin-tight jeans that hug every inch of her curves. 'Get real, pretty girl. You know I never get nervous.'

'You look nervous,' she repeats, dragging her bottom lip between her teeth.

I trace my finger across her red lips. 'You look a little nervous yourself.'

She nips playfully at my finger, startling me and turning me on. 'I'm only nervous for you.'

Ever since we left New York, our relationship has been on a strict friends basis. She seemed to close the door when we returned to our real lives so I backed off, even though I didn't want to.

'Did you come back here just to psych me out?' I joke to cover up the sexual tension. I rake my hands through my hair and glance over my shoulder at the people pouring in through the front door. 'Because that is very mean of you.'

She throws her arms around my neck and bites at my earlobe. 'I'm feeling very mean tonight.'

Gently pushing her back by the shoulder, I notice her eyes are glossy and dilated. 'Are you drunk?'

She bobs her head up and down, looking cute as hell. 'I had a rough night so Lila gave me some shots of Bacardi.'

'Lila gave you Bacardi?' I question with a doubtful arch of my eyebrow. 'She doesn't seem like the Bacardi type.'

'Well . . . Ethan gave it to her.' She teeters to the side, falling toward the floor, and my arm snakes around her waist.

I help her recompose her balance and keep a hand on her side. 'Are you going to be okay?'

'I'll be fine . . . ' Her eyes drift to the middle of the room where people are dancing beneath the bright lights. 'We should dance.'

Suppressing a laugh, I scoot us to the side when a group of rough-looking guys walks by. I turn her back to the wall and she leans against it while I brace a hand possessively beside her head. 'Ella May, I have to play in, like, five minutes. I can't dance right now.'

She pouts out her bottom lip, sulking and batting her eyelashes. 'Pretty please.'

'Ella . . . ' I start through a laugh and then my shoulders jerk upward as one of her hands rubs up the front of my jeans over my hard cock. I snag her hand before she can stick it down the front of my jeans. 'Baby, I think you might be a little drunk, so take it easy, okay?'

Her free hand begins to seek the same area when Ethan and Lila appear in the doorway. Ethan's carrying a beer in his hand and Lila has a phone up to her ear, talking really loudly over the noisy room behind us.

'So she found you,' Ethan calls out with a smirk. 'Thank God. She wouldn't shut up about you.'

Ella burrows her face into my chest. 'I'm tired.'

'How much did you let her drink?' I ask Ethan, annoyed. 'Too much, obviously.'

Ethan shakes his head and tips his head back to take a swing of his beer. 'She chose to drink. I left them out in the living room for, like, fifteen minutes while I was taking a shower, getting ready for this little shindig. When I came out, there was a half a bottle of our Bacardi missing and these two were in the kitchen drunk off their asses.'

Lila stumbles in her heels and supports herself with a hand against the wall. 'Well, I don't really give a shit what you do,' she says into the phone. 'I don't want you coming over.'

A big grin rises across Ethan's red-tinted face as he points at Lila. 'She's breaking up with some dude over the phone. It's fucking hilarious.'

'Are you drunk?' I accuse, stumbling backward as Ella puts all her weight against me.

Ethan nods his head. 'Maybe a little.'

I smooth Ella's hair away from her face. 'Who drove?'

'We took a taxi.' Ethan gulps down his beer and sets the empty bottle down near the wall with many discarded bottles and glasses. 'I'm not stupid enough to drive drunk.'

Ella cups her hand around my ear and whispers, 'But he didn't pay the cab driver. He made us jump out and run.'

I sigh and put my arm around her lower back. 'Let's go get you three seated, so I can focus on what I need to do.'

I choose a booth in the far corner and ask the waitress who showed me where everything was to keep an eye on them and not serve them any more alcohol. They're trashed — beyond trashed and it's only going to lead to trouble.

Ella rests her head on the table with a sad, puppy-dog look on her face and I brush her hair away from her sweaty forehead.

I crouch down beside her and ask in a low voice, 'Did something happen tonight that upset you?'

She shakes her head and turns her face away from me. 'Nothing happened. I just want to go home and go to bed.'

She's lying, but I can't pick her brain right now. Even though it nearly kills me, I leave the table and head for the backstage area to collect my guitar. When I step out onstage and into the light, the room quiets down a little, but it's still not the best scenario. The place is a real shit-hole, and for once I'd just like to play somewhere where people aren't wasted.

I strum a chord, put my lips up to the microphone, and pour my heart out to a roomful of strangers who aren't listening.

★   ★   ★

After the performance some big, bald dude corners me backstage in the hallway and hands me a card with his name and phone number on it.

'Hey, that was an awesome performance.' He's got a scar running down half of his arm and a gold chain around his neck.

'Thanks,' I mumble, reading the card. 'Mike Anderly.'

'And you are . . . ' He waits for me to tell him.

'Micha,' I say, excluding my last name on purpose.

'Look, I'm gonna get straight to the point.'

He talks with his hands out in front of him. 'I'm a music producer. I work for a pretty small but good, honest company out in San Diego. I like your sound and I'd love to talk to you about what your future plans are in the music business.'

I stare at the card. 'My future plans?'

He nods. 'Yeah, with your music.'

I pick up my guitar case. 'Yeah, I'm not sure what my plans are.'

'Well, when you do decide, give me a call,' he says and turns for the main room. 'Like I said, I'm really interested in your sound.' He walks away and I figure he's probably just some weirdo.

But what if he's not? What if it's some random act of luck? I may not have said I know what I want to do with my music, but I do. I want to play in a place that isn't shitty, where people listen and understand. I want to be a musician.

★ ★ ★

I feel like a parent, getting the three of them home, and by the time we're stumbling into my apartment, I'm ready for all of them to pass out. I pick up Ella and carry her back to my bed because she can barely walk.

'Keep your dick in your pants,' I advise

Ethan as he ambles into the kitchen with his arm around a very intoxicated Lila. 'And don't drink anymore.'

He waves me off and Lila giggles as she opens the fridge, knocking over bottles. I descend down the hall and back to my room with Ella in my arms. Her breathing is soft and she keeps murmuring something about wanting it all to go away. It's scaring the shit out of me.

Without putting her down, I kick my boots off into the corner with the rest of my shoes and carefully lay her down on my bed. The lights in my room are off, but the moonlight gleams through the window and onto her face, her plump lips, her beautiful, flawless pale skin.

She snuggles into my pillow and murmurs, 'I'm sorry.'

I pull the blankets over her. 'For what, baby?'

She sighs, disheartened. 'For ruining your first performance.'

'You didn't ruin my performance, pretty girl.' With a small smile on my face, I kiss her cheek. 'I love you. Now go to sleep.'

By the time I get my shirt off, she's passed out. I take a quick shower, washing the icky feeling of the night away. I'm not thrilled to have to play in places where people barely listen. I want more, and even though the guy was sketchy, I wonder if maybe he could be legitimate.

When I return to the bedroom with a towel wrapped around my waist, Ella is sitting up on the bed and the lamp is on. She has a musing look on her face, like she's about to start some trouble.

'You're supposed to be asleep,' I tell her, tossing my dirty clothes into the hamper and grabbing some clean pants from the top dresser drawer. It's clear she's checking me out, which would be great, except she's drunk and I can't do anything with her without feeling bad.

'I'm bored.' Her speech is slightly slurred and her eyes are red. 'Can we do something?'

I climb into bed and sit down next to her. 'I think we should go to sleep. It's late.'

'Ethan and Lila are still awake.' She retrieves a bottle of Jack that was hidden behind her back, twists off the cap, and flicks it to the foot of the bed. 'They're playing strip poker.'

My eyes enlarge. 'Right now?'

She bobs her head up and down. 'They've already both taken off their shirts.'

'Were you just out there?'

'Yeah, where do you think I got this?' She shakes the bottle in front of my face and my hand darts out to steal it away, but she jerks her hand back, laughing. 'Uh-huh. No way, Micha Scott. Not until you play with me.' She kneels up in front of me and swings her leg over my lap, tipping her head back to take a gulp. She gags, before her face turns serious. 'You remember that time . . . that night my mom died?'

My body constricts. 'How could I forget that night?'

There's a mischievous look in her green eyes, and I wonder where the fuck this conversation is heading. 'You remember how you kissed me before climbing down that tree?'

I nod, wrapping my fingers around her waist. 'Of course I remember, but I'm surprised you do.' Because she was just about as drunk that night as she is now.

She licks her lips seductively. 'It was a nice kiss, wasn't it?'

I remove the bottle from her hands and force down a big swig, knowing I'm going to need it. I've never seen this side of her and even though she's drunk, I am really fucking curious what lies ahead. 'It was a very nice kiss.'

She leans forward and places her hands on my shoulders. 'We should do it again.'

An internal struggle develops inside me

over what's right and what's wrong and she softly presses her lips to mine. She rarely kisses me first and it's a nice change, to know I'm wanted.

'You're so sexy.' Her finger draws along my stomach muscles and my breath hitches. 'I used to secretly stare at you all the time when you would work on cars with your shirt off.'

I try not to laugh at the secret she's divulged and playfully trail kisses down her jawline to distract her from her confession. 'How about we go see what Lila and Ethan are up to.'

Giggling, she leaps off the bed and knocks the lamp over. Not bothering to pick it up, she backs toward the hall. 'If you want me in bed, you're going to have to come get me first.' She takes off running.

I slip on a pair of jeans and a shirt, grab the bottle of Jack, and go out into the kitchen where Ethan and Lila are sitting at the table with their shirts off and cards out in front of them. Ella slumped over the fridge door, digging noisily through the beers.

Ethan drops the cards down on the kitchen table and surrenders his hands. 'Lila talked me into it.'

Lila gazes up at me with little recognition. 'It's true. I did.'

I drop down in the seat between them and

take a shot. 'All right, I'm giving up on trying to stop this regrettable night.' I collect the cards and shuffle them. 'So don't come crying to me when you're all naked and cold.'

Ella

I didn't plan on drinking this much, and I feel guilty for dragging Micha and everyone else into my mess. But I wanted to forget for two goddamn seconds that my father is going home for Christmas and invited Dean and Caroline back to the house for the weekend, but not me. I had to hear what was going on when Dean called and asked me where the keys to the Cutlass were because he was planning on fixing it up and selling it or some shit — I hung up on him before I heard the full story.

Then the letter arrived from my dad. The freaking letter that I just couldn't open, because it felt like whatever was in it could potentially crush my world into a billion pieces.

By the time we showed up at Micha and Ethan's house, I was verging on a panic attack and I'd forgotten to take my medication that morning.

When Ethan had gone to take a shower,

Lila pulled out a bottle of Bacardi and ordered me to spill my guts over a few drinks. A few turned into a very long blurry line and suddenly it's several hours later. I have cards in my hand, a beer up to my lips, and a very intense game of strip Texas Hold'em going on. My shirt's on the floor, along with my socks and boots.

Ethan and Lila left the house to go make a beer run. Micha made them give him the keys to the truck so he knew they would walk instead of trying to drive. Micha and I keep the game going, both of us determined to win. My drunken state has simmered down since I switched to beer, but my ability to make good choices is hindered.

Micha sits across the table from me, mulling over his cards. 'I think I'll raise you your bra.'

I shake my head with my eyes narrowed at him. 'No way. Only one article of clothing per hand.'

He flicks his lip ring with his tongue, trying to seduce me and play dirty. 'And who made up those rules?'

'I did.' I circle my finger above my head. 'See this invisible crown right here. That means I'm the Queen of Poker and therefore I get to make up any rule whenever I want.'

An off-pitch laugh bursts from his lips.

'That motion you made is for a halo, not a crown, and an angel is something you're not.'

My jaw drops and I throw a chip at him, hitting him in the chest. 'I am so an angel.'

'Ow.' He rubs his nipple where the chip scraped. 'That was vicious.'

I nip my teeth at the air and then laugh, taking a drink of my beer. 'Now back to the game. What do you have?'

He taps his fingers on the table, eyeing his cards and then targets an inside-melting gaze on me. 'I want to up the bet,' he says, and when I start to gripe, he adds, 'If you win you get my signed Silverstein shirt, but if I win you have to get naked.'

My heart thumps deafeningly in my chest. 'I thought you said you'd never give me that shirt — that it was your pride and joy for getting it signed.'

He gives a blasé shrug. 'I'm making an exception right now.'

I measure the pair of queens in my hand and the one laid down on the table, but there is also a pair of aces dealt. Shit. 'I don't know . . .'

'Come on, Ella May,' he says, wiggling his eye-brows up and down. 'Loosen up.'

From over my cards, I glare at him. 'I'll tell you what. If you lose you give me the shirt, but if I lose I'll take off my bra and jeans, but the panties are staying on.'

Micha chuckles and takes a shot. 'That's not very fun.'

I roll my eyes. 'I've seen you play poker with girls like this before and you never offer up anything this rewarding unless you have a good hand and know you'll win.'

'And I've seen you play enough times that I know you won't back down from a good challenge,' he retaliates, slamming the bottle onto the table. 'So come, pretty girl, are you in or out?'

I consider it, but not for very long, and lay my cards down on the table. 'I'm in. Now what do you have?'

A soon as his lips turn upward, I know how it ends. He slaps his cards down on the table. 'Get naked, Ella May.'

'You had the fucking ace.' I smack some of the cards off the table and they float to the floor. 'I knew you had it.'

He continues to grin. 'And yet you kept playing. Now get naked.'

I stare inanely at him. 'That wasn't fair. You tricked me.'

His eyes hold mine powerfully as he pats his hands on the table. 'That was a totally fair hand and you know it, so stop being a baby and hand over your losings.'

Staring him down, I come to the

conclusion that there's no point in fighting. Keeping my eyes on him, I get to my feet and carry my chin high.

He raises a finger as he shoves the chair away from the table. 'Just a second.' He saunters into the living room and disappears out of my sight.

Confused, I start to head for the doorway to find out what he's doing, but as soon as my foot inches forward, the stereo clicks on and I stop as 'Closer' by Nine Inch Nails clicks on.

'You have got to be kidding me,' I mumble as Micha struts into the kitchen with a pleased grin on his face as he rubs his hands together. 'No way. Music was not part of the deal.'

He braces his hands on the door frame and the light highlights the muscles on his chest and the shameless blaze in his aqua eyes. 'Now, most guys would have gone with some sexy song you had to dance to, but I'm a lyrical man myself and I think this song fits perfectly.'

The lyrics make my cheeks heat. 'In no way, shape, or form did I offer up a striptease.'

His tongue slips slowly out of his mouth and when he pulls it back in, he draws his lip ring with it as his fingers comb through his disheveled hair, leaving strands sticking up.

'Pay up, pretty girl.'

Pressing my lips firmly together to bury my nerves, I reach around to the back of my bra and unclasp it. Wavering temporarily, I inhale an insecure breath, release the fabric from my fingers, and allow it to fall to the floor.

His eyes drift to my chest, unashamed, as he sips a beer. When he pulls the bottle away from his lips, he makes a motion with his finger. 'Continue.'

I want to smack him upside the head, but I unbutton my jeans. With my knees shaking, I step out of my pants and stand vulnerable in the spotlight, something I despise. Thankfully, I'm wearing boy-cut panties so at least my ass is covered. His eyes lazily move up my long legs, across my bare stomach, finally resting on my eyes.

'You can sit down now,' he says like he's the boss.

Proving a point, I walk across the kitchen and steal a beer from the fridge. 'I don't have to sit down just because you tell me to — '

Warm fingers grip my side and reel me around, snatching the beer from my hand as my back presses against the fridge door. Micha stands only a sliver of space away from me, eyes fierce, lips tantalizing, his expression yearning with need.

He leans in to kiss me, but my hand pushes

at his chest, and his bare skin is warm as I hold him back. 'No way. You didn't win anything but a show.'

Lowering my head, I duck under his arm, but he snags my wrist and pins it above my head kind of roughly. We're drunk and neither of us is thinking rationally, but my interest in what's coming renders me motionless.

His pupils are so large only a ring of aqua is left. His breath is hot against my cheek as he takes my other arm and confines it above my head so my body is exposed to him. It seems like I should be nervous, but excitement bubbles through my very starved body.

He inclines toward me and his chest brushes my tingling nipples. 'Do you want me to stop?' His voice is husky.

I shake my head with honesty. 'No.'

The thumb of his free hand travels down my side and along each rib before settling on my hipbone. Wetting his lips with his tongue, he moves his mouth toward my breast and my eyes close as he takes my nipple in his mouth.

'Oh my God,' I moan as ecstasy shoots up between my legs and coils through my stomach as my back curves into him. 'Micha . . . '

He releases my arms, and before an objection departs my lips, he picks me up and smashes his lips into mine. I vice-grip my legs around his hips and my lips open willingly, allowing his tongue to enter my mouth for a heart-stopping kiss. Backing toward the sofa blindly, his hands feel all over my skin, leaving a trail of heat everywhere.

'Not on the couch,' I murmur. 'Lila and Ethan could be back at any moment.'

He gives a glance at the front door and then turns us in the direction of the hallway. His fingers sneak up the bottom of my panties and cup my ass as he kicks his bedroom door open hard with his foot and the doorknob bangs into the wall. Without our lips parting, we fall onto the mattress with a bounce. Giggling, my fingers slide down his hard chest and to the button of his jeans, but he halts my hand with his.

'Ella, maybe we shouldn't,' he says, blinking dazedly through the alcohol.

I manage to slip my other hand down the front of his jeans and his breath falters. 'You don't want me?' I ask.

Sucking a sharp breath through his nose, his head slumps forward as I rub him and drive him crazy. 'Trust me, that's not it. I think we . . . '

I hit the right spot and all his thoughts drift away. His lips pursue mine again and he kisses me freely as his hand slides down my stomach and to the edge of my panties.

Hooking his finger into the top, he yanks them down my legs and when they reach my feet, I kick them off.

Instead of his lips returning to my mouth, they endeavor to my stomach just above my belly button. Smoothing kisses down my skin, his warm tongue licks a path all the way down and my legs open up so his tongue can slip inside me and my mind becomes even foggier.

$$\star \quad \star \quad \star$$

When my eyes open, sunlight filters into the room and my head is pounding. A blanket is bunched up over me and my pores feel icky. Wiping the sweat from my cheek, I sit up and glance down at the signed Silverstein T-shirt covering my body.

A smile breaks through as I spot a folded-up piece of paper on the pillow beside me and pick it up. Micha's handwriting is scribbled across the lines in red ink.

Hey beautiful,
So that was quite the drunken night . . . never done one of those with you before. I think I might have a new song to add to our list.
Anyway, don't get all worked up. I stopped it before it got too far, in case you

can't remember. I didn't want you to have to suffer through a drunken mistake. Trust me, I'm an expert at them and they're not fun.

I hate to bail on you, but I got to go to work. I'll stop by your place later. And you can keep the shirt. It looks better on you anyway.

Love you more than life itself, more than the sun and the air.

You own my soul, Ella May.

Micha

Still smiling, I climb out of bed and slip my jeans on. Leave it to Micha to sign a letter like that. He's always had such a poetic way with words and his beauty shines with each letter.

Grabbing my shirt off the floor, I depart for the front door, folding up the note carefully and tucking it safely into the back pocket of my jeans. I feel light, even though I'm hungover. I don't regret what happened, although it would have been nice if we were sober. The feeling is strange, but maybe that means I'm getting better at dealing with life.

The living room is trashed, beer bottles all over the floor and coffee table, and there's an empty Bacardi bottle on the table, along with scattered poker cards. Getting a garbage bag from the kitchen drawer, I rack my brain for where my phone and purse are. I remember being at the club, Micha playing on stage, and then coming here and his hands all over me. My eyelids drift shut as I remember every moment of it.

'Only One' by Yellowcard begins playing from somewhere in the room and my eyes snap open. With my ears perked up, I follow the sound, which guides me to the couch. Under a frayed throw pillow is my phone. My eyebrows scrunch as I scoop it up, not recognizing the ringtone. When I glance at the screen, however, it makes sense.

I answer the phone. 'Did you change my ringtone for you?'

His laughter fills the other end of the line. 'It seemed fitting this morning.'

'It seems like you're trying to send me a message through your notes and your song choice.' I collect a bottle from off the top of the television and drop it into the bag. 'You know I'm not mad about last night, right? I was sober enough that I can remember stuff . . . You don't have to feel guilty.'

'I don't feel guilty,' he assures me over banging in the background. 'I'm glad last night happened. The note and the song were my way of sending you a message.'

Bending down, I pick up an empty beer

carton and toss it into the bag, then tie it shut and drop it outside the front door, leaving the door open to grab my purse, which is near the television. 'What message?'

'That's for you to figure out.'

'And what if I can't figure it out?'

'You will,' he responds. 'But whether or not you say it out loud is a whole other story.'

He's right. I already have it figured out, but saying it out loud is something I can't quite do.

'You're being very cryptic.' Stepping outside into the warm sunshine, I shut the front door and drag the garbage bag down the stairs with the bottles clinking together. At the bottom, my eyes scan the parking lot. 'How am I supposed to get home?'

'You could stay there until I get home,' Micha offers. 'Or better yet, you could just move in.'

My lungs compress, reducing the flow of oxygen as his heavy words crumble my mood. 'I have to get home. I have a class tonight.'

'Since when do you have class at night?' he questions. 'Are you just saying that because of my little moving-in remark?'

I don't bother picking up the bag as I trudge toward the Dumpster and heave it inside. 'No, I really have class,' I lie. 'I'll call you a little bit later, okay? I need to find a ride home.'

'All right.' His tone is clipped. 'I'll talk to you later, I guess.'

He hangs up before I can and it leaves me feeling hollow, like a part of me has been removed. Shaking the sensation away, I punch Lila's number into the keypad.

'Well, look who decided to finally wake up,' she answers with humor radiating from her voice. 'Did you do the walk of shame?'

'Micha and I didn't have sex, Lila,' I respond in a snippy voice and then, feeling terrible, apologize. 'I'm sorry. I'm just hungover or something. And I need to get home and lay down, but I don't have a ride.'

'You could take the bus.' She pops a bubble into the phone. 'Although I wouldn't recommend it.'

'How did you get home?' I press my fingertips to the brim of my nose as my headache from hell surges.

'Ethan gave me a ride.' A door slams and I hear keys hit the counter. 'I was actually just out to lunch with Parker.'

'I thought you were done with him.'

'Hey, he insisted.'

I start toward the exit that is situated near a brick wall. 'All right, I'll track down a bus.'

'Good luck with that. And watch out for the licker,' she jokes with an evil laugh. 'Keep your elbows tucked in and stay away from the back of the bus.'

'Ha-ha, you're a freaking riot,' I say

derisively. 'Talk to you later.'

I drag my exhausted legs toward the Starbucks at the corner of the street. After I have some caffeine in my system, my brain turns back on. But by the time I reach the apartment and recollect what made me drink that much in the first place, all I want to do is go to my room, turn the lights off, and sleep for an eternity. The letter from my dad still lies on the coffee table, unopened.

'Are you ever going to open that?' Lila appears in the doorway, dressed in a blue dress and heels that match. Her blonde hair is curled around her face and pinned by a few diamond barrettes.

Slipping off my sandals, I drop down on the couch and stare at the white envelope addressed to me. 'I haven't decided yet.'

Clipping an earring in, she sits down beside me on the couch. 'Ella, can I ask you something?'

I shrug and cross my feet up on the table. 'I guess.'

She picks up the letter and flips it over to the back. 'What are you so afraid of? With this letter? With Micha? With life?'

'Feeling it all — losing it all,' I say and her face twists. 'It's nothing. I'm just not sure what my dad is going to say and it kind of worries me.'

Lila doesn't know about what happened with my mother. She knows she passed away, but not the circumstances leading to her death. Only my dad, Dean, and Micha know that haunting secret and I plan on keeping it that way.

I tear the envelope, taking a deep breath, and unfold the paper, telling myself that I can handle whatever's in there. That I'm stronger than I used to be.

Ella May,

I want to start off by saying I'm sorry for everything. And I mean that. I've been sober for almost a month now and they took me off the meds. My head's clear and I don't like what's in it, especially everything related to you.

My therapist had me write down everything I regretted in therapy yesterday and it all seemed to be about you. It was like we all piled our garbage on you to clean up and it never should have been that way. The more I wrote, the more I realized you never really had a childhood. All those times I spent at the bar, I was being nothing but selfish. I'm a terrible father who put everything on his daughter, for no other reason than I didn't want to be an adult.

That night was not your fault. You were seventeen and I was the adult. I should have been home with her, but Jack Daniels was much more important and easier to deal with.

I knew how bad she was, more than you'll ever understand, and deep down I knew I was wrong when I left you in charge that night. Now that my head is clear, I can imagine how hard it must be for you to deal with. All the pain you have to be feeling. I keep thinking about the pain in your eyes the last time I saw you and it eats away at me.

I'm sorry, Ella. For ruining you childhood, for taking away your happiness, and just for messing up your fucking future.

I love you.
Dad

'What the fuck am I supposed to do with this?' My hands shake as I clutch the letter in my hand. Tears pour out of my eyes as I force my lungs to breathe in and out as a wall around me crashes to the ground.

15

Micha

I don't know why I got so pissed off at Ella this morning on the phone, other than sometimes things between us feel hopeless. I love her and I know she loves me, but sometimes I don't think she does as much. It hurts when I analyze it.

That night, I pack and go to bed early, feeling down that Ella isn't coming with me. We've spent the holidays together every single year since we were five. It was the only way to celebrate, since her family was never really into it and my mom couldn't afford to do much. She tried though, by decorating the house and making Ella and me a nice breakfast. She'd always wrap a few presents up for the both of us. It wasn't much, but it was still nice.

Long after I fall asleep, my phone wakes me up. My hand fumbles across my nightstand, knocking over the lamp, until it finally brushes my phone. Still half alive, I blink my eyes into focus and see Ella's names on the screen.

I answer it quickly. 'What's wrong?'

She sounds hoarse. 'Can you come let me in? I didn't want to ring the doorbell and wake Ethan up.'

'You're at my house?' I rub my eyes and check the time on the clock.

'Yeah, I'm standing in front of the door.'

I stumble out of bed and hurry to the door in my boxers, with the phone still held up to my ear. Flipping the porch light on, I swing open the door. The light hits her swollen eyes and the red streaks on her cheeks from the dried-up tears. She's wearing a pair of striped shorts, with flip-flops on her feet, and her hair is pulled up in a messy bun. She has no bra on under the thin tank top she's wearing and I can see her nipples through the fabric.

'What are you doing?' I haul her inside the house to hide her barely covered body away from the eyes of anyone else. Her skin is ice cold and she's shivering. 'Did you walk here?'

She shakes her head and hugs her arms around herself. 'No, I took the bus.'

My gaze skims her bare legs and her perky nipples. 'Dressed like that?'

She shrugs and sinks down into the couch, grasping an envelope in her hand. 'There was hardly anyone on it.'

Turning the lamp on, I sit down on the couch and put my arm around her shoulder, desperate to make her feel better. 'What happened? And what's that in your hand?'

She gives me the crinkled envelope with her name and address on it. 'This came in the mail yesterday.'

I turn it over, noting that she's opened and read whatever is inside. 'Who's it from?'

She taps the return address with her finger. 'It's from my dad.'

Shit. 'What did he say?'

She stares at the floor, her eyes enlarged. 'That he was sorry and that what happened to my mom wasn't my fault. That it was his because he was the adult and he never should have left that kind of responsibility on a child. That he should have been home taking care of his family instead of at the bar . . . and that he loves me.' Tears flood her eyes and stream down her cheeks as her breathing becomes erratic. 'I've wanted him to say that forever.'

The ache in her voice almost makes me cry. She climbs onto my lap and buries her face into my chest, sobbing as she clutches desperately onto me. I scoop her up in my arms and carry her back to my bedroom where I lie down with her.

With each tear shed, she steals more of my heart, until she owns it completely. I realize that even through the hard times I'm sure we'll face, I'll never be able to walk away from her.

I wake up with Ella's head pressed into the crook of my neck and her arms clasped firmly around my waist, as if she feared I'd sneak off in the middle of the night.

She bawled her eyes out until she passed out and my heart nearly broke in two. Even though it makes me feel horrible, I sometimes hate her fucking family. They took a beautiful girl who was full of life and who could have done amazing things and crushed her into pieces. Although she's fixable — I can see that now — she is still so broken and vulnerable.

'Rise and shine. We gotta hit the road.' Ethan bangs the door open, and when he takes in the situation, his face drops. 'You are still going, aren't you?'

I nod as Ella snuggles closer to me. 'Yeah, give me like fifteen minutes or so.'

'Whatever, man. Just hurry your ass up.' He walks away, leaving the door wide open.

'Baby, are you awake?' I whisper in her ear and kiss the sensitive spot on her neck.

Her shoulder shivers upward as she nods her head with her eyes closed. 'How could I sleep through Mr. Loud Mouth?'

I nibble at the tip of her earlobe and breathe in the scent of her hair. 'I have to get ready to go . . . Are you sure you don't want

242

to come with us? I really want you to.'

Her leg hitches around my hip and her body bows into me. 'I think I — I want to come with you guys, but I have to go back to my place and pack a bag real quick. And I have to stop by and do a quick visit with my therapist. We have to see if Lila will go with us too. I don't want her here alone.'

My body stiffens from her intimate touch. 'All right, but you know Ethan's gonna complain the entire time.'

She rolls on top of me, props herself up on her elbows, and peers down at me through her puffy eyes. 'I know, but he'll just have to deal with being a few hours late to wherever it is he thinks he has to be.'

Knotting my fingers through her hair, I tug at the roots and bring her face close to mine, loving how her eyes roll back. 'Are you sure you're okay? Last night you had me worried.'

'I'm fine, Micha.' She kisses my lips softly. 'Last night was a good thing, even though it was intense . . . and I think I need to go back home. If nothing else than to talk to my father.'

She begins to recoil, but seizing her hips, I trap her in place and entice her lips back to mine. I slip my tongue inside her mouth and she lets out a quiet moan. When I let her go, our breathing is ragged. She backs off of me and I try not to think about our unbalanced love for each other. She'll get there eventually, once she understands what love is.

When I call out 'I love you' as she heads for the hallway and she returns it with only a smile, it stings a little.

Ella

Ethan lectured me the entire time I packed my bag and then his face got really red when I announced I had to go see my therapist before we took off. I need to talk to her, though, about my revelation last night. Ever since I was a little kid, I thought love wasn't real. Then Micha showed me differently, but I still couldn't love him like he deserved.

Whether intentional or not, my dad's letter released me from some of the burden I'd been carrying. Not all of it, but some, and last night when I was curled up beside Micha, I envisioned something I'd been blind to.

A hope for a future.

Anna is locking up her office door when I arrive. 'I thought I was supposed to meet you.'

She whirls around, pressing her hand to her heart, her eyes amplified as her keys fall from her hands to the floor. 'Good God, you scared me.'

I scoop up the keys and hand them to her. 'I'm sorry. I just thought we had an appointment today.'

She drops her keys into her purse. 'I was actually getting ready to call you. I got a call from my sister and she needs me to come over a couple days early. She's very worried about hosting Christmas dinner for everyone.'

We make our way down the hallway of the school and push out through the doors, which latch shut behind us. It's a cloudy day and the violent breeze cools my skin and stings my cheeks.

'So I guess I'll see you when you get back,' I say, getting ready to leave her and cut across the grass toward my apartment.

She turns for the parking lot, but stops at the curb. 'Of course, first thing on Monday. And make sure to call me if you need anything.'

Ethan's lifted truck drives up to the sidewalk and he lays on the horn. Anna's eyes dart toward it and the heel of her shoe catches in the grass, causing her to trip.

I sigh and redirect my direction to the truck. 'Sorry about that. He just gets kind of antsy.'

'Are you going somewhere?' She frees her shoe from the grass and steps back up onto the sidewalk.

I nod. 'I decided to go with Micha and

Ethan back home.'

She does the buttons of her navy blue jacket up. 'That's good. I'm glad you decided to go.'

I shield the wind from my face with my hand. 'Why? I thought you said you weren't sure if I should.'

'No, I said only you would know if you should.' She pauses and wisps of her short hair flap in the breeze. 'Ella, can you do something for me on this vacation?'

'Sure, what?'

'Stop worrying so much and have fun. It's what you need,' she says with a smile.

'I do have fun . . . sometimes.'

'Well, try to have fun the entire time.'

I pluck bits of my hair out of my mouth as I take in her words. 'You remember what you said about being in a relationship with Micha and that only I would know when I was ready. Well, I think I'm ready. I know it's really soon and everything, but last night, well, I saw a glimpse of a future with him that I really, really wanted. And that's never happened to me before.'

She doesn't look upset, like I'd expected she would. 'That's good. I'm glad you were able to see that. But remember to take things as slow as *you* need to. I want you to focus on yourself.' She waves and walks across the grass toward the parking lot. 'Have fun, Ella, and I mean it. You deserve to.'

Fun? Is that the magic cure to repair my mind? I tuck my chin in and fight against the wind, heading toward the car — heading home.

⋆　⋆　⋆

Road trips with Ethan and Micha are a pain in the butt. I forgot about the guys' 'no bathroom stop' rule: they'll only stop, like, every four hours for a break. If there isn't a restroom close by, then they consider a bush a good substitution.

It doesn't bother me that much, but poor Lila isn't used to their crap. We're sitting in the back of the truck on opposite sides and she's bouncing up and down, jiggling her legs to hold it in.

'Just pull over.' I slap the side of Ethan's arm for being an asshole and refusing to pull over. 'She's not going to pee off the side of an off-ramp.'

'I'll back the truck up, so it blocks her,' he replies, stunning Lila. 'No one will see.'

'I don't think . . . ' Lila presses a look at me for help.

I unbuckle my seatbelt and lean over the seat to pinch Ethan's arm. 'Pull the damn truck over now,' I threaten. 'If not for me, for her.'

'Ow, you're always so evil,' Ethan complains and then taps the brakes hard, sending me flying over the seat. 'But I'm much eviler.'

I summersault over and my legs hit the dash as the shifter stabs me in the back. Sitting up straight, I smooth my hair into place and extend my hand toward him to do something equally as sinister, but Micha snags my elbow and pulls me onto his lap.

'Easy, you two,' he says, hugging me close and conforming his lap against my backside. 'We have a long drive ahead of us still.'

Shooting me a dirty look, Ethan swerves the truck off the nearest off-ramp that leads directly to a truck stop. Semis line the chain-link fence that borders the building and there's a flashing marquee promising everyone ten cents off each gallon when paying with cash.

He pulls up to an empty gas pump and silences the engine as he zips his plaid hooded jacket up. 'But just so you know, this is for Lila, not you.'

I glare at him as Lila hops out of the truck and dashes toward the entrance of the building. She's wearing a white dress and pearls around her neck, looking completely out of place at the truck stop. When I asked her why she was overdressing for a road trip, she shrugged and said she was used to having to dress up for days related to holidays.

Micha gets out of the car and offers his hand to help me out. The cool air hits my bare legs as I stretch my arms above my head.

Micha eyes me with amusement as he ruffles his blond hair into place so wisps are dangling across his forehead. 'You know you give Lila crap for overdressing, but you kind of undressed.' He gestures at my jean shorts and purple T-shirt. 'What were you thinking when you put that on?'

'Hey, it was hot when we left,' I argue, adjusting the bottom of my shirt back over my stomach. 'And I wanted to be comfortable.'

He unzips his black hoodie, and his T-shirt rides up a little, showing a glimpse of his abs. 'Put this on before you freeze to death.'

'I'll be okay,' I assure him, enclosing my arms around myself.

He urges the jacket at me with persistency. 'Take it, because I'm not putting it back on.'

I take the jacket and give him a quick kiss on the cheek before sticking my arms through the sleeves and zipping it up. It smells like his cologne mixed with a scent that belongs only to him and I inhale deeply, relishing it.

'Did you just smell my jacket?' he inquiries

with a cock of his eyebrow. 'Is that like some kind of weird ritual or something?'

'It smells like you,' I explain and pull the front of the jacket over my nose to shield it from the cold. 'And I like the smell of you.'

He seems pleased with my odd response and tugs the hood over my head. 'Smell away.'

Smiling, I turn for the gas station as a red Mustang, the same year's as Blake's, inches up to the pump two rows down. I shrug it off as coincidental, until Blake gets out of the car. He has on a gray beanie and a hoodie over a blue shirt. His jeans don't have paint smudges on them and he has gloves on his hands. Micha and Ethan are distracted by a blonde who has her butt sticking out as she attempts to fill up the oil in her car. Ethan is saying something vulgar about her ass while Micha encourages him to go help her 'fill up her tank.'

Rolling my eyes, I mosey over to Blake as he slides his credit card into the slot.

'So this is a freakishly weird coincidence,' I say, startling him and he drops his card onto the ground.

'Shit, you scared me.' He squats down to retrieve the card and then stands up straight. 'What are you doing here?'

My gaze flicks to Micha laughing at Ethan

attempting to hit on the blonde, who rolls her eyes and slams the hood down, uninterested.

'I'm headed home for the holidays.' I redirect my attention to Blake. 'What about you? What are you doing all the way out here? Don't you know California's the other way?'

The corners of his mouth quirk at my lame joke. 'My mom lives in Cali, but my dad lives over in Colorado.'

'Oh, so you're about to break to the east,' I say. 'I see.'

After punching some buttons on the credit card machine, he removes the nozzle, puts it into the car, and the gas gurgles.

He leans back against the car and folds his arms. 'So you're on the road with your boyfriend,' he says with an underlined meaning.

I flinch with guilt. 'Yeah, about that night at the restaurant, I've been meaning to track you down and say sorry.'

His eyebrows lift with skepticism. 'That's funny, because it seems like you've been avoiding me.'

I sigh. 'Was it that easy to tell?'

He shakes his head. 'Ella, you practically ran away from me when I shouted out to you after class, but I just wanted to talk.'

I blow out an uneven breath as I fiddle with the zipper on my hoodie. 'I'm sorry. I just didn't know what to say. He was drunk that night and upset about some stuff.'

He glances over his shoulder at Micha removing the receipt from the pump and Ethan who's digging out some soda from the cooler in the back of the truck. 'He seems intense.'

'But that's the thing. He's not,' I say, defending him with irritation surfacing in my voice. 'He's normally not like that.'

'Okay, if you say so,' he says tolerantly.

I rest my butt on the top of the hood, letting my legs dangle over the side as I change the subject. 'How come you didn't bring your girlfriend with you?'

The gas pump clicks and he turns to take it out. 'We broke up.'

'How come?' I ask, surprised. 'You looked so happy.'

He rips his receipt from the machine and shoves it into his back pocket. 'I don't know. The last time I was there, things just were off.' He rubs his hand over his face. 'We've been dating since we were fifteen and I think it only went on for that long because we were both too afraid to be without something we've had forever . . . We were together because we were attached to the idea of us.'

My mind wanders to Micha and myself. We've known each other forever. Is this how it will turn out? Anxiety grasps at my chest. I don't want to lose Micha. Ever.

'Well, if you need anything, you can call me whenever.' I hop off the hood and my sandals splash in a rainbow-tinted puddle. 'I'm not going to be doing anything except for probably getting into trouble.'

He chuckles as he rounds the back of the car. 'You don't seem like much of a troublemaker.'

A laugh sputters from my lips and I shuffle over to the driver's side. 'That shows how very little you know me.'

He opens the car door. 'You're right. I hardly know you, except for that you love to draw, don't have a car, and think Professor Marlina's watercolors look like paint-by-numbers.'

'They do,' I tell him in a serious tone. 'I swear to God she copied them from one of those books.'

He grins, glances over in Micha's direction, and then his gaze lands back on me. 'So I have a question.'

I hesitate. 'Okay.'

He wavers, considering something with his hand resting on top of the door. 'So say I'm hanging out at my father's house and I get really bored. Can I call you? Just to talk.'

I shift uncomfortably, putting my hands up

into my sleeves. 'Yeah, if you want.'

He winks at me and my uneasiness shoots up a notch. How the hell did things shift so fast? 'I'm going to hold you to that.'

I give him a tense smile as I step back so he can shut the door. Waving, he backs out and drives out of the gas station parking lot. As I turn for Ethan's truck, my body smacks into someone.

'Are you having fun?' Micha asks in a condescending tone, with eyes as cold as snow.

'We were just talking.' I move backward and then to the side to walk around him, but he sidesteps me and barricades my route.

'Ella May, I'm sorry to break it to you, but the guy was totally hitting on you.' He lowers his voice to a protective growl as he leans in and his eyes darken. 'And if I see him do it again, he's going to get punched in the face.'

'No violence,' I plead with a heavy-hearted sigh. 'Why do guys always have to hit each other?'

'As opposed to knocking someone down to the ground and pulling their hair until they cry?' He edges out of the way of a car pulling in and tugs on my sleeve to drag me along with him.

'I did that once when I was twelve.'

'Or biting them on the arm?'

I huff a frustrated breath and wrench my arm away from him. 'All right, do whatever you want. I'm removing myself from the situation.'

As I march by him, his fingers grip my hip and he yanks me against him. Folding his arms around my shoulders, he walks behind me to the truck, freeing me only to open the door.

'I only want to hit him because I love you,' he says with a frown developing at his lips. 'It pisses me off how he looks at you, like that night at the restaurant. You may not see it, but even through my drunk eyes it was completely obvious.'

I take in the jealousy written all over his face. 'You're jealous of Blake?'

'Of course I'm fucking jealous.' He gapes at me like I'm a moron. 'He gets to be around you all day because you go to the same school. Plus, who knows how many times you hung out with him while I was on the road.'

'Twice outside of class.' I hurl myself into the back-seat and accidentally bump the top of my head on the ceiling. 'And once was because Lila needed to get off campus for a day.'

'You're breaking a code even talking to him,' he tells me with sternness.

My jaw drops. 'A *code*? Are you crazy?'

He props his foot on the sidestep of the lifted truck and puts his hand on the back of the seat. 'Scoot over.'

I move over into the middle of the seat and he scoots into the backseat beside me. Folding my arms, I aim an irritated look at him. 'So about these codes, you might need to let me know what they are. I mean, am I breaking some kind of *code* by being by myself in the backseat?'

He blinks, unentertained. 'Argue all you want, but you didn't see the way he was looking at you.'

'Micha, I'm not some prize everyone wants.' I inch toward the door to put more distance between us. I'm pissed off at his accusations and the fact that he doesn't seem to trust me. 'I'm a brat who has mental issues and who can't make up her mind about anything.'

'Just the fact that you can admit that out loud,' he says as he slides closer me with his arm draped over the back of the seat, 'makes you something special. Do you know how many people won't admit their flaws and the things they need to work on — how many people can't even see themselves?' He sneaks his hand between my thighs, his eyes forceful as he lures me back over to him and my heart leaps inside my chest. 'You're fucking special and if I want to act all possessive over you when some stupid art guy hits on you right in front of me, I'm going to. Either that or I'm going to have Ethan chase him down right now so I can punch him in the face.'

I clamp my jaw shut to stop my smile from appearing. 'You're funny when you're like this.'

He kisses my temple. 'Well, I'm glad you find my pain so entertaining.'

I peer up at him through my eyelashes. 'I just have to say that I've seen you flirting with girls many times, making out with girls, taking them to your bedroom.'

He winces at the last part. 'But what did I always say when you asked me about it?'

A smile breaks through. 'That you were just buying time until I came around.'

'Exactly.' He rubs his lips together and all I want to do is lick them, take his lip ring into my mouth, and stroke his tongue with mine. I want to do a lot of dirty things to him right now.

'Your mind's going into the gutter, isn't it,' he mocks arrogantly. 'I can see lust written all over your face.'

I direct my concentration to the window, laughing under my breath. 'You know, for someone who's so sure of himself, you worry an awful lot about losing me.'

'That's because I'd be lost without you.'

'Total player's line, Micha Scott.'

Fixing a finger under my chin, he angles my head back toward him, so our lips are inches apart. 'Remember the pact. You and I are in it for the long haul.'

'What pact?' Lila asks as she jumps up into the passenger seat, breathless from the climb into the tall truck. She has a large bag of Skittles and a bottle of water in her hand.

'A secret pact.' He beams a grin at me.

I'd almost forgotten about the pact made by two children trying to seek something that they could never really have — normalcy.

Ethan gets into the truck and spins the tires as he drives away from the gas station, racing toward the freeway, cranking up 'Silhouettes' by Smile Empty Soul.

'I think we need a drink,' Micha declares, reaching for the back sliding window, so he can get into the cooler.

I seize his hand and hold it against my chest over my heart. 'Not while we're driving.'

Daggers shoot from his eyes as he scowls at my hand over his. 'Why not? I'm not the driver.'

My lips part, about to confront him about his drinking, but I hear Anna's warning echo in my head and I chicken out. 'I just don't think we should start drinking yet when we know we're going to be doing that for most of the weekend.'

He withdraws his hand and rotates in the seat. 'Excellent point. Although, it would help pass the time.'

I gaze at the window as the land progressively changes from green to white, lost in my thoughts. Will I ever be stable enough to help people instead of cause them problems?

Micha

It's late when we arrive at Star Grove. The sky is black and the stars are covered by clouds. A thick layer of snow blankets the streets, the houses, and the yards, and red and green Christmas lights flash around the trimming of my house.

Lila is asleep in the front seat with her head relaxed against the window. Ella fell asleep in my lap and with her face so close to my cock that my mind has been filled with dirty scenarios almost the entire drive. But I boxed up my sexual tension, not wanting to relive another episode where Ethan overhears us doing naughty things.

When Ethan parks the truck in my

driveway, Lila wakes up and stretches her arms above her head like a cat. 'Where are we?' She blinks her eyes at my two-story house and then at Ella's house next door. There are no tire tracks in the snow in the driveway of her house, which means no one is home.

My mom's car is parked out in front of the open garage where the back end of the Chevelle sticks out. Ethan jumps out, leaving his door wide open, and tramples through the snow to the back of the truck. Lila follows, letting the cold air in, and meets Ethan at the tailgate. They begin to get the frozen suitcases out of the back.

Ella is nuzzled in my lap, fast asleep, and I just can't help myself. Nibbling on my lip ring to stifle my laughter, I gently pinch Ella on the rib, right below her boob. She jumps up from her deep sleep, green eyes wild and glowing in the dim cab light.

'What the hell?' She smacks my arm, blinking the weariness out of her eyes. 'That was the meanest way to wake me up ever.'

I rub my arm where she hit me. 'It was actually one of the funniest things I've ever seen.'

'A jerk move.' She leans forward toward my neck, but at the last second heads south and bites at my chest through my shirt.

I wince, but smile. 'You know that turns me on more than anything.'

She brings her bottom lip in between her teeth. 'You've been turned on for most of the drive. I could feel it pressed against my cheek.'

Ready to end the battle, I finish with a winning line. 'That's because your mouth was only inches away from my cock.'

Her cheeks heat up as her lip pops free, all red and swollen and so tempting. I get out of the car into the freezing cold and offer my hand to her. She takes it, about to jump out in the snow in her flip-flops.

'Wait a second.' I retract my hand and turn my back to her. 'Hop on or else you're going to freeze your toes off.'

She mounts my back willingly and I carry her to the porch. Icicles dangle from the trimming and the ice on the steps has been sprinkled with salt. My breath laces out in front of me as I reach above the porch light and retrieve the house key hidden below a clay pigeon. I lower Ella to the ground, hand her the key, and dismount off the steps into the driveway, my boots crunching in the snow.

'Unlock it and go inside,' I instruct, backing toward the car. 'I'll get our stuff.'

She watches me, her skin like porcelain

beneath the porch light. 'Who said I was staying here?'

'Who said you weren't?' I smirk. 'Now quit being a pain in the ass and get your butt inside where it's warm.'

Before she turns away, a trace of a smile reveals itself on her lips. She unlocks the door and goes inside while I get our bags. Ethan decides he's going to crash on the couch, which he's done a lot since we were kids. Lila takes the bed in the spare room. That leaves Ella in my bed, something I'm thrilled about, although she probably won't share the feeling.

After I show Lila where the room is and toss Ethan a blanket, I carry the bags to the bedroom. The light is on and Ella is lying in my bed on her stomach, flipping through the pages of . . .

'Where the fuck did you get that?' I lunge for the notebook, but she rolls to the side, laughing and hugging it to her chest.

'Oh my God . . . is this like your little black book?' She flinches as I leap on top of her and steal the notebook away from her hands.

'It's not a little black book,' I practically growl. 'It's just a . . . '

'Journal that keeps track of all the girls you've slept with.' She slaps her hand over her mouth as she laughs so hard her face turns red. When she recomposes herself, she kneels up in front of me. 'You know, I thought I knew everything about you, but I was wrong.'

I toss the notebook into the trashcan. 'Where did you find that?'

She shrugs, lies back on her stomach, and slides her hands underneath the pillow. 'It was under here.'

I kick the bags under my computer desk and turn on a lamp before shutting the ceiling light off. Then I shuck off my shirt and lie down in bed with her.

She's shivering because the room is ice cold, but that's how my mom likes to keep it to reduce the power bill. 'There were a lot of names in there . . . more than I thought.'

I release a slow breath and rub my hand across my face. 'Ella, I don't know what you want me to say . . . I never wanted anyone to find that. It was just for my own personal thing, so I could . . . ' I tense. 'Keep track.'

She watches me expressionlessly and the level of awkwardness is maddening. 'My name wasn't in there.'

I rotate on my side and look into her eyes. 'That's because I knew I wasn't going to have to keep track anymore. There's been no one since you and there never will be again.'

Her breathing accelerates and she starts to

get up. Thinking she's going to leave, I reach to stop her, but all she does is discard her shoes onto the floor and shimmy out of her shorts. I instantly get excited at the sight of her ass sticking out of her panties.

She leaves my jacket on and climbs beneath the covers. 'It's cold,' she states with unreadable eyes.

I unbutton my jeans, slip out of them, and get under the covers with her, wincing when my feet brush hers. 'Your feet are fucking cold.' I place a hand on her hip. 'God, you're cold everywhere.'

She wiggles her feet between my ankles and snuggles closer. 'I guess you'll have to keep me warm.'

I set my chin on top of her head. 'You confuse me sometimes, pretty girl. You really do. One minute you're mad at me and the next minute you seem to want me.'

She buries her face into my chest and her hot breath warms my chilled skin. 'I confuse myself sometimes.' She pauses. 'I think there's something really wrong with my head, because reading that list just makes me want to have sex with you.'

Every muscle in my body freezes. 'What did you just say?'

'You heard me right.' Her finger tickles circles around my nipple. 'Like I said, I think

there's something very wrong with my head
. . . It just made me want to take claim of you
or something.'

'Then do it.' I hold my breath, waiting for
her reaction.

She slants back and looks me in the eyes.
'Not tonight. I'm tired, but you do have a
birthday coming up in a few days.'

'Well, just to get things clear now, I want
you wrapped up in a bow and nothing else.
Well, maybe high heels. Those fucking gorgeous legs of yours look ridiculously sexy in
heels.'

Smiling, she rests her cheek back on my
chest and tangles her leg with mine, opening
herself up to the top of my thigh and I can
feel the warmth flowing off her. 'Maybe that
can be arranged.'

I embrace her and inch my legs closer,
rubbing gently against her. 'You seem to be in
a good mood.'

Her breath catches from my touch and she
rocks her hips slightly. 'I'm just trying not to
worry. Doctor's orders.'

My hands slip around to her backside and
I rest my palm on her thigh. 'So does that
mean that the old Ella May just might
return?'

'No . . . ' Her eyes close as my finger traces
a line back and forth along her soft skin. 'I

265

don't think she can exist anymore, but I'm pretty sure I can give you the real, current me . . . if you want.'

'Of course I want.' I grip her ass, shut my eyes, and breathe her in. 'I want it all.'

16

Ella

I wake up to the smell of bacon and eggs. It's been a while since I had a good breakfast and my mouth instantly salivates. Stumbling out of bed, I pull a pair of jeans on, noticing that Micha took the garbage out, probably to get rid of the notebook.

'It should bother me,' I say to myself, slipping a long-sleeved thermal shirt over my head. 'But it doesn't. God, is my head really that messed up?'

I wander out into the kitchen. Micha's mom is cooking over the stove as pans sizzle. Her blonde hair is in a bun and she's wearing a pink sweatpants suit. A guy, at least ten years younger than her, is at the table reading the sports section of the newspaper and drinking juice. His brown hair is thick except for a small bald spot on the top and he has dark circles under his hazel eyes.

'Good morning, sweetie,' Mrs. Scott greets me with a cheery smile. 'Would you like some breakfast?'

I glance at the stranger at the table, who

makes me nervous as he evaluates me. 'Umm . . . where is Micha and everyone else?'

She stabs the bacon with a fork and turns it over. 'They went outside. Micha's really excited that his dad paid to get his car fixed, I think . . . It was really nice of him.'

'Shit.' I don't mean to say it aloud and Mrs. Scott looks at me perplexedly.

'Are you all right?' she asks, scraping the eggs around in the pan with a spatula.

I snatch one of Micha's jackets off the hanger near the back door and step outside, not answering her. There is no way in hell he could be excited about that.

Outside, the air is below freezing and sends me into a shivering frenzy. My boots crunch against the snow as I hike to the garage where the Chevelle is parked. The once smashed in side is now as smooth as silk, repainted a smokin' black, with a cherry red racing strip down the hood. It's in racing condition but only because of Micha's father.

'Can you believe he fucking did this?' Micha's sharp voice surprises me and I whirl around, nearly falling on my ass as my shoes slip on a patch of ice.

Micha's hand snaps out to catch me, but he slants sideways, losing balance. I grab the hem of his jacket and get my footing for the both of us.

Clutching onto my shoulder with one hand, Micha grasps the beer in his hand like it's the most important thing in the world. 'My father thinks he can pay me off.'

'What do you mean?' I ask, letting go of his arm and turning back to the car.

He strolls around me and jumps up from the ground, knocking some icicles off the trimming of the garage roof. 'He sent my mom some money after I helped him out with his little thing to fix up my car as a thank-you.'

I'm unsure how to approach the situation. 'Well, I guess it was kind of nice of him. I mean, at least he did something good.'

His aqua eyes are as cold as the ice beneath our feet. 'I'd rather have him call me, at least then he'd be acknowledging my existence. But instead he sends my mom a fucking card.' Wrestling a piece of paper out of his pocket, he throws it in my direction, but it makes it only halfway between us and falls to the snow.

I swipe it up, dust the snow off it, and open the card. *Please use this money to fix Micha's car up like we talked about on the phone and tell him thank you for helping me. It was a very nice thing he did, and my family and I are grateful for it.*

'His family and he are grateful.' He kicks

the tire with the tip of his boot and chucks the beer bottle at the wall, and it shatters all over the cement. 'He's a fucking asshole. Like I'm not his family.'

I set the card down on the hood and open my arms to give him a hug, but he backs away. 'I just need a moment, okay? Can you go inside or something?'

He's more wasted than I thought. Up close, the red lines in his glossy eyes are visible and his cheeks are flushed. His hair is sticking up, like he's dragged his hands through it multiple times. There's anger in his eyes that only an excessive amount of alcohol can bring out.

'Okay, I'll be inside if you need me.' I trek for the door, but pause at the steps, noticing that Ethan's truck is gone. I turn back to Micha to ask where he went, but he's shutting the garage door as he pulls out another beer from the pack on the shelf, locking away the world as he buries his pain in alcohol.

I think about confronting him — about his drinking problem and pushing me away — but when I make it to the bedroom, exhaustion overtakes my body and I fall onto the mattress, wondering why I came here in the first place.

★ ★ ★

Depression and anxiety are the devil. Anything can trigger them and flip my mood in a heartbeat. Luckily, Anna taught me to notice when I'm sinking into the hole of despair that can turn into a bottomless pit. She taught me how to realize when it's taking over and how to fight the darkness. If I work at it, I can get ahold of the light again. But it's all about pushing through my dark thoughts and not giving up.

About thirty minutes later, I push my way back into the light and storm out of the house, marching straight for the garage. Ethan's truck is in the driveway and there are footprints leading to the garage.

I shove open the door and step inside. Ethan and Micha are sitting on the hood, with their boots propped up on the front bumper and beers in their hands. Lila is talking on her phone in the corner with her finger pressed to her ear as she attempts to block out their chatter.

Micha's eyes connect with mine and the rawness in his face almost shies me away. 'Hey, where'd you go?' He stumbles off the hood and, with his long legs, strides toward me.

He's wearing a gray thermal shirt with a tiny hole in the hem and his black jeans are secured around his hips with a studded belt. His hair's a mess, his eyes lost, and the smile on his face means trouble is about to start.

His hand seeks my waist, but I edge back. 'We need to talk.'

Ethan glances at me with his black hair in his eyes and his face carries a warning. 'Ella, just let it be.'

'You don't know what I'm going to say,' I tell him. 'So stay out of it.'

'Yeah, but you've got that tone like you're about to bring up something personal and he can't deal with personal right now.' He shoves the sleeves of his green shirt up and lies back on the hood with his hands behind his head.

Micha blinks confusedly at me. 'Wait, what's up?'

Ethan's made me nervous so I back down and head for the cooler. 'It's nothing. I can't even remember what I was going to say.'

He grabs my elbow and reels me into his chest. 'Let's go do something really, really fun.'

I try to squirm away. 'I don't want to.'

His forehead furrows as he scratches the back of his neck. 'Why are you acting funny?'

'I'm not.' I bend my arm out of his grip. 'I just don't like that you're drunk.'

'Why? I've been drunk plenty of times.'

'I know and that's the problem.' I bite down on my tongue. 'I'm sorry. I didn't mean that.'

His eyes burn with rage. 'You get drunk just as much as I do.'

I shake my head. 'That's not true.'

'It's completely true,' he snaps and the loudness of his voice causes me to jump. 'You drink as much as I do, whether it's for fun or because you're trying to bury something. It's what we've all been doing since we were fourteen.'

'Hey, don't bring me into this,' Ethan argues, climbing off the hood. 'I cleaned up my shit.'

'No, you didn't.' Micha trips over the laces of his boots and slams into one of the shelves, knocking tools and car parts to the ground. Lila's eyes bulge as she hangs up her phone. 'You still drink when you feel like shutting down — all of us do.'

A silent moment builds around us as our breath fogs out and we take in the realization that he's right. We all started drinking around the age of fourteen. It began as curiosity, but the older we got, the more we used it as an escape from the reality of our lives.

'Well, I'm done,' I finally say, surrendering up my hands as I back toward the door.

'I'm done with you too!' he yells, red-faced. 'I'm sick of your fucking mind games and problems. I'm sick of it and I want out.'

My hands fall lifelessly to my side. 'I meant

I was done with drinking, but it's nice to know where you stand.'

'Ella, he didn't mean that. He's just drunk, so stop acting crazy and get over it,' Ethan interrupts, shaking his head at Micha. 'You better get your shit together right now, man.'

Micha glares at Ethan. 'Stay out of this.' He turns back to me, but I'm already out the door.

He doesn't follow me as I run down the street. The wind blows in my hair and stings at my cheeks as I try to flee from the hurt and pain, but anxiety nips at my heels.

Micha has never gotten that mad at me. Ever. It's like a knife to the heart and I don't know how to pull it out. It hurts everywhere.

When I reach the corner, I slow down and try to regain control of my thoughts. I take my phone out of my pocket and dial Anna's number.

She answers after four rings and a piano plays in the background. 'Hello.'

'Hi, Anna, this is Ella.' I feel bad for calling her when it's obvious she's with her family.

After a few seconds I hear a door close and the noise quiets. 'What's wrong?'

I stare up at the graffiti on the street sign. 'I did something you told me not to do . . . I confronted Micha about his drinking problem.'

'And what happened?'

'He said some . . . stuff.'

She pauses. 'What kind of stuff? Hurtful stuff?'

'Lots of stuff. And yes, it hurts.' I press my hand to my aching heart as I hunch over. 'Really bad.'

'And what does the pain make you want to do?' she asks as a car drives by and splashes slush up from the street. 'Ella, where are you?'

'I'm standing on the corner of the street and all I want to do is run,' I admit. 'I want to cry . . . I want to scream.'

'So scream,' she encourages. 'Go ahead. Let it all out.'

'But I'm on the street.' I glance up the road at an older couple walking down the sidewalk. 'And there are people around.'

'So what?' she says. 'Don't worry about them. Just let it all out — let the worry and pain go. Don't hold it in, Ella. We've talked about that.'

Feeling like an idiot, I open my mouth and let out a quiet scream.

'You can do better than that,' she insists. 'Really scream, Ella.'

Sucking in a deep breath, I give it all I got, letting it all out, and it echoes for miles.

★　★　★

After I clear the congestion out of my chest, I walk down the road toward Cherry Hill where the cemetery is located, thinking about the people I've lost. My mom and Grady, both were taken out of my life way too early.

A crisp layer of snow coats the tombstones and trees, the grass is buried, and icicles hang from the fence. Walking up to the leafless tree in front of my mother's grave, my shoes fill with snow and my nose turns pink. I bend down and brush a bunch of snow from the top of her grave.

I read out loud the words that are far too simple to sum her up. 'Maralynn Daniels, loving mother and wife.' There was no mention of her struggle or how she got dealt a shitty hand at life.

My thoughts drift back to a conversation she and I had when I was about fifteen. We were watching television, although she was dazing off a lot and not paying attention.

'Why do you think I'm this way?' she asked abruptly with a contemplative look on her face.

I turned the volume of the television down. 'What do you mean, Mom?'

She stared at the wall as if it had held the answers to life. 'Why can't I escape the dark thoughts, like everyone else? Why can't I think the same as everyone?'

I racked my brain for a good answer to give her. 'I don't think everyone thinks the same, Mom. Everyone's different.'

'Yeah, but why do some people get it easy?' She looked at me and her green eyes were huge, like she was hypnotized. 'They just walk through life without problems.'

I let out a slow breath, knowing my words were going to be important to her. 'Everyone has their problems, Mom. It's just that some people's are harder.' I inched toward her and the fear in her eyes began to subside. 'I think the people who go through more can end up stronger in the long run. They have insight in to what a lot of people don't have and a better understanding — they can be more open-minded.'

The corners of her mouth tipped upward and she gave me a rare smile. 'You're a smart girl, Ella May, and I believe that one day you'll grow up to do great things . . . I really hope you do.'

The knots in my stomach began to unwind. I'd said the right thing and she was relaxed and happy, which had been my goal. I thought I'd made an impact on her, but it turned out I was wrong.

'I'm sorry, Mom,' I whisper to her grave. 'I really am . . . Sometimes I feel like I owe you my happiness.'

The wind rustles around me, whispering through my hair. I sit down in front of the tombstone and sit with her grave in silence, promising myself I'll come back and visit often, vowing she won't be forgotten.

★ ★ ★

I don't see Micha for the rest of the night. I sleep in the same room with Lila and then sneak out of the house before Micha wakes up from his drunken stupor. I'm not really mad at him anymore for drinking. What he said was true. We all do it to hide our pain and we all need to stop. But his harsh words still haunt me.

Lila and I go out to my garage and I start up my dad's Firebird so we can go get some lunch. My dad keeps a spare key under the visor, but the car's been sitting for so long that it takes forever to start. Finally I get the engine to roar to life and then let it run for a while as I tromp through the snow looking for a way to get into the house.

Lila follows me, zipping up her coat, and then she slips on her gloves. 'It is so cold here.'

'I know.' I peer up at the frosted window of the kitchen, noticing that it's not completely shut. 'Well, I think I found our way in, although it's going to be equally as cold in there since the damn window's probably been open for months.'

I step back from the window and my phone beeps from inside my pocket, alerting me that I have a text message.

BLAKE: Whatcha doin?

I hesitate then text back.

ME: Trying to break into my house.
BLAKE: Sounds fun.
ME: Not really.
BLAKE: I'm just kidding. So what else are you doing? Anything fun? I was thinking of bailing out on my dad a few days early and going back to the campus. When are you going back? Maybe we could meet up and get some coffee or something.

★ ★ ★

'Who is it?' Lila peers over my shoulder at the screen and her nose scrunches. 'Oh my God, is he seriously texting you?'

I sigh, locking the screen so it shuts off. 'I told him he could.'

Lila *tsks* me with a wave of her finger. 'El, I'm warning you now to back off this supposed friendship with that guy. You're only going to end up in a mess.'

'It is just a friendship.' I move away from the window and toward the car. 'And besides, you encouraged it once so you could get a ride from him.'

'And I regret it.' She follows after me, slipping on the ice a few times. 'I saw him talking to you at the gas station and there was nothing but lust in his eyes . . . and now he doesn't even have a girlfriend so there's nothing stopping him.'

'You know, I'm regretting telling you that,' I say. 'And it doesn't matter anyway. Even if he did like me I would never do anything with him.'

She grabs my arm and forces me to look at her. 'Walk away from this right now. Blake is hot and you two have that whole art thing going on. You may not think anything could happen, but sometimes stuff just does. Trust me.'

'Are you speaking from experience?' I ask as my phone beeps with another text message.

★ ★ ★

BLAKE: I didn't scare u off, did I . . . look, I know you have a boyfriend, so I'm not proposing a date. Just going to get coffee as two fellow artists who love coffee.

'I've had plenty of experiences with this crap,' Lila continues, letting go of my arm. 'I've had many guys *accidently* get caught up in the moment and *slip up*. And I know plenty of girls who have done it too. And you're so lucky, Ella. You really are. Please, for the sake of all women, just get away from Blake and focus on the beautiful relationship you have in front of you.'

'After what happened yesterday, you still think it's beautiful?' I ask doubtfully.

'You two fighting makes it more beautiful.' She sighs and her breath fogs out. 'I also know that right now you're mad and the last thing you want to be doing is texting some guy who has a crush on you. You might do something stupid.'

'I'm not mad at Micha. Just upset with . . . stuff.'

'Same difference.'

Sighing, I text Blake back.

★ ★ ★

ME: I'm going to be here until the end of winter break. Maybe I'll c u when I get back.

★ ★ ★

281

He doesn't respond and Lila and I get into the car with the heater blasting at our faces. I don't really care whether Blake texts me back or not. He was a nice friend, but that was it. My thoughts revolve around a much bigger issue: when I face Micha and tell him it's over.

Micha

Something wet hits me in the face and I jump up with my fist raised in front of me.

'Settle the fuck down.' Ethan stands over me with a cup in his hand. 'It's just water.'

I wipe my face with the sleeve of my shirt. 'What the fuck are you doing?'

He sets the cup down on top of my dresser. 'Well, you've been asleep for about fourteen hours and so I thought I'd make sure you were still alive.'

Clutching my throbbing head, I check the time on the clock mounted on my wall beside the window. It's early morning and snow flutters outside.

'What happened?' I swing my legs over the side of the bed, preparing to get up, but a bitter taste in my throat forces me to lie back down.

'Well, you drank practically all the alcohol

282

in the house,' Ethan says, crossing his arms. 'And then you ruined your relationship with almost everyone you know, besides me, but that's because I don't give a shit.'

I rake my hand through my hair and roll to my side. 'What about Ella?'

'That one is probably the worst.' He messes with an alarm clock on my nightstand, rotating the knob on the back.

I turn back around. 'Why? What'd I say?'

He makes air quotes and says, ''I'm sick of your fucking mind games and problems.''

I drape my arm across my face as I shake my head. 'Goddammit. What was I thinking . . . God fucking damn it!' I punch the headboard and then wince when my knuckles pop.

He props the clock up beside the lamp. 'You were drunk, which was the reason the fight started. Ella doesn't want you drinking so much anymore and I have to agree with her. Yes, we all drink, but it seems like you do it more as a coping mechanism than the rest of us. In fact, you've kind of been doing it a lot lately.'

I peer up at him from underneath my arm. 'Dude, what the hell have you been reading? You sound like a psychiatrist.'

He backs up toward the doorway with a grin on his face. 'How to clean up your best friend's drunken mistakes. Now, get your ass out of bed, so you can go patch things up with Ella before she runs away again.'

I kick the blanket off me and sway to the side as I get to my feet. 'She ran off . . . She's gone?'

'Calm down.' Ethan rolls his eyes. 'After you yelled at her, she ran to the end of the street, but came back. She bunked up with Lila last night. I guess she doesn't have a key to her own house, which is weird.'

'It's not weird.' I signal at him to get out as I grab a pair of clean jeans from my dresser drawer. 'Her dad and brother are assholes.'

Giving an agreeing nod, he leaves the room and shuts the door. My stomach aches and my head feels like it's going to explode, but most of the pain lies in my heart.

I was the only one in Ella's life who'd never done anything to intentionally hurt her, but now I'm not.

★   ★   ★

'She's not answering her phone,' I mutter, pacing the living room floor. The carpet is old and brown and has holes in it, and the walls are this icky shade of green that resembles puke. 'What if she's run off again?'

'Dude, settle down.' Ethan peels open a

cheese stick and sinks back into the leather sofa that's missing an arm. 'I texted Lila and she says they're just out getting some lunch.'

Rubbing my forehead, I plop down into the recliner and kick an empty soda bottle out of the way so I can put my feet up on the table. 'God, why is our relationship always so up and down?'

Ethan peels at the string cheese and rolls his eyes. 'Because you both have problems, yet you won't talk to each other about them because you want to spare one another the pain.'

I steal a handful of candy from the dish my mom set out on the coffee table. 'Again, what have you been reading? Because you're seriously on a roll today.'

He crumbles the wrapper up and tosses it onto the table. 'I've just been around you both forever and I have eyes. Plus, my mom does that shit all the time with my dad. She lets him get away with anything just because she's afraid of confrontation.'

'Is that what we do?' I mull it over.

His eyes widen in mockery. 'Um, yeah. It's what you've been doing since you were kids.' He stands up, dusting some crumbs off his jeans. 'Maybe if you two would just be completely honest with one another for once, you'd be okay. I have to go. My mom wants

me to pick up a fucking ham for dinner.'
Sliding his keys out of his pocket, he departs
for the back door. 'It's the day before
Christmas, for God sakes. I don't know how
she thinks I'm going to find one.'

'You're a wise man, Ethan,' I call out,
knowing I'm going to annoy him and myself a
little, but it needs to be said. 'Thanks for
spelling it out for me.'

'Don't get all weird on me because I said
what I think.' He steps outside and then the
door slams.

I flip through the channels, restless, until
the back door creaks open. My mom and
Thomas walk in.

'Hey, man, what's up?' He nods his head at
me as he takes a seat in the sofa. He has a
pair of cargo pants on, brown work boots,
and there's a stain on his white shirt. 'Are you
watching the game?'

I toss the remote down on the coffee table.
'Do I look like someone who would be
watching the game?'

He looks at the tattoo on my arm, the
piercing in my lip, and my black shirt and
jeans. 'Umm . . . I don't know.'

Forcing back an eye roll, I leave the couch
and meet up with my mom in the kitchen.
'Okay, so I don't get it.'

She's unloading a sack of groceries into the

fridge and peeks up over the fridge door. 'Don't get what?'

I motion my thumb over my shoulder at the living room where Thomas is channel surfing. 'He seems like an idiot.'

'He's really nice, Micha.' She rummages around in a plastic bag on the counter and takes out a few cans of pumpkin. 'And he makes me happy.'

I eye her white button-down shirt that's tied at the waist and her jeans with diamond studs on them. 'He's making you dress weird.'

'So I'm dressing younger.' She lifts her chin up with confidence. 'I lost a lot of my youth and if I want to have fun now then I can.'

'Because you had me?' I steal a bag of chips from her hand. 'Or because of dad?'

She shakes her head as I pop the bag open. 'No, you were the best thing that ever happened to me. I lost my youth because of my choices, but now I'd like to make the choice to get some of it back and enjoy life a little.'

I cast a glance back at Thomas, who's laughing at something on the television. 'With him?'

She closes the cupboard. 'With him.'

I grab a handful of chips, making a mess on the floor. 'Fine, if that's what you want right now then I'll back down.' I pop my knuckles. 'But if he hurts you, I'm punching him in the face.'

She ruffles the top of my head tolerantly like I'm still a kid, then takes out two beers from the fridge and heads for the living room. 'And if you're wanting to make up with Ella, you should know that I just saw her climb inside the window to her house.'

I pick up the chips I dropped on the ground. 'How did you know we were fighting?'

She laughs. 'Honey, when you two fight the whole world knows.'

I have no idea what she means, but I slip my jacket on and step outside into the freezing cold. Snow drifts down from the sky and coats the ground as I hike over to the chain-link fence. The metal freezes the palms of my hands as I hop over it and knock on the back door.

After two knocks, Lila answers. She has on pink boots with fur on top, a coat, a hat, and a scarf. 'Yes.'

'Cold?' I joke, trying to lighten the mood, but all she does is frown. 'Sorry, not the best time for jokes, huh?'

She crosses her arms, her blue eyes very unwelcoming. 'You know how much I encouraged her to let you in — that you loved her so much and would never hurt her? You've basically crushed her and I look like a liar.'

'I'm going to make it better,' I insist, stepping toward the threshold, hoping she'll move over and let me through.

She stays still, blocking the doorway. 'Before I let you in, you have to promise no more drinking when you're upset and no more hurting her. I swear to God if you continue to hurt her, I'll rip out your lip ring.'

I put a hand over my mouth to protect my lips. 'I promise, never again.'

She moves back to let me in and then shuts the door behind us. 'She's upstairs in her room.'

I head for the stairway. 'You know, Lila, you're pretty hard core. Not many people would dare threaten the lip ring.'

'Well, I'm not most people,' she calls out. 'Ella's my best friend and she needs protecting. Something you usually do, only this time you were the cause of her needing it.'

I leave her in the kitchen and climb the stairs. The house is freezing and the sound of music flows through the air: 'One Thing' by Finger Eleven. The door to the bathroom where her mom died is wide open and there's something colorful all over the tile.

'Ella,' I say, walking toward the door. 'Are you up here?'

She walks out of her room with a handful of markers and her eyes widen when she sees me. 'How did you get in here?'

'Lila let me in,' I explain, my breath fogging out in front of me. 'Didn't you turn the heat on?'

She shakes her head and dismisses me, heading to the bathroom. She has her leather jacket and fingerless gloves on. When she reaches the bathroom, she crouches down and scribbles something on the floor.

I approach the scene with caution, knowing it has to mean something important. 'Pretty girl, what are you doing?'

She sketches a black line along the tile. 'I'm making a shrine . . . And don't call me pretty girl, please.'

I squat down behind her and hold my breath as I set my hands on her shoulders. She doesn't shrug them off, but tenses under my touch. 'You have no idea how sorry I am.'

She traces a circle around a woman with wings and a cupcake in her hand. 'You don't need to be sorry. I'm not mad at you.'

My brow knits with perplexity. 'Then what's wrong?'

She shades in the eyes of the angel and then fills in the flame of the candle in the cupcake. 'That I was right — about everything.'

I brush her hair to the side as she writes *I love you* below the angel's feet. 'Right about what?'

She writes, *I love you, Mom, and happy belated birthday.* Clicking the cap back on the marker, she stands up and turns to face me. 'That I ruin you.'

My eyes snap wide as she squeezes by me and rushes into her bedroom. That was not what I expected at all.

I catch up with her right as she's about to shut the door and brace my hand against it, shoving it back open. 'You don't ruin me, Ella May. How could you ever think that?'

'I think it because it's true.' She chucks the markers onto her dresser. 'My problems do anyway.'

I bite at my lip, working to maintain a steady voice. 'You know as well as I do that when people are drunk they say hurtful things they don't mean.'

She swallows hard. 'But sometimes they mean them.'

'I didn't mean it. I promise. God, I wish I could have, like, a redo or something, because I'd slap myself for even thinking those words.'

'Redo's don't exist,' she breathes softly. 'And I don't think I should do this anymore

— I wasn't even supposed to be doing this to begin with. I was supposed to stay out of relationships until I got my shit together, but every time I'm around you, it's impossible. All you do is look at me and I feel like I'm drowning.'

'I'm not sure what you mean,' I say with caution. 'Is that a good thing or a bad thing?'

She puffs out a frustrated breath, collapses onto her bed, and buries her face in her arms. 'It could be a good thing, if I wasn't so messed up . . . When I'm with you, every part of me is consumed by you.'

I climb onto the bed with her and place a hand gently on her back. 'You know that's the most honest thing you've said to me.'

She peeks up at me through her veil of auburn hair. 'I know.'

I brush her hair out of her eyes. 'Ethan suggested a weird thing to me today. That maybe you and I need to be more honest with each other, instead of always trying to protect each other.'

'I think you were pretty honest in the garage,' she replies coldly. 'Micha, if you want to walk away, then do it now because if things get any deeper, I swear it's going to kill me next time.'

'You have no idea how important you are to me.' I get off the bed and hold my hand out to her, knowing it's time to pour our hearts out to each other. 'Will you come somewhere with me?'

She eyes my offered hand suspiciously. 'Where?'

'That's a secret.' I wink at her, acting calm, even though I'm terrified she won't go with me — that I've ruined everything I've worked so hard at with her. 'But I promise, it'll be good.'

She sets her hand in mine, trusting me, and I can breathe again. I make a silent vow that I will never hurt her again.

17

Ella

'Okay, so sometimes I really don't get you.' My gaze scans the park full of bent and broken bars and empty dreams. It's the playground we grew up going to, but there were more drug dealings going on than children playing. The merry-go-round is crooked and the teeter-totter is missing a seat. The chains of the swing are rusted and the slide is buried in snow.

He tugs me toward the swing set with a big grin on his face. 'I can't believe you don't remember.' He dusts off the snow from the seat and sits down. 'It's like one of the best memories of my childhood.'

I brush the snow off the swing beside his and drop down in it, wrapping my fingers around the cold metal chains. 'You mean when we made the pact? I remember that.'

He runs backward and picks up his feet, soaring up toward the sky. 'Yeah, but do you remember what we were doing before the pact was made?'

I twist back and forth as snow falls from

the links. 'We were playing truth.'

Braking with his shoes, he halts the swing and twirls to face me. 'So you do remember.'

'Of course I remember.' I roll my eyes and spin around once with my legs stretched out in front of me. 'It was the day you made me admit that I had never kissed anyone before.'

His grin broadens. 'And the day I took your first kiss.'

I clamp my jaw shut to keep from grinning. 'Only because I was too naïve to see that you were totally playing me.'

'I was fourteen,' he says. 'I wasn't playing you. I was just curious what it would be like to kiss my best friend, because all the other girls I'd made out with just weren't doing much for me.'

I nudge his foot with my toe. 'You are such a liar.'

He crosses his heart with his finger. 'I'm totally being truthful here. Ethan kept yammering about all his awesome make-out sessions and I just didn't get it. Every time I was with a girl, it felt like there should be more.'

I suppress a laugh. 'And did the kiss fulfill all of your wildest dreams?'

'Oh yeah.' He grins haughtily. 'I couldn't stop thinking about how soft your lips were for, like, days.' His eyes shadow over. 'But what I really think added fuel to my developing obsession with you was that, like, a year and half later I saw you walking around naked in your room.'

I prod him in the shin with my foot. 'You did not.'

He smiles proudly and motions a finger at the swings we're sitting in. 'Oh no, I'm not. These swings are a no-lying area, remember?'

I let the swing sway back and forth. 'Well, while we're telling the truth, I once had a naughty dream about you.'

In a faint glow of the lamppost, his eyes sparkle like the snow. 'What exactly happened in this naughty dream?'

I pump my legs, taking the swing higher as I lean back freely. 'That's a secret I'll never tell.'

'Then I call bullshit.' He kicks off, joining me in the sky. 'Come on, pretty girl. You just made my night. Do you know how long I've thought that this was a one-sided crush?'

I laugh to myself as my cheeks heat at the memory of the dream. 'Micha, it's way too embarrassing.'

He catches the chain of my swing and plants his feet down in the snow, abruptly jerking us to a stop. 'Come on, it's going to drive me crazy.'

Our faces are only inches apart and his breath is hot against my cheeks.

Staring down at the ground, my hair falls to the side of my face. 'I had a dream that you and I had sex on the hood of your Chevelle.'

He sweeps my hair back and the look on his face tells me I'm in for it. 'Were you on your back or did I have you bent over?'

My frozen cheeks start to burn. 'I was on top of you on the hood.'

He rubs his jawline, letting out a low laugh. 'We are so doing that while we're here.'

I swat his arm. 'We're supposed to be taking things easy . . . and after what happened in the — '

He puts his hand over my mouth. 'That's why I brought you here — to tell you the truth. You need to understand how I feel about you and I figure this is the perfect place since it's where it all really began.'

'You want to play truth again?'

'I want to play truth again.'

We stare out at the quiet street. There is something about the holidays and the snowfall that shuts everyone up in the neighborhood. It's nice and was my favorite time of the year as a kid.

'Do I make you miserable?' I ask suddenly.

He shakes his head swiftly. 'Never. Not one single time. Sad, yes. Miserable, no.' He takes a deep breath. 'Have you and Blake ever done anything?'

My head whips toward him. 'That's your question?'

He shrugs. 'I need to know.'

'No. Not once did I ever even think about it,' I say. 'What about you? Did you ever do anything on the road?'

He rolls his eyes like it's the most ridiculous question he's ever heard. 'Even when I thought you cheated on me and I wanted to go back to my old habits, I just couldn't get there.' He pauses. 'Although, Naomi did try to kiss me.'

My jaw tightens as anger trickles through me. 'Lila was right.'

He draws his hood over his head and tucks his hands into his sleeves. 'About what?'

'That Naomi had a thing for you.'

'Was that where all that bitchiness came from in LA?'

I nod. 'Yep, she overheard Naomi talking crap about me.'

'Why didn't you say anything?' he asks.

'Because I trusted you.' I shrug. 'And I didn't want to start trouble.'

He traces my lip with his chilled finger and it sends a shiver coursing through my body. 'I want you to be more honest with me. I don't want you to be afraid to tell me things.'

'You keep things from me,' I remind him. 'Because you don't think I can handle stuff.

And I need to learn how to handle stuff, otherwise, explosions happen.'

He moves his hand back to the chain. 'Like your panic attacks?'

I swallow the giant lump in my throat. 'Yeah, like those . . . and you need to really consider if you want to deal with that shit for the rest of your life, because I may be able to get it under control, but sometimes stuff will trigger it.'

'For the rest of my life?' His voice softens. 'Do you want that, Ella May? Do you want me eternally, infinitely, forever, till death do us part?'

My chest pressurizes with the heaviness of his words, so I make a joke. 'Have you been reading the thesaurus again?'

'No jokes.' He rolls up the sleeve of his jacket, and reveals the black lines of the infinity tattoo. 'I'm not asking you to marry me, but I want to know if you see us together forever, because I sure as hell do.'

My insides quiver at the honesty in his aqua eyes. 'But I'm broken.'

His gaze never wavers from me. 'I know what I'm getting into and I want it more than anything, but the question is, do you want me?'

My heart thumps fitfully inside my chest as I let the shield around it evaporate into dust and listen to it wholly for once, shoving away the worry. 'Yes.'

It feels like the sky has opened up and the sunshine has been freed from the clouds.

Micha lets out a gradual breath as he stares off at the road. 'Fuck, I've been waiting for you to say that for forever.'

I lean over to kiss him, but he pulls away, and instead holds up his hand. 'Now we need to make the pact again.'

'I'm not going to spit in my hand,' I say with disgust. 'And then let you mix your spit with it.'

'Why? You did it before.' He spits in his hand. 'Besides, we've done a lot dirtier things than this.'

I know once I do it, I'm making a commitment. 'We have so many problems.'

'I'll ease up on the drinking if that's what you need. Hell, I'd cut my fucking arm off if you'd just let me be with you,' he says. 'But, Ella, we can wait around, wasting years, hoping we'll reach perfection in our lives. But it doesn't exist. We'll always have problems, but as long as we work through them *together*, I think we'll be okay.'

'There are so many problems.' I pull off my glove and spit in my trembling hand. 'But if this is what you want, then I'm in. Although, I have to say that cutting your arm off would be a disgusting gesture.'

'Fine, if you really want me to, I'll keep my arm.' He jokes, then hesitates, edging his hand away. 'Is this what you really want though? Because all I want is for you to be happy.'

I search my brain for the truth. 'I want it more than anything, just as long as you promise me one thing.'

'And what's that?'

'That if at any time it gets to be too much for you, you'll leave me — walk away and get out.'

'That will never happen,' he guarantees me. 'You need to give me some credit. You left me, ripped out my heart, and then came back acting like a robot, and you know what? We made it through. You and I, good or bad, belong together. We make each other whole.'

Tears threaten to spill out and my heart nearly stops. To anyone else, it would sound like a line, but I know it's the truth. I lift my hand up with my palm facing him. 'I need you to promise, just so I can have peace of mind.'

'Fine.' He says tolerantly. 'I promise that if things get too bad, I'll walk away.'

I let out a breath of relief. 'Then I'm in.'

It's the exact words I said during our last pact when we promised to run away together, get a nice house, good jobs, and have a happy life.

'So am I.' He spits into his hand again. 'Gotta make sure it's nice and slimy for you.'

Snorting a laugh, I press my palm to his and I swear the earth stops, because this moment is the beginning of forever.

'Now we have to kiss,' Micha says, leaning in. 'It's tradition.'

I meet him halfway and brush my lips to his. His hand cups my cheek and he instantly intensifies the kiss, stroking his tongue with mine. Our breaths collide and swarm around us as the swings' chains clink together with our movements.

Pulling away slightly, he captures me by the waist and aids me over to his lap, so I'm facing him with my legs tucked through the space on each side of him.

'No flinging us out onto the ground,' I order, putting my glove on before winding my hands around the chains. 'Last time I nearly broke my arm.'

A devious look masks his face as he picks up his feet and soars us off into the sky. It's cold as hell and there are dogs howling in the background as someone starts to shout, but I can still feel it — the lightness that comes with letting someone love you completely.

18

Micha

Early the next morning, Caroline called to ask Ella if she would mind doing the shopping for Christmas dinner. Ella agreed and Caroline gave her a list of stuff. I was kind of annoyed, since Ella used to have to take care of this shit all the time when we were growing up. Dean should have offered her a break. So after we cleared out all the alcohol from the house in preparation for the arrival of Ella's father, we went to the local grocery store.

'I have a confession,' I announce as we walk up the frozen-food aisle. The store is crowded and picked over since it's Christmas Day and everyone in the damn town has rushed to buy last-minute stuff.

'I'm not sure I want to hear your confession,' she responds with a smile as she scans the list. She's wearing a tight pair of jeans that hug at her hips, and every time she bends over to grab something off the bottom shelf, I get a nice view of her ass. 'Things have been going so well.'

'But it's kind of important and it's been

bugging me since our game of truth yesterday, because it should have been said.' I pause. 'I want you to know that I talked to this music producer down in San Diego.'

Her eyes slowly lift from the paper. 'When did this happen?'

'It happened, like, a couple of days ago.' I inch the cart out of the way as an old woman nearly runs into the back of me. I have my hood over my head and she looks at me like I'm going to rob her, so I charm her with a smile, before returning my attention to Ella. 'And it's not really a big deal. Some guy came up to me and handed me his card when I was playing at The Hook Up. I don't even recognize his name or anything, although I Googled him and he does work for a small studio.'

'Did you call him?' She opens a freezer door to get a bag of frozen peas.

I nod, taking the bag from her hand and tossing it into the cart. 'Yeah, he wants me to come out for a meeting in, like, a couple of weeks.'

She wraps her leather jacket tighter around her with a puzzled look on her face. 'And what happens if it works out for you? Then you'll move to California?'

'Maybe . . . I don't know,' I lie with hesitance. 'I haven't let myself think about the what-if's too much.'

She adds another bag of frozen peas to the cart and starts walking down the aisle. 'But what if something happens? Because it could. You are amazing after all.'

'Well, if something does happen . . . ' I clear my throat, feeling like a total pussy over the fact that I'm nervous. 'Then I was thinking that maybe you could move there with me. They have a couple colleges nearby that you could transfer to so you don't have to give that up.'

Her eyes widen just like I anticipated. 'And we would just, what? Live together?'

'Well, I wasn't thinking we'd move out there and live separately.'

'Live together,' she repeats. 'Like, with you?'

'Calm down, okay? You don't have to answer now.' I toss a bag of chips into the cart and push it forward. 'Just think about it.'

She scratches off an item on the list with the pen. 'Okay . . . I'll think about it.'

I opt to end the conversation there, right on a good note, because it will keep me in a good mood all day.

Ella

I unpack the groceries and read through the many past-due bills that were piling up in

305

the mailbox. One in particular is a notice that the house is about to go into foreclosure. My chest tightens as I read it and the paper shakes in my unsteady hand.

'What's wrong?' Micha asks, coming up behind me.

'It's nothing.' I stuff the letter back into the envelope and set it down on the kitchen table. 'Just bill stuff that I have no idea what to do with.'

I head to take a shower. I've been frozen since we arrived and the hot water sounds great at the moment. Plus, I need a minute alone to mull over his declaration that he wants us to live together. *Live together.* My mind can barely grasp the idea of it.

Micha trails after me toward the stairs. 'You should let me get in with you,' he says with a captivating smile on his lips. 'It could be for my birthday.'

'Your birthday isn't until tomorrow,' I remind him, stopping at the bottom of the stairs. 'And besides, I have to take a quick shower and get dinner started.' I glance at my watch. 'Everyone is going to be here in, like, four or five hours.'

He presses his hand to his heart with the most appealing look on his face. 'I'll be quick. I swear.'

'What exactly do you think's going to

happen during this shower?' I ask as his fingers spread across my hips, just below the hem of my shirt, and he guides me against him. 'Because I plan on getting clean.'

He shakes his head slowly with fire blazing in his eyes. 'No way. Showers are made for dirty things.' He backs me around the banister and into the wall, tangling his fingers through my hair forcefully and dipping his voice to a husky whisper. 'Think about the last time you and I showered together. How good it felt.' His hand comes up between my thighs, not stopping until it reaches the top. Even through the fabric of my jeans, heat devours my skin.

Something between a moan and a whimper escapes the back of my throat and he takes that as a yes, colliding his lips into mine. I suck his tongue deep into my mouth as I unbutton the front of his shirt and rip it off.

'I don't have any clean clothes,' I murmur against his lips as he backs us toward the downstairs bathroom.

'We'll figure something out.' Kicking the door open, we stumble in and he locks the door before returning his lips to mine. Trailing soft kisses down my jawline, he unfastens the button of my jeans and I slip them off, then tug off my shirt and shake out my hair.

The desire in his eyes nearly melts me and my body craves him inside me so badly. I quickly unclasp my bra, then grab the waist of his jeans and haul him toward me. When my nipples brush his skin they instantly perk up and his eyes close as his lips find mine. Desire pours through me as his hands glide around to my backside, searing hot as he enfolds our bodies together.

Reaching behind my back toward the tub, I manage to turn on the water and steam slowly engulfs the room. My skin dampens and my thighs tingle to be touched. I start to take off his jeans and he helps me out enthusiastically. Once the rest of our clothes are off, we climb into the shower and he draws the curtain closed. I can't help but smile at the memories that surface.

Water drips from his blond hair, beads across his lips, streams down his lean chest. His hand travels down my side and along my stomach, but before he can slip his fingers inside me, I jump up and link my legs around his waist, surprising him.

'I want you inside me,' I whisper, letting my reservations go. 'Right now.'

His eyelids open and his lashes flutter against the splashes of the shower. My confession shocks us both and without any more hesitation, he braces a hand on the wall and thrusts inside me.

My breath comes out ragged and my legs tighten around his hips as he pushes deeper into me. I can barely breathe . . . barely think. It feels so good. When he hits the right spot, I moan and grip my fingers into his shoulder blades.

'Micha, I love you,' I murmur between breaths and realize that this is what I want. Forever.

Micha

It startles the shit out of me when she says she wants me inside her. She has never been so upfront about what she wants and it turns me on so badly that my cock actually hurts.

Once I'm inside her, it feels so goddamn good, and I'm probably not going to last long. Water runs down our bodies and makes everything slippery, which is an added bonus. Bracing against the wall with one hand to keep us from falling, I rock into her over and over again, driving her to the edge. When her head tips back, the flow of the shower streams along her tits and I can't help myself. I want a taste.

I lower my mouth to one of her breasts and suck the water off while tracing her nipple with my tongue until she groans. Her fingers knot through my hair and she guides my mouth closer, seeking more. And I give it to her. Hard. Until she screams out my name. Her hair is soaked and water beads on her eyelashes as her head angles back against the wall and her green eyes glaze over. Moments later I join her, breathing loudly as I struggle to hold us up.

Once we've both caught our breath, I slip out of her, turn off the water, and we climb out. She wraps a towel around herself and I tie one around my waist. I feel so alive right now there are no words.

She chews on her lip as she slants back against the wall. 'What are you smiling about?'

I shrug, rolling my tongue to retain the smile from getting bigger. 'I didn't know I was.'

She kisses me on the cheek. 'You have this big grin on your face, so just tell me what you're thinking about.'

'You really want the truth?' I question. 'Because it's intense.'

She nods her head and her wet hair drips water down her shoulders. 'I want the truth.'

I kiss her lips lightly and whisper in her ear, 'I was thinking how we could do this every day when we have our own place.'

Her faltering breath hits my cheek and I worry she's going to freak out. 'I think we should start trying some different places besides the shower.'

My grin enlarges as I lean back and search her eyes. 'I could throw you down on our table. Or better yet, I could bend you over the banister.'

'I don't picture us having a banister,' she replies thoughtfully. 'I think I just want a small apartment. It's easier to keep clean.'

'You're getting me excited, Ella May,' I proclaim.

'I'm glad. I want you to be excited.' She bites down on her lip. 'I'm scared though. I mean this is huge, you know.'

I'm glad she admits it to me. 'Me too, but then I think about how we're going to have the 'no clothes on inside the house' rule and I just get happy again.'

She rolls her eyes and combs her fingers through her hair. 'If you don't end up moving to California, then what are you going to do?'

'We are going to get our own place eventually no matter where we live,' I say and kiss her forehead. 'You may think it's fast, but you got to remember that technically you and I have been living together since we were kids. I mean, we barely left each other's side since we were six.' I pause as tears abruptly fill her eyes. 'Baby, what's wrong?'

She wipes the tears away with the back of her hand. 'It's nothing. I just really want it to work out.'

Hugging her against me, I rest my chin on top of her head and gently rub her back. 'It will, and you want to know why?' I ask and she nods. 'Because most people go into this blind. They don't know the bad side of the person they're with. But we know each other's flaws and cracks — we know what we're getting into and that makes us stronger.'

'I really do love you.' She tightens her arms around me.

'I love you too,' I reply, trailing kisses down her neck. 'More than anything.'

19

Ella

I'm proud of myself for telling the truth to Micha and for not worrying too much during the trip, at least so far. By the time I'm dressed and walking out of my room, I'm feeling kind of happy. When I enter the kitchen, however, my good feeling deflates.

Caroline is by the stove, with her black hair wound up out of her face, stirring a pan with an apron tied around her waist. Micha is over by the microwave waiting for the butter to heat up, wearing a pair of jeans that hang loosely at his hips and his blond hair is a little damp still from the shower. Dean is at the table, in slacks and a button-down shirt, and he's peeling off the husk of the corn on the cob.

'We brought them with us,' he explains when he notices me staring at the corn. 'Caroline wanted them.'

'Oh. Okay.' I turn to Caroline. 'What still needs to be cooked?'

She shoos me away with her free hand. 'You are not cooking anything.'

I pick up a spoon off the counter. 'I always cook Christmas dinner.'

'Which is why it always sucked,' Dean remarks under his breath as he tosses a husk into the garbage.

'I did my best,' I say. 'And it's not like I wanted to. No one else would. And half the time no one would eat it.'

Caroline turns the stove's temperature down. 'You are not cooking this year. It's not right that you've spent your whole life taking care of everyone else.'

I glance over my shoulder at Micha. 'What have you been telling her?'

The microwave beeps and he opens the door. 'I didn't tell her anything.'

Perplexed, I look at my brother. 'Did you . . .'

Rolling his eyes, he tosses a cob into a large crock-pot on the table. 'Look, all I did was mention that you cooked for us almost every day while I was growing up.'

Caroline smiles as she covers the pan with a lid. 'He's been seeing someone about his anger issues.'

My eyes dart back to Dean, waiting for him to snap at her, but he just shrugs and grabs another corn on the cob that needs to be shucked.

'We'll cook dinner.' Caroline signals for

Dean to add something.

He lets out a frustrated breath. 'You should go out and do something fun. Be a kid for a change or whatever. We'll get things ready for when dad arrives.'

'How is he even getting here?' I ask, setting the spoon down on the counter. 'He doesn't have a car.'

'His counselor is dropping him off,' Caroline explains, plugging in the mixer. 'I guess he lives about an hour away from here.'

She starts to hum as she mixes some orange stuff in a bowl. Dean focuses on the corn and I stand there unsure of what to do with myself. Finally I glance at Micha for help.

'We could go out to Back Road and spin some doughnuts,' he suggests, setting the butter down on the counter.

'Your car's not made to spin doughnuts,' I say as he walks toward me. 'Hence the last time we got stuck.'

'I got chains we can put on it if it gets stuck.' He steals a marshmallow out of an open bag on the counter. 'Besides I need a few dents in that tainted car to make it whole again.' He tosses a marshmallow at me and I open my mouth to catch it, but it pegs me in the forehead.

'But I love your car.' I pick up the

marshmallow and toss it into the trash. 'I don't want to see it ruined.'

'I loathe it now,' he annunciates. 'My father has officially tainted it.'

'If you want to ruin it,' Dean chimes in, 'there's a sledgehammer in the garage.'

'That's okay,' Micha replies in a clipped tone as he snatches the bag of marshmallows and tugs me toward the door. Micha has never liked Dean very much. 'I got another idea.'

I grab my jacket off the door hanger and giggle as he hauls me toward the fence. He hops over it effortlessly, and then he picks me up by the waist and lifts me over easily.

'What's your big idea?' I say breathlessly as he leads us toward the garage and snow fills my shoes. 'Running it into a wall, racing it until the engine explodes?'

He lets out his evil villain laugh as he opens the garage door. 'We're going to spin dough-nuts dangerous style.'

I shake my head quickly. 'No way. Last time, I almost got a concussion when you rammed the snowbank.'

'Well, you better man up.' He opens up the passenger door for me. 'Because it's gonna get intense.'

I duck my head into the cab and drop into the seat. 'I don't man up. I'm a dainty little girl.'

He snorts a sharp laugh. 'Okay, if you say so.'

He slams the door and circles the front of the car. His gaze fleetingly lands on the twelve pack nestled on the shelf between the toolbox and oil. When he spots me looking at him, he grins and gets in the car, pushing the garage door opener latched onto the visor. Punching the gas, he peels out down the driveway, skidding from left to right and fishtailing it when we hit the icy road.

'Can you do me a favor?' I ask as he cranks the wheel.

'I'll do anything you want,' he answers, straightening out the car.

'Can you try not to kill us?' I say, cranking up the heat. 'Now that we've started planning a future, I kind of want to have one.'

★ ★ ★

Ethan and Lila follow us up to Back Road in Ethan's truck. The sky is cloudy but silent from the snow drifting to the ground. About halfway up to the old racing spot. Micha has to get out and put the chains on the tires. Watching him bend over and get them on is very entertaining because his pants keep slipping down on his hips. When he catches me checking him out, he winks at me and waggles his eyebrows suggestively. I turn in my seat, smiling to myself.

After we make it to the end of the road, Micha gets out and takes the chains back off so we can 'spin doughnuts dangerous style,' as he put it. Ethan parks his truck near a snowbank and Lila and he climb into the car with us. The area in front of us is open and packed with snow. Icicles hang from the branches of the trees that border around us and the roof of The Hitch, a rundown brick building that was once a restaurant, has caved in.

With his hand on the steering wheel and his eyes locked ahead, Micha pumps the gas and a cloud of smoke puffs out the exhaust. The tires spin and I cover my eyes with my hands.

'What's wrong?' he wonders with humor. 'Where's my dangerous girl tonight?'

'I'm having a hard time with the fact that you're going to destroy the car.' I peek between my fingers. 'It's just too tragic.'

'I'm not going to destroy it.' He picks up his iPod and hands it to me. 'You want to do the honors?'

I take it and scroll through the selection, finally clicking on 'Face to the Floor' by Chevelle.

Micha grins. 'Excellent choice.'

My hand instantly shoots for the side of the seat and I prop my foot up on the dash as I slouch down.

'El, what are you doing?' Lila peers around the seat at me. 'And what the hell is this music?'

'It's Chevelle,' Ethan says like she should know.

She arches her eyebrows as she sinks back in the seat. 'Okay . . . '

'Just put your seatbelt on,' I instruct as Micha laughs, revving the engine.

She obeys, quickly clicking it on and Ethan leans forward, resting his elbows on the console. 'Don't hit the fucking snowbank like last time. I don't want a concussion again.'

Ethan and I trade looks because the concussion involved him and me smacking heads upon impact.

'I got this,' Micha assures us confidently, shifting into drive. 'At least I think . . . if anyone wants to bail out, now is the time.'

We target an assumption at Lila.

'Hey, I'm not a wimp.' She places her hand over her heart, offended. 'And I'm staying in.'

Micha pushes the gas pedal and the tires spin. We lunge forward, slowly speeding up and swerving all over the place as the car battles against the deep snow. Frost flurries around the car as he shifts into a higher gear and accelerates, heading for the end of a road that's blocked off by a massive snow hill. Shutting my eyes, I wait for it because I know it's coming. It happens every single time.

'Everybody hang on,' Micha instructs, before he jerks on the e-brake.

The car spins out of control, like a carnival ride. With my eyes closed it feels like I'm flying. I want to stick my hands out and bask in the freeness. Moments later, the car smacks into the bank and the abrupt impact sends me flying for real. I land on top of Micha, banging my head on his as the car jerks to a stop.

'Oh, motherfucker,' Ethan moans. 'Fuck. Lila, are you okay?'

'I'm fine,' she assures him with terror in her voice. 'But why didn't anyone warn me?'

I open my eyes and look into Micha's aqua blue eyes. 'Hi.'

'Are you okay?' He delicately touches my head with his fingertips. 'We hit heads pretty hard.'

I press the heel of my hand to my head. 'I think you did that on purpose, so I would end up in your lap.'

'Maybe just a little.' He leans down and kisses me passionately, sucking on my bottom lip before pulling away, leaving my body suffocated in warmth. 'Actually I was aiming for a nice slide in, but I choked at the last second and didn't pull the brake quick enough.'

I start to sit up, but he holds me down by placing a hand on my chest. 'I think you should just stay there for a while. It's a good place for you.'

My head is resting in his lap and I can feel the bulge through his pants. 'Really? Even in this situation.'

His eyes sparkle with delight. 'Again, your face is, like, inches away from it.'

'You two better shut the hell up with that,' Ethan warns sharply from the backseat. 'It's seriously getting annoying and I don't have the stomach for it.'

Micha kisses me again, making an over-exaggerated moan to irritate Ethan more. The car door slams as Ethan removes himself from the car and Micha helps me sit up.

'I'll be back in a second,' he says. 'I'm going to get the tow strap out of the trunk.'

As soon as he's out of the car, Lila dives over the console and into the passenger seat. 'So let me get this straight. He got his car stuck only so they could tow it out?'

I waver, cranking up the heat to full blast. 'He got his car stuck to make a statement to his father about fixing his car.'

'But his father's not here.'

'Yeah, it's more for himself.'

She doesn't get it and I don't try to explain it to her. If this makes Micha feel better, then I'm glad. It's what he deserves.

★ ★ ★

About an hour later, the car is unstuck. Micha got the tires wedged in really deep and we finally had to bring out the snow shovels Ethan had in back of his truck.

It's not the only time we've been stuck out here and we learned our lesson the first time we got stranded to always be prepared with a snow shovel, tow strap, and chains. Otherwise, it's a long walk home in below-freezing weather.

After the car is back in the shallow end of the snow, Micha takes the tow strap off and winds it around his hand as he proudly takes in the scratches and dents on the front fender.

'I'm going to ride home with Ethan,' Lila tells me, reaching for the handle of the door.

'Wait, I have to ask you something.' I hesitate and rotate in the seat to face her. 'Are you sleeping with Ethan?'

Her blue eyes round as she ties the scarf around her neck. 'No, we're just friends. God, Ella, I don't sleep with everyone.'

'It's not that,' I tell her. 'It's just that you two seem close . . . and I mean, what do you guys do when you're alone?'

She pushes the door open and steps out, her feet sinking into the snow. 'We talk.'

I lean over, wondering what the two of them could possibly have in common. 'About what?'

'Life.' She shuts the door, tramples to the back of the car where Ethan's truck is running, and climbs inside.

One day, I'll get her to confess to me what it is they do. I turn up the music and sing along as I wait for Micha to get in. When he opens the door, a gust of wind blows in and chills the cab.

He pokes his head in, his cheeks pink from the cold and snowflakes speckling his hair. 'What? Are you driving?'

I run my hand along the top of the steering wheel. 'I was thinking about it. Why? Are you not going to let me?'

'I will totally let you.' He laughs. 'But there's something I need to do first.'

With my shoulders slumped, I swing my leg over the console and sit down in the passenger seat. 'What do you need to do?'

He shuts the door, pausing as he nibbles at his lip ring and stares pensively out the windshield at the sky, which is getting darker.

'I'm still deciding.'

'We really should be getting back,' I say, checking my messages. 'Dean texted me, like, five minutes ago and said dinner is in an hour. I guess my dad is there now and your mom and her boyfriend are going to be over soon.'

'You seem sad that your dad's there,' he states, looking at me intently.

I stare up at the cloudy sky and the snowflakes falling from the sky. 'I'm not sad, just nervous.'

'But I thought the letter made it better,' he says. 'That he let you know it wasn't your fault.'

My breath puffs out unevenly. 'Micha, I'll always carry that night with me, whether my dad says it's my fault or not.'

'Ella, it wasn't your fault.' Panic flares in his eyes; he's worried I'm reverting. 'You have to start believing that.'

'Micha, I'm okay.' I place a hand on his as a comforting gesture. 'It's when I don't say these things aloud that there's a problem.'

His Adam's apple bobs up and down as he swallows hard. 'Okay.'

We sit in silence, watching the snowflakes land on the hood and drift through the beam of the headlights.

When he looks at me again, the lust in his

eyes forces me to suck in a sharp breath. 'All right, no more drowning in our sorrows. It's confession time again.'

'Haven't we done a lot of that over the last day?' I thread my fingers through his. 'I think I might be all confessed out.'

'I have this dream,' he says, ignoring my request. 'Well, it's more like a fantasy . . . But anyway, you and I have sex in my car. We are in the driver's seat, with you on top of me.'

'That sounds an awful lot like the dream I had.'

'That's because great minds think alike. But having sex on the hood in this weather doesn't seem like it would work, so I'm going with inside.'

I glance over my shoulder at the road. 'You want to have sex in the car? Right now? What if someone comes up here?'

'Hardly anyone comes up here in this kind of weather. You know that.' He stares at me, biting on the damn lip ring and my body burns hot with longing. Without even thinking, I maneuver over the console and straddle his lap.

His lips quirk. 'I really thought it would take more persuading than that.'

He considers something, and then moves me over to get out of the car. Popping the trunk, he grabs something before hurrying back in, shivering from the cold air. There's snow on his shoulders and a blanket in his hand. 'Just in case someone does show up then we can at least be covered.'

'You keep a blanket in your trunk?' I say. 'Man, you are prepared. How many times have you had sex in your car?'

He pulls me back onto his lap and wraps the blanket around us. 'This is a first for me, pretty girl.'

'You've never done anyone in the car before?' I question with cynicism.

His face is humorless as he tucks a strand of hair behind my ear. 'I know you saw me with a lot of girls, but I think you totally mistake how much effort I put into it. Doing it in a car is going to be fucking complicated. Besides, I've been saving this place for you.'

Rolling my eyes, I fasten my arms around the back of his neck. 'And what would have happened if we'd never gotten together? Then you would have never lived out your fantasy. And what if I wasn't into it?'

He squeezes my ass. 'Oh, I knew you'd be into it. As much as you get embarrassed about stuff, cars have always turned you on. I remember the first time I took you for a ride in The Beast. It was a piece of shit back then, but it could still kick it. You were sitting in the passenger seat with your hand out the window and you had this look on your face — you were getting so turned on. It turned me on so badly, I had to take care of myself when I got home.'

'I wasn't getting turned on,' I lie. 'I was enjoying the moment.'

An artful smirk curves at his lips. 'If I would have pulled over and asked you to do me, you totally would have.'

I shake my head in protest. 'No, I wouldn't have. You would have freaked me out if you'd asked me.'

The intensity in his face switches to solemnity. 'I actually know that. You know, when it came to doing crazy things like jumping off roofs and fighting, you were good to go. But challenge you to face your feelings and you'd run away like you were on fire.'

'That's because I didn't understand them,' I utter quietly, staring off into the darkness outside. 'Anna . . . my therapist, thinks it's because no one ever hugged me or whatever. I don't know . . . She says weird stuff like that all the time to me, like she thinks it's my childhood that made me this way.'

Silence encases us and finally I dare a glance at him, fearing I've probably freaked him out with my confession. 'I'm sorry. I should probably keep that stuff to myself.'

'I want you to talk to me about stuff, Ella,'

he says. 'I'm just surprised you did. You've never said much about what goes on in therapy.'

'That's because it's personal.' My chest rises and falls as I breathe soundly.

He cups my cheek and runs his thumb underneath my eye. 'You do realize we've crossed the line of things being personal.'

He's right, so summoning confidence, I continue. 'She says I didn't get hugged enough and I told her you hugged me all the time, but she didn't seem that impressed.'

He laughs softly. 'I remember the first time I tried to hug you . . . I think we were, like, eight or something. You'd scraped the shit out of your knee trying to climb up a tree and I wanted to make you feel better, so I went to hug you.'

I wince at the memory. 'And then I punched you in the arm. I remember . . . you scared me. I'd never had anyone approach me like that.'

'I know.' He bushes his lips against mine as his finger traces my cheekbone. 'The next time I made sure I was a little more careful, although I did sneak in a few arm wraps and pats on the back.'

'It was weird for me when you did it,' I confess. 'But there were too many people around and I didn't want to look nuts by running away from your celebration . . . God, I can't believe I was that old the first time I can remember being hugged.'

'What were we, like, thirteen?' Micha recollects, dazing off as he coils a strand of my hair around his finger. 'I was so fucking excited that I'd won that stupid bet.'

'It was a stupid bet.' My eyelids flutter as his hand runs through my hair and tugs at the roots. 'We all knew Danny was afraid of heights. I have no idea why he even tried to jump off the cliff into the lake.'

'I held my breath the entire fall.' I clutch onto his shoulders. 'I think I was scared you'd hurt yourself or something.'

'That's because you loved me. You just didn't know it yet.'

'You didn't know it either. You were just as blind as me.'

'I know, but I can remember swimming out of the lake totally stoked because I'd won two hundred bucks. Plus I was so hyped up on adrenaline. When I saw you standing on the shore in the cut-off that showed off your long skinny legs' — he pinches my ass and I shake my head — 'I wasn't even thinking. I just went over, picked you up, and latched on to you.'

'You nearly squeezed the life out of me,' I recollect. 'And you got my clothes all wet

. . . but I did like it.'

He crooks an eyebrow. 'It didn't seem like you did.'

'I did.' I latch onto his gaze, needing to look at him. 'It was scary, but nice. Everything with you is scary, but nice.'

His expression changes at my honesty and he leans in to kiss me fervidly, ending the conversation. I eagerly unzip my jacket and toss it into the backseat. He pulls my shirt over my head and quickly unfastens my bra with one flick of his finger. His gaze instantly lowers. Cupping one with his hand, he brings his mouth to my breast and I fall backward, bumping the horn. It honks into the night, but I'm too lost to care as his hand glides down my stomach and delves inside my jeans. Once his fingers are inside me, my eyes seal shut and warmth ripples through my body. The horn keeps honking and 'Don't Wait' by Dashboard Confessions flows from the speakers.

'Micha, I want you,' I moan as he sucks kisses along the hollow of my neck and I can hardly breathe. 'I really do.'

He draws back slightly, his eyes penetrating mine. When his lips return to mine, it's not just about lust or desire — it's about making us whole.

Rising my hips upward to take my jeans

and panties off, I accidentally bang my head on the roof. Laughing softly, he steers my mouth back to his forcefully as I fumble to undo the button of his jeans and then he wiggles them down. Seconds later he's inside me and I hover forward to stop the horn from honking as I open my mouth, allowing his tongue to devour me. The windows fog up as he thrusts into me and I cling onto him like he's what keeps me thriving. Because he is.

20

Micha

I smile the entire drive home. Not just because she let me do her in the car, but also because so much has changed. She opened up to me and her eyes lost a little bit of the sadness in them.

When I pull the car up to the front of her house, however, my gut wrenches at the idea that all the progress could be taken away in a heartbeat if Dean or her dad decides to bring painful things up. I decide before I get out of the car, that if they do, I'll hurt them.

Dean's red Porsche is in the driveway, along with Ethan's truck. As we walk toward the back door, holding hands, snow falling from the sky and crunching under our shoes, neither one of us speaks. When we reach the door, I pause before opening it.

'You sure you want to do this?' I ask. 'Because we could take off right now, just you and I and go wherever you want.'

She stands on her tiptoes to kiss my cheek and then nods. 'I think I have to.'

Reluctantly, I open the door and we walk

head-on into the lion's den. At the table, Ella's dad, Lila, and Ethan are sitting quietly around bowls and plates full of corn, stuffing, chicken, peas. There are rolls and butter and much more than both of us are used to seeing. Keeping a hold of Ella's hand I walk over to the table and we take a seat side-by-side.

'It took you a long time to get back,' Ethan mutters under his breath with an accusing laugh. 'What, did you get stuck again or something?'

'Knock it off.' I take a roll as Ella grips my hand under the table with her eyes fixed on the tablecloth. Her dad looks awkward sitting across from us, cutting a piece of chicken into absurdly thin slices.

'Hello, Ella,' he says formally, without making eye contact. 'How have you been?'

My muscles tense waiting for her response.

It takes her a second. 'Good. Really, really good.'

I exhale and the heaviness and worry of the night alleviates for the moment. Dean enters with a box in his hand and a confused look on his face.

'Who drew on the bathroom floor?' He drops the box on the counter.

Ella raises her hand. 'I did.'

'Okay.' His tone holds annoyance. 'Well, next time close the damn door. You know how I feel about it being open.'

I grit my teeth, trying not to say anything as Ella raises her chin and looks at her father, who seems obsessed with the chicken. 'Dad, I think the chicken is cut.'

'Oh.' He sets the fork down to the side of the plate and sighs. 'I didn't even realize I was cutting it.'

'Be nice,' Caroline hisses at Dean from behind us. 'Or I swear to God you're sleeping alone tonight.' She appears at the table with a plate of crackers and cheese. She's wearing a red dress with a skeleton on the bottom and a cross around her neck. 'All right, who's hungry?'

We all dig in like we're starved animals and my mom and Thomas come waltzing in right on time. My mom has a green dress on that's a little too short and Thomas has a polo shirt and cargo pants on. Ella's dad stands up to give my mom a quick kiss on the cheek, and then they take a seat at the opposite end on fold-up chairs.

After everyone is seated, Caroline clinks her fork against her cup. 'Okay, so my family has this tradition where we all go around and say one thing that we're thankful for.'

'Baby, I don't think that's such a good idea,' Dean says, reaching for the gravy. 'Not here, anyway.'

She swats his hand away from the food. 'I don't really care what you think. I think we should do it.'

We wait for him to react because the Dean we used to know had a fucking hell of a temper on him. Back when we were kind of friends and played in a band, he would get pissed over everything and he broke a lot of drumsticks.

He rubs his hand tensely on the back of his neck. 'Fine, I'm really grateful for you cooking this delicious dinner for everyone.'

Caroline beams at him. 'And I'm grateful everyone showed up.'

My mom chimes in. 'I'm grateful the kids could make it here. It's been so lonely without them.'

Thomas glances around the table, looking lost. 'Umm . . . I'm grateful the Vikings won the game.'

I roll my eyes and Ella covers her mouth to hide her laughter. My mom scowls at us, but then Ella's dad clears his throat, seeming nervous.

'I'm grateful for being sober,' he says and sips on his water. 'This is the first Christmas I've not been drunk in as long as I can remember.'

Ella lets out a shaky breath and her eyes water over, like she's going to cry. No one speaks for a minute and finally Caroline looks at Ethan.

'What about you?' she asks.

He contemplates it with a smirk on his face. 'I'm thankful for red lacy bras that have an easy-access clasp in the front.'

I restrain a laugh as Ella's head falls onto the table, her shoulders shaking as she laughs under her breath and Lila and I join in.

'Ethan Gregory,' my mom warns. 'That was uncalled for.'

He surrenders his hand in front of him. 'Hey, I was just being honest.'

My mom rolls her eyes. 'What about you, Lila?'

Lila twists a strand of her blonde hair around her finger with a twinkle in her blue eyes. 'I'm thankful for candy canes.'

Ella raises her head up and smoothes her hair into place, looking as mystified as everyone else, except for Ethan.

He winks at Lila, who blushes a little. 'That's a good thing to be thankful for.'

Ella remains quiet for a while with this strange look on her face, like she's thinking deep, and then she glances at me. 'I'm grateful for Micha.'

I lean over and kiss her in front of everyone. 'I'm really grateful you said that.'

'Wait,' Dean interrupts, gaping at us with a

disgusted look on his face. 'Are you guys dating?'

'Yep,' Ella says indifferently, scooting her chair closer to the table. 'Now, can we please eat?'

We eat the rest of the meal making small talk. Ella keeps biting her lip and assessing everyone, but she doesn't look sad, just genuinely interested in what everyone is doing and saying. There are even a few moments where she looks happy.

It's a good look for her.

Ella

Dinner is as about as awkward as possible, especially when Caroline makes us admit what we're grateful for. At first I try to think of something meaningful, but then I just listen to my heart. When dinner is over, we clean up in a drama-free environment. It isn't anything special, but it's normal, which is something I've wanted since I was a little girl. No drunken fathers, no screaming, no working my ass off to cook a dinner that no one will eat.

I help Caroline clean up and wash the dishes while my dad goes up to his room to unpack. Dean disappeared somewhere and

337

Micha went home for a while because his mom had a present for him. Lila and Ethan are in the living room, attempting to put a small pine tree up that Dean cut down in the front yard.

When I take the trash out back, a cloud of smoke engulfs my face when I round the porch. Dean is leaning against the house in the shadows smoking a cigarette and wearing one of his old heavy flannel jackets with the hood pulled over his head. I have a flashback of when I was fourteen and caught him smoking something else in the garage.

'What are you doing out here?' I open the garbage lid and drop the bag into it.

He scratches his head and takes another drag. 'Do me a favor and don't tell Caroline I'm out here. She thinks I quit. And I did. Kind of.'

Nodding, I hug my arms around myself and turn for the house.

'So it's weird, right?' he says abruptly.

I backtrack and squint through the dark to look at him. 'What's weird?'

He blows out a puff of smoke. 'Having him here sober.'

Through the window of the house, Caroline is talking to my dad. He has a striped shirt on and a pair of slacks. His brown hair is combed neatly and his face is freshly shaven.

'It is weird,' I agree, returning my attention to Dean. 'And he looks so clean.'

Dean bobs his head up and down. 'I know . . . I swear there was, like, a year where he didn't shower.' He takes another drag and kicks his shoes at the snow. 'Did he . . . did he write you a letter too?'

'Yeah . . . ' I trail off at the awkwardness of standing here talking to him about personal stuff. 'I'm guessing he wrote you one.'

'I think his therapist or counselor or whatever made him.' The end of the cigarette glows in the dark as he inhales from it. 'I'm not really fucking sure what I think of it yet.'

'Me neither.' I rock from side to side to keep warm. Without a jacket on, my skin is numb and probably turning purple. 'I like that he did it, but it doesn't erase the past.'

'Nothing can erase the past,' he states bluntly. 'But we can fucking move on, which is what I've been trying to do for a while.'

'Me too.' I wonder if we're going to go down that path again; the one where he tells me it's my fault this all happened.

Snow floats down on top of our heads as I stare out at the street, where the lights from the streetlamp illuminate the ice on the sidewalk.

'She inherited the car,' he admits. 'That's where she got it.'

I whip my head back toward him. 'What?'

He takes a long drag. 'The Porsche. I guess she had, like, this rich great-aunt or something who no one knew really, and when she died, she left every single one of her relatives something and that's where she got it from.'

'Did Mom tell you that?'

'Yeah, a couple of weeks before she . . . before she died. It was the same time she told me that when she was gone, I could have it. I thought she was being weird at the time, but now that I look back I wonder if she was, like, preplanning her death.'

I force down the massive lump in my throat. 'Are you sure she wasn't lying, because she told stories sometimes. Like how she and dad met at a train station when they both missed their train, when really they just dated each other in high school.'

'The train story was better,' he says with a small smile as he ashes the cigarette. 'And yeah, she was telling the truth. I could tell because it was one of her normal days.'

I let out a wobbly breath, thinking about her infrequent normal days. Those days clutch at my heart because I know there won't be any more.

Dean offers me a cigarette. 'It'll calm you down. Trust me.'

I pinch it in my fingers and take a hit. 'You know it tastes as bad as the last time you gave me one,' I say with a cough, covering my mouth with my hand.

Smiling, he drops the butt into the snow and puts it out with the tip of his shoe. 'Yet, you still took it again.'

Shaking my head, I trample through the snow toward the door, but it swings open and my dad steps out, tugging his hood over his head. 'Jesus, it's cold out here.'

'Well, it is December,' Dean remarks with an arch of his eyebrows.

My dad pops a cigarette into his mouth and lights the end of it. 'It seems like we should have decorated the house or something. We never really did that, did we?'

'We did once,' I say, scuffing the toes of my shoes along the snow. 'But you weren't here. I think it's when you took off with Bill for that couple of weeks to go ice fishing. Mom wanted us to do it . . . ' I trail off and we all get quiet.

'Well, maybe we should start making it a tradition.' He exhales a breath of smoke that floats toward my face. 'Maybe we can all come back here during Christmas, decorate the house, and have a nice dinner like we just had.' He pauses, seeming nervous. 'What do you two think?'

Dean flicks a glance at me and then shrugs. 'Whatever. Sounds good. Although I'm not promising anything. I've got a life of my own.'

My dad doesn't respond and it gets quiet again. I laugh under my breath. This is probably how it's going to be with us, at least until we can all get over our issues. Things will be weird, we'll have a hard time being around each other, and we'll probably say things that are hurtful.

But what makes me able to handle it is the fact that I have people in my life who are there for me. I have Lila. And Ethan. And Micha. I can tell him about everything and I know he'll make me feel better, he'll listen, and he'll be there for me.

I back toward the fence. 'I think I'm going to go next door for a while.' I climb over the fence and they watch me, perplexed. 'And I like the idea, Dad, about the Christmas thing. It sounds good. Count me in.'

He nods and continues with his cigarette as Dean leaves him and goes into the house.

I enter Micha's house without knocking, just like I did when I was a kid. He's sitting at the kitchen table eating a piece of pie he must have snatched from my house before he left. His blond hair hangs in his beautiful aqua eyes, and the way his mouth moves makes me want to kiss him.

He sets the fork on the plate as he looks up at me and his eyes widen. 'God, you look like you're freezing. Your cheeks are all red and your lips are purple.'

I press my lips together to warm them up. 'I was standing outside for a while talking to Dean and my dad.'

He pulls a face as he puts his plate in the sink. 'How'd that go?'

'Okay.' I shrug and walk across the kitchen to him. 'No one said anything mean, so that's always an added bonus.'

He rinses off the plate and then turns the faucet off. 'Are you okay?'

I wrap my arms around him and embrace him with everything I've got. 'I am now.'

His arms fold around me and he tilts my chin up to give me a soft but succulent kiss. When he pulls away, his eyebrows are knit. 'Did you smoke?'

I bit my bottom lip to hide my guilty conscience. 'Umm . . . kind of.'

He waits for me to explain and when I don't he kisses me again, probably enjoying the taste. 'What do you want to do for the rest of the night?' he murmurs against my lips.

I consider his request. 'I want to lay in bed with you.'

He takes my hands and leads me down the hallway, giving me exactly what I want.

Micha

I have a surprise for her for Christmas, but I'm not sure how she's going to take it. My mom actually gave it to me tonight as a present. At first, I thought she was fucking insane, but she assured me she was indeed sane.

'I think you should give it to Ella,' she said, handing me a little black box. We were sitting on the couch across from each other while Thomas sat next to her, drinking a beer. 'It was your great-grandmother's.'

Thomas wrapped his arm around her shoulder, pretending to be interested. 'Yeah, girls love that shit.'

I opened the box and it was exactly what I thought. 'Not Ella . . . she's going to fucking flip if I show this to her.'

'Micha Scott, watch your language,' she warned, waving her finger at me. 'And I think Ella loves you more than you think.'

'I know she loves me.' I snapped the box shut and shoved the box back in her direction. 'But she's not going to like this.'

She declined to take the box, crossing her legs as she leaned back into Thomas. 'I've never told you the story of your great-grandmother, have I?'

I sat the box down on the table and crossed

my arms, slouching back into the chair and propping my boots up on the coffee table. 'No, but I have a feeling you're about to.'

'You're such a wise child.' She sighed. 'Whenever my mom used to talk about her, she'd refer to her as the lucky one in the family. I don't know if you know this or not, but I come from a long line of women whose hearts were broken.'

'That isn't helping you with your point,' I told her, and Thomas chuckled as he fidgeted with one of the ornaments on the tiny Christmas tree balanced on the end table.

She rolled her eyes and opened the box, so the ring was staring at me. 'The point of the story isn't the women who didn't find love, but the one who did. Your great-grandmother Sherri, and my grandmother, was happily married for fifty-three years to a guy she met when she was a teenager.'

'You're so full of shit right now,' I say, shaking my head. 'But I have to give you props for making up the story.'

'It's not a story, Micha Scott. It's the truth.' She picked up the box from the coffee table and balanced it in the palm of her hand, urging me to take it. 'You're one of the lucky ones who did find love. People envy you and Ella — hell, I envy you.'

'That's because you were married to a

douche bag for six years.'

'What you have isn't the same as your father and me. I barely knew him when I met him.'

Giving up, I decided to tolerate her and took the box from her hand. 'I'll think about it.'

She smiled, leaning back into Thomas, who whispered something in her ear. The longer I stared at the ring, the more my reservations crumbled. In the end, I had an idea.

As Ella and I lay in my bed with the lamp on, we cuddle close to each other because of the icy temperature. The neighbors' red and gold Christmas lights flash through the window and light up my room. Ella has on the Silverstein shirt without a bra on and her hair smells like vanilla mixed with smoke. I love the smell.

'What are you thinking about?' She rolls onto her stomach and rests her chin on my chest, batting her eyelashes at me. 'You're being really quiet.'

I stare into her eyes, considering my next words carefully. 'I'm thinking about giving you your Christmas present.'

Her head tilts to the side. 'Since when do we do the Christmas present thing? We've never done it before.'

'Well, I'm thinking about starting a new

tradition.' With a deep inhale, I reach for the box on my nightstand and balance it on my chest right in front of her face. 'Actually a few new traditions maybe.'

Her green eyes amplify as she quickly retreats and kneels on the bed. 'What is that?'

Collecting the box, I sit up. 'It's what you think it is. However, before you go freaking out, let me get through my speech, okay?'

Her chest heaves as she breathes in and out. 'Okay.'

I'm shocked I even got an okay from her, so I swiftly push forward. 'So, my mom told me this story about my great-grandma who apparently was, like, the only woman in the family lucky enough to ever find love.' I pause, trying to pick up her vibe, but in the low light, her eyes look black and her face is barely a shadow.

I kneel in front of her, taking her hand, which trembles. 'She also explained to me how lucky we are and that she kind of envies us.'

She stifles a smile. 'Your mom envies a couple of teenagers?'

'Hey, tomorrow I'm officially out of that category,' I remind her in a light tone.

She swallows hard and her eyes flicker to the box in my hand. 'Which means I should be giving you the presents.'

'Oh, you will,' I assure her with a grin as I clutch the box tightly in my sweaty palm, struggling to hide my nervousness. 'But tonight is about you and me and our future.' Her lips open with an objection, but I talk over her and her eyes drift to the door. 'The thing is, I knew when my mom suggested it that you aren't ready. I get you, Ella May, that much.' I cup her cheek and compel her to look at me. 'Like how I know that right now you want to leave. Not because you don't love me, but because you're scared. Scared you can't do it. Scared you'll hurt me. Scared you'll actually be happy about what I'm going to ask you.'

She bites down on her bottom lip, looking torn, her eyes wide, her chest heaving with each unstable breath. 'Sometimes I think you're a mind reader.'

I smile. 'I actually am. I just don't tell anyone because it would freak too many people out.'

She rolls her eyes and sits down on the bed, settling my nerves a little. I sit in front of her and position the box between us.

'I'm not going to ask you to marry me,' I say and her eyebrows furrow as she raises her gaze from the box to me. 'I'm going to make a proposition.'

'A proposition?' she asks, confounded.

'What kind of a proposition?'

I'm thoroughly enjoying myself now, knowing she's curious. I take her hand in mine and open her palm to set the box in it. 'I want you to wear it, not on your ring finger but on some other finger and then you can move it to your ring finger whenever you're ready.'

She gapes at the box fearfully. 'And what happens when I move it? We just get married?'

'Yeah,' I say simply. 'That's kind of the point.'

Her gaze connects with mine, her pupils magnified. 'But then we'd be married — like, really married.'

'It's not happening right now, so calm down.' I massage her hips to try and relax her. 'Now, are you going to open it, or stare at the box all day?'

She stares at the box for what seems like an eternity and then tentatively flips the lid open. Her breath catches. 'Holy shit,' she says and drops the box.

Trying not to laugh, I pick it up and remove the ring, holding it out to her. 'What do you say, pretty girl? Are you in or out?'

I wait for what seems like forever and then she slips an unsteady finger through the band. 'I'm in.'

It's on the ring finger of the wrong hand, which means we're not quite there. But one day we will be. And that's all I need at the moment.

21

Ella

I feel so strange the next day, in ways that are unexplainable. I have a ring on my finger, the diamond band twisted in knots that swirl up to a black stone in the center of glistening studs. It's actually the most perfect ring for me, not girly with a big flashy diamond on it, like a lot of girls want. It's dark, different, and has some scratches on the surface, like me.

The more I think about it, it's downright perfect.

I decide to wake him up with a nice birthday present for being the greatest person that has ever graced my life.

At the crack of dawn, when the sunlight is barely peeking through the curtain, I sneak out of bed and over to my house, which is soundless. Lila is fast asleep in my bed and I tiptoe to my closet. Searching through my old clothes, I find what I'm looking for.

I remember when I wore it for Halloween. I was sixteen and decided to act like a girl for the night. Usually, I did something scary, but that year I put on a leather dress and some stilettoes that made me tower over almost everyone at Micha's party. My hair was done up and I had some bright red lipstick on. It had been a rough day at my house that day. My dad had wrecked the car and my mom had yelled at him for hours, so I was relieved to be leaving and getting a break.

When I showed up, the party had been in full mode. The music was cranked, people were wasted, girls were half naked, and furniture had been broken. Micha was talking to a girl with curly brown hair, wearing a dress equally as short as mine, but she had a lot more cleavage that nearly fell out of the top. He was dressed in a black T-shirt with a red skull on it and there were skulls all over his belt that held up his black jeans. He had sprayed black streaks in his hair and there were leather bands around his wrists.

They were in the kitchen next to the keg and I had walked up casually as if nothing was out of the ordinary.

'You know someone's broken your mom's ceramic plate, right?' I told him reaching for a plastic up. 'Out on the back porch.'

He was fully engulfed in the brunette. 'Well, I'll clean it up . . . ' When his eyes landed on me his voice trailed off and the brunette gave me a nasty look. His gaze skimmed my costume and he didn't look happy. 'What the fuck are you wearing?'

I sipped my beer. 'A Halloween costume.'

He gaped at me. 'What the hell are you supposed to be?'

'A slut,' I say, cutting a glance at the brunette. 'Which seems to be a theme tonight.'

She glared at me and then smiled sweetly at Micha. 'I'm going to go dance. Do you want to join me?'

He waved his hand at her dismissively. 'You can't walk around like that.'

'Why not?' I was thoroughly enjoying how upset he was over the dress. 'It's how everyone else is dressed.'

He leaned to the side and checked out my backside. 'Your ass is basically hanging out of it . . . and girls dress like that when they want to get fucked, so go home and change.'

I started to get pissed. Knocking back the entire beer, I crumpled the cup and tossed it on the counter. 'You're acting like a jealous boyfriend and it's weird.'

'I'm trying to protect you, Ella May,' he retorted loudly over the music as I marched toward the living room where everyone was dancing. 'From all the other guys out there who are thinking the same dirty thoughts as I am.'

For a brief moment, his words excited me,

but I smothered the feeling. 'You have no right to try and stop me from doing anything, when you do whatever you want and whoever you want all the time and I don't ever say a word.'

He glared at me and I scowled back, before backing away into the crowd with my chin held up defiantly.

About an hour later, I was pretty drunk and dancing with some guy with brown hair and bloodshot eyes, who smelled like pot. He was cute, but I wasn't into him. Every time he tried to touch me, I inched out of his reach with panic soaring through me.

Finally, he grabbed my waist, digging his fingers into me roughly, and forced me to get closer to him. Anxiety had seized my throat as his fingers spread around my hips and I was just about to knee him in his special place when he was yanked away from me.

'Get the hell out of here.' Micha shoved him back, then clenched his hands into fists.

The guy stumbled into a few people, regained his footing, and came back at Micha with his fists out. But the threat in Micha's eyes made him rethink it and he shied away into the crowd.

When Micha aimed his gaze at me, I was thrown off by the intensity. 'Go into my room and lay down, before you end up doing something you'll regret.'

'Fuck you,' I replied, hating to fight with him, but he was being possessive and it was getting on my nerves. 'You're acting like a controlling asshole.'

His expression softened and he offered his hand to me. 'I'm just trying to protect you from stuff. You're drunk and you're dressed like . . . ' His eyes strayed up my body and then he shook his head, blinking his eyes. 'Just please come lie down with me.'

I snatched hold of his hand and he steered me up in front of him to walk behind me with his hands on my hips. He didn't let go of me until we reached his room.

He shut the door and he sucked on his lip ring, appearing uneasy, which was very unlike him. 'Do you want one of my shirts to sleep in?'

'You're acting really, really weird.' I sat down on the bed, unfastened the strap of my shoe, and wiggled my foot out, before starting on the other one. 'What's wrong with you tonight? Did a girl blow you off or something?'

'I never get upset over a girl, unless it's you.' He released his lip ring from his teeth and began unclipping the bands on his wrists. 'I think I should be the one asking you what's wrong. I've never seen you dress like that.'

'I'm fine.' I slipped my foot out of the shoe and turned around to climb into his bed. 'I just wanted to do something different.'

I turned around to get under the covers and when I faced him again, he had an amused smile on his face.

'What?' I asked, pulling the blanket over me. 'Why are you looking at me like that?'

He signaled for me to scoot over as he slipped his shirt off. 'It's nothing. I just can't believe you showed up wearing that.'

Fuming, I rolled to my side and put my back to him. 'What's-his-face from the dance floor seemed to like it.'

He got into bed with me, pressing his body closer to mine than he normally did. 'I didn't say it was a bad thing . . . it's just surprising. That's all.' He placed a hand lightly on my hip and my stomach fluttered, which it had never done before.

A loud breath escaped my lips and I winced. Sealing my lips shut, I crossed my fingers he hadn't heard it. He edged nearer, so his chest was touching my back and his warm breath feathered my skin.

'Ella?' He sounded choked up.

It took me a second to compose myself enough to speak. 'Yeah.'

The silence that followed drove me crazy.

'Sweet dreams,' he finally said and kissed

the back of my neck before rolling over.

Looking back at the memory now, I can't help but smile, realizing what was really going on.

Stuffing the dress and shoes into my bag, I hurry downstairs and run into Caroline in the kitchen. Her black hair is sticking up all over the place and she has a set of striped pajamas on. She pours herself a cup of coffee, yawning, and when she sees me, she smiles.

'Oh, I thought you were in bed,' she says. 'Are you an early riser too?'

I swing the bag onto my shoulder. 'Not usually. This morning was just an exception.'

She collects her cup of coffee and pulls out a chair at the table. 'Did you want some coffee?'

'Sure, why not.' Setting the bag to the floor, I pour myself a cup and join her at the table, breathing in the steam. 'God, I love caffeine.'

She adds some milk to her coffee and takes a gulp. 'I'd like to take some pictures of you and Micha later today, if you don't mind. I always take pictures around the holidays.'

'Okay,' I say. 'I have to ask Micha, but I'm sure he'll be okay with it.'

She gives a prolonged pause. 'I'd like to take some of you, Dean, and your dad too.'

My expression plummets as I lower my cup

back to the table. 'What did Dean have to say about that?'

'He said he'd do it.' She gets up to put the milk in the fridge. 'As long as you two agreed to it.'

I strain a smile. 'All right, well, I guess that's fine with me.'

She returns to the table, appearing hesitant. 'Dean's a little different than he used to be. I think anyway. I think his therapy sessions are really helping.' She pauses to take a drink. 'You know it took him forever to completely open up to me . . . about everything.'

I stare at the cracks in the table, getting uncomfortable. 'Oh.'

'Don't worry, Ella. I'm not looking to talk about it,' she says kindly. 'I just wanted to let you know that he's different and that maybe you could let him in a little more.'

My gaze rises to her. 'I let him in as much as he wants me to let him in.'

She gathers her empty cup and sets it in the sink. 'That's not true, although he probably won't admit it. He doesn't really admit anything, unless you force him to — he holds a lot in.'

Confusion swarms my head. 'He's always said whatever he thinks when he's around me.'

'No, he says things to push you away.' She pats my arm and then heads for the doorway, the sunlight streaming in from the window to the side of her. 'But that's something you two will need to talk about one day in the far future . . . when you're both ready. In fact, you know what you should do?'

'No.' And I'm not sure if I want to.

'You should come stay with us for the summer,' she says, glancing over her shoulder at me. 'Maybe for a few weeks.'

'I'm not sure that'd be a good thing.'

'Just think about it, okay?'

I nod and she leaves the kitchen. After I finish my coffee, I grab my bag and head out the door and into the freezing cold, mulling over my future.

Micha

I'm woken up to someone sucking on my neck and the scent of vanilla. I decide I might not open my eyes and just let Ella go to town.

'Rise and shine, birthday boy,' she whispers in my ear as she nips at my lobe and her leg slides over me so she's straddling me.

'No way,' I reply with my eyes shut, feeling the skin between her legs brush against my stomach. 'You're going to have to suck on a lot more things to bring me out of this deep sleep.'

She laughs and slants back. I open my eyes and I'm instantly glad I did. She has on a short leather dress that barely covers up her body and high heels that match. Her auburn hair is done up with stray pieces hanging loosely around her face and her lips are stained red.

'I've seen that outfit before.' My hands pursue her hips. 'In fact, I remember that day very clearly.'

'You were so mad.' She runs her finger through my hair. 'I thought you were going to punch that guy on the dance floor.'

'Oh, it took a lot not to,' I assure her, pressing her down against my swollen cock. 'I was so pissed that he tried to touch you.'

'Why, though?' she asks with curiosity. 'Guys had tried to hit on me before and you never did anything.'

'That's because you usually beat me to the punch. But that night you acted like you were asking for it,' I say. 'Do you know when you were climbing into bed, I got a full view of those naughty little panties you had on — they barely covered anything.'

Her lips part. 'Is that why you were smiling?'

'Fuck yeah.' I sneak my fingers up her dress

and squeeze her firm ass. 'I got an eyeful and I was so turned on.'

'Oh my God.' She covers her mouth with her hand, shaking her head. 'That's so embarrassing.'

'Why? I've seen everything now. Hell, I've been inside you.' I jerk the top of her dress down, surprising her, and lure her breast down toward my mouth. 'I've kissed every single part of you.' Taking her breast into my mouth, I roll my tongue along her nipple until she moans.

'I had a plan,' she says, breathless. 'I was going to . . . ' She trails off, whimpering as I suck with just enough force to drive her body crazy and she quivers against me.

Letting her go for a second, I slip her panties down her legs to her ankles. 'Keep the dress and the heels on.'

A smile touches her lips as she kicks off her panties and gradually lowers herself onto me. I meet her halfway and push into her. Her breath hitches as her head falls back and some of her hair slips out, falling along her shoulders.

'Micha . . . ' she moans as I thrust into her again. 'Oh my God . . . '

I kiss her fiercely as my hands move down her bare shoulders, along the side of her leather dress, and rest at her hips where I grab tightly ahold of her. Our skin begins to dampen with sweat as our movements start to match each other's. When she cries out my name, with her eyes glistening, she loses it completely and I join her. Once we regain our breath, I kiss her jawline and incline away, slipping out of her. Circling my arms around her, I roll to the side, pull her close, and look into her eyes.

'Best birthday present ever,' I say and gently kiss the palm of her hand, feeling the ring on her finger. 'I don't think any birthday will ever top this one.'

She smiles contently. 'You don't think so?'

I run my finger along the edge of the ring and it sends a rush of adrenaline through me, knowing she's close to being mine forever. 'No, I know so.'

★　★　★

It's late in the afternoon when we finally get out of bed. Ella complains about being sore and it makes me proud.

She scowls at me when I tell her this as she puts her T-shirt on. 'So what do you want to do for the rest of the day?'

'Make you sorer,' I say, tugging a long-sleeve shirt over my head.

She sighs, letting her arms fall to her side.

'Can't I have just a tiny little break? Pretty please. Maybe just like an hour.'

'Fine.' I frown, disappointed, and search for something else to do. 'Okay, I know what I want to do.'

She wiggles into her jeans and does up the button. 'What's that?'

I back for the door, scooping up a lighter my dad left behind when he bailed out on me. 'I want to burn all the stuff that ever reminded me of my dad.'

I wait for her to lecture me, but she picks up her jacket and zips it. 'We should probably do it in an open area, like the driveway,' she says, unfazed. 'Just to be safe.'

'There is no one else in the world who can get me like you do, pretty girl.' I take her hand and we head outside to build a fire.

The sun is actually out and shining down, but the air is still cold. Everything is concealed in frost and the driveway has been plowed.

Ella hunts for the lighter fuel and some wood while I go into the garage and collect some things that belonged to my dad. When I return to the driveway, she has a small fire going and a relaxed look on her face as she stares at the flame with her head tilted to the side.

I start throwing things into the flames one

by one, starting with an old work shirt that was left in the garage. 'I've decided I'm not going to talk to him again.'

She takes the lighter and tosses it into the flames. 'But what if he calls and really wants to be in your life again?'

I chuck one of his old screwdrivers into the fire, even though it won't really burn. 'He's going to have to do a hell of a lot more than call.' I take a deep breath and stare at the photo of my dad and me in front of his old Dodge Challenger parked in the garage. We used to work on it every day. It was our thing, until he bailed and took the car with him, and all that was left was an empty garage full of bullshit memories.

I crumple up the photo and toss it into the fire, watching it singe. 'He'll have to earn it.'

Her fingers grab mine and she squeezes my hand. 'Good, because he doesn't deserve you.'

With the next thing I try to add, she quickly tries to stop me.

'What are you doing?' she asks, snatching ahold of my wrist to stop me from throwing the six-pack of beer into the fire.

'I'm getting rid of my baggage.'

'Micha, I didn't say you had to stop drinking, just that you should stop trying to deal with your problems that way.'

364

'I know,' I say. 'But right now, I think this is what we both need.'

Looking into my eyes, she nods and lets go of my arm. I chuck the pack into the flames, which rush up toward the sky excitedly as the bottles break. As we stare at the blazing flame melting away at the snow, Ethan's truck pulls up and he and Lila hop out.

'Okay, I so want to know what this is for,' Lila says, stuffing her hands into her coat pockets, the glow of the fire reflecting in her wide eyes.

'We're saying good-bye.' I swing my arm around Ella's shoulder and draw her closer.

'Good-bye to what?' Ethan asks, zipping up his coat and pulling the hood over his head.

Ella and I trade a secret glance.

'To the past,' she says, and I smile, because that's exactly what it is.

22

Ella

The next few days are relaxing and filled with long drives and small conversations. Caroline takes her pictures of us out in the front yard. We all manage to smile in some of them, but it's much easier in the pictures of just Micha and me. When we're getting ready to leave to go back to our lives, she assures me that she'll send me copies.

Lila and Ethan returned back to Vegas the day before and Micha and I are taking the dinged-up Chevelle back home. Micha is waiting in the car while I say a quick good-bye to everyone. Dean gives me a halfhearted pat on the back and Caroline gives me a real hug, throwing me out of my comfort zone.

When she pulls back, my anxiety is pounding through my chest, but I mentally talk myself down and approach my dad, who's standing on the back porch with a heavy brown coat on. 'Are you sure you don't want me to stay for a few extra days and help you get the house all set up? Or go with you to your first AA meeting?' I don't really want to, but I worry he won't go if someone isn't watching him.

'I'll be fine,' he assures me, dragging his hand along the railing as he steps down from the top step. His hair is combed and his eyes have life in them. I'm not sure how long it will take me to get used to his new look. Probably a while, since I can't remember him ever looking this healthy. 'Can we talk for a minute, though?'

Perplexed, I nod and follow him out back. Frost glazes the entire yard as the sunlight sparkles down on it. He dithers in his thoughts for a while, staring at the garage as if it holds the answers to life.

'I want you to know that I meant what I said in that letter,' he finally says with an uneasy tone. 'Sometimes it's just hard for me to express myself out loud.'

I nod, understanding as I scrape my boots at the snow. 'I get it. I really do.'

He rubs his hand across his face. 'Would you consider coming back here for spring break, just to visit, not to look after me or anything?'

'Dad, you know the house is about to enter foreclosure, right?' I ask nervously. 'Didn't you see any of the bills on the table?'

He nods, raking his hands through his hair. 'I did and I might have to let it go. But the thing is, Ella, it's not for you to worry about. That's kinda what this is all about. You need to go live your life and I'll live mine. I'm learning how to do that now.'

The feeling makes me nervous, yet frees me at the same time. It's confusing and new, but so is everything really. 'Okay, I'll try.'

'Good.' He hesitates and then opens his arms to give me a hug.

Scratching the back of my neck, I move in awkwardly for a hug and his arms wrap around me. Never can I remember him hugging me. Not once, even when I was a kid. It's weird and unnatural, but I'm glad it happened. And when it's over, I wave good-bye and head for the driveway, letting go and moving on.

When I climb into the car, Micha grins at me, sets the iPod down in the console, and laces our fingers together. 'Are you ready?'

I nod as a smile breaks through. 'I'm more than ready.'

Returning my smile, he backs out of the driveway and onto the slush-covered road. As we drive away from our houses, I can feel myself moving forward toward the beginning of my own life.

Epilogue

Six months later

Ella

It's June and the Vegas heat is stifling even though I am wearing a tank top and short shorts. Lila and I stand underneath the shade of the carport at Micha and Ethan's apartment.

'Oh my God, I'm going to miss you so much.' Tears flood from Lila's eyes and she folds her arms around me, giving me a hug.

A lot of people have been doing that lately and I'm getting used to it. Although sometimes it's just strange, like when Ethan hugged me. He was drunk, but still.

'I'm going to miss you too.' I hug her back the best I can and then we pull away. 'But you'll see me in, like, a week when you and Ethan bring out the rest of the stuff.'

'But it's not the same. You won't be right across the hall.' She dabs her eyes, wiping away the running mascara, and sniffles. 'I can't believe you're leaving me here alone, to go live in my hometown.'

'You could always come back,' I say, hopeful. 'I bet you could even talk Ethan into coming.'

'Hey, I'm not a fucking pushover,' Ethan calls out as he tosses the last box into the trunk of the Chevelle. 'And no girl is going to ever get me to up and change my life.'

'Yeah, yeah, we'll see,' I state with an attitude I know is going to annoy him.

He makes a face as he slams the trunk and then leans against the door, folding his arms and staring out at a tree. His hair has grown out and he looks kind of scraggily and he's added three more tattoos to his collection.

'He's sad his best friend's leaving him. And you,' Lila whispers with a small smile and she fixes a strand of her blonde hair that's fallen out of a clip. 'He admitted it to me last night when he was drunk.'

We giggle quietly so we don't piss him off more.

Lila's expression turns serious as she taps the ring on my finger. 'Oh yeah, and let me know when that changes fingers. In fact, I better be the first person you call when it does.'

I smile at the idea, which is no longer scary but exciting. 'All right, I promise I will, and let me know when you and Ethan finally hook up.'

She rolls her eyes. 'Never going to happen.'

We wait by the car silently until Micha trots down the stairs with the phone up to his ear. He has on a gray T-shirt and a pair of black jeans, and wisps of his blond hair dangle in aqua eyes.

As soon as we got back from winter break, he started talking to the music producer out in San Diego on the phone. At first it went nowhere, so he went on with his life, playing at The Hook Up and other places and working his job in construction. But then he got a call back. He took a leap of faith and went out there for a meeting. They loved him and I wasn't surprised when he said he was moving out there. Then he proceeded to tell me I was coming with him. I hid out in my apartment for about a day.

'Pretty girl,' Micha had called out through my door. 'Just let me in so we can talk. You've been in there for a while and you're starting to worry me.'

I paced the floor with my hands on my hips, inhaling and exhaling. 'I'm fine, but I can't talk about it yet.'

There was a soft thud. 'We already talked about this, remember? You knew it was coming.'

I stopped in the middle of my room and turned in a circle, looking for my phone. 'Just give me some time, okay. I . . . I promise I'll come out in just a bit.'

It took him a second to respond. 'Okay, but I'm just going to be out in the living room.'

I waited until I heard him leave and then dialed Anna's number. As soon as I heard her pick up, I sputtered out, 'Micha wants me to move to San Diego with him.'

'Now calm down, Ella,' she said. 'You knew this may have been coming — you've been talking to me about it since you came back from Christmas break.'

'I know.' I sunk down onto my bed. 'But now it's real. And real is scary sometimes.'

'I know,' she replied. 'But you can't run away from it.'

'I'm not,' I said. 'I just don't know what to do.'

'You could make a list,' she suggested. 'Of the pros and cons and how you feel.'

I glanced at a notebook and pen on top of my dresser in the corner. 'That's your advice?'

'That's my advice,' she said, and someone talked in the background. 'I have to go, but make a list like I said and then call me later and we'll talk.'

'Fine.' I sighed, hung up, and did what she told me to do. In the end, the list told me what I had known all along, but I was just too afraid to admit it aloud without some encouragement.

I applied for some jobs online in San Diego and we made a trip out there a couple weeks ago for job interviews. We picked out a one-bedroom apartment in a decent area. It's scary as hell, but with Micha by my side, I know I can handle it.

'You ready?' Micha asks as he approaches me with his hand extended.

My anxiety bubbles as I slip my hand into his. It's the first time we'll be living together and I'm interested how our story will go.

Lila gives me another hug while Ethan and Micha give each other a guy pat on the back and pound fists. Micha and I get into the car and he turns the engine on as I balance a photo on the dashboard.

Caroline had sent the picture to me not long after Christmas. Micha and I had been standing beside each other out on the front porch and his head was turned toward me instead of at the camera. He had whispered a perverted comment into my ear and I had laughed right as Caroline snapped the shot. It was the perfect picture, because even though we weren't looking at the camera we were genuinely happy and we were making each other feel that way.

The backseat is full with bags and boxes, so

Micha uses the side mirror to back out. I give a quick wave to Lila, who's sobbing and Ethan comes up and puts an arm around her.

Once we reach the exit, my phone rings and I answer it. 'I'm going to be fine. I promise.'

'I know you are,' Anna says. 'But I wanted to make sure that you called that therapist number I gave you.'

'Yes, and I have an appointment in a few weeks with her,' I say, buckling my seatbelt. 'And I'll make sure to go, just like I told you I would yesterday.'

'Good.' She pauses. 'And if you ever need anything, and I mean anything, don't hesitate to call me.'

'I will,' I promise. 'And Anna, thank you for what you said the other day — about me being a different girl than the one who first came in. I know I've changed, but it's nice to hear.'

'I only said the truth, Ella. You have changed and I think you'll do fine in life. You just need to remember that asking for help isn't a bad thing, so make sure to do it, because there will be times when you need it.'

I smile at Micha, who's observing me with curiosity. 'I will.'

'Good,' she says. 'Remember to have fun and don't worry so much.'

'I will.' I hang up and Micha threads his fingers through mine.

'Who was that?' Micha asks, halting at a red light.

'Anna.'

'What'd she have to say?'

I glance up at the sunlight sparkling in the sky. 'That she thinks I'm going to be okay.'

★ ★ ★

A few hours later, we pull over into a rest stop for a quick bathroom break and to get some snacks out of the trunk. We park along the turnout on a rocky cliff that overlooks a lake. Just a ways to the side, people are cliff-diving into the water. It's not very high and they look like they're having fun. While I'm waiting on Micha, I inch over to the edge and peer down at the water rippling in the sunlight, remembering the bridge and how badly I wanted to jump that night.

'What are you doing?' Micha's worried voice abruptly rises over my shoulder and his hands grip my waist.

I stare at a woman as she summons up the courage to jump off the ledge. With her eyes shut and arms flying, she soars downward, free as can be. Seconds later she splashes into the water.

'I think we should jump.' When I meet Micha's eyes, he doesn't look happy.

'I don't think that's a good idea.' He tugs me by the hand away from the cliff. 'We need to hit the road.'

I squirm from his hold, slip off my shoes, and put my hair up with an elastic band from around my wrist. 'Come on, it'll be fun.'

'I'm not going to do it.' He stuffs his hands into his pockets and shakes his head. 'Not with this.'

I cross my arms. 'Why not?'

'Because . . . ' He shrugs, kicking the tip of his boot at the dirt. 'The idea of you jumping freaks the shit out of me.'

I take his hand and move closer to the cliff. 'It's not about that. It's about letting go. I want to do this.'

He wavers, glancing out at the shimmering lake. 'Fine, you win. I'll do it, but only because I love you and have the hardest time saying no to you when you look at me like that.' He shucks off his T-shirt, revealing his lean muscles and the tattoo on his rib cage. He unlaces his boots before slipping them off and then takes his wallet and change out of his pockets. 'But you're holding my hand the entire time.'

I grin, excited. 'Okay, it's a deal.'

We walk to the edge, hand in hand. The

cliff is straight down with only a few jagged ledges, a doable fall, unlike the bridge back home.

He dithers, sucking his lip ring into his mouth, and then a smile creeps up on his face. 'Whenever you're ready, pretty girl.'

I take a deep breath, shut my eyes, and whisper, 'I'm ready.'

He counts under his breath. 'One . . . two . . . three.'

We dive off the cliff, holding hands. The fall is brief, yet it feels like it lasts forever before we hit the water together. With his help, I break back through the surface of the water in an instant.

Panting loudly, I glance back up at the cliff, which doesn't seem as high. My clothes cling to my body and my chest feels weightless. 'That was fun.'

He laughs as he wipes droplets of water off his skin, his lips, his long eyelashes. His blond hair is slicked back as he runs his hand over his head. 'I'm glad. Now can we swim back to shore and hit the road? I want to get there before dark.'

I look into his liquid-blue eyes. 'What's the rush? We could stay out here all day, floating around in the water, just you and me.'

He pulls me close to him and paddles us backward toward the sandy shore nestled near the bottom of the cliff. 'That's what you want to do? Float in a lake all day?'

'No, I just want to see if you'll do it for me.' I hook my arms around his neck and fidget with the ring until it slips off my finger and into my palm, still deciding.

'You know, if you ask me to do anything, I'll do it.' He kisses me and I suck the water off his lips. 'Because I'm a sucker for those sad-puppy eyes you give me every time you want something.'

I move my hands away from his neck, fastening my legs around his waist to hold myself up. I still hesitate, but then finally I let all my reservations go. 'And now I want to give you something.'

He cocks an eyebrow, confused until I lower the ring onto my other finger. It feels right, like it's belonged there forever. At first his expression is stoic and I worry he's changed his mind about marrying me.

'I can take it off,' I say quickly. 'If you don't want me to put it on there yet.'

'Take it off?' He gapes at me like I'm crazy and brings me closer, so every inch of our wet bodies touch while he keeps us afloat by kicking his legs. 'Why the hell would I ever want you to do that? I never want you to take it off. Ever.'

'But you look like you're upset or something.'

'I'm shocked. I thought it was going to be years and years and years before you ever put that thing on your other finger.'

A smile emerges at my lips. 'You want me to keep it on?'

'Of course I want you to keep it on.' Happiness fills his eyes, as blinding as the sunlight behind him. 'And you're never allowed to take it off.'

I nod and he crashes his lips into mine, kissing me with everything he has and I return his passion equally as we kiss our first kiss of our forever.

Other titles published by
The House of Ulverscroft:

THE SECRET OF ELLA AND MICHA

Jessica Sorensen

Ella and Micha have been best friends since childhood, until one tragic night shatters their relationship and Ella decides to leave everything behind, including Micha, to start a new life at college. But now it's summer break and Ella fears everything she worked so hard to bury might resurface, especially with Micha living right next door. Micha is sexy, smart, confident, and can get under Ella's skin like no one else can. And he's determined to win back the girl he lost, no matter what it takes.

LADY SARAH'S REDEMPTION

Beverley Eikli

When Lady Sarah Miles becomes the sole survivor of a shipwreck, she assumes the identity of her ill-fated travelling companion to avoid an arranged marriage. Masquerading as governess to the daughter of dashing Roland Hawthorne, the mutual attraction between Sarah and her employer quickly turns to love. But Sarah's past returns to haunt her, revealing more secrets than just her false identity. Determined to redeem herself in Roland's eyes, she unwittingly plays into the hands of an unexpected adversary. With Sarah's honour at stake, can Roland's daring plan succeed? Or will the woman he loves be lost to him forever?

FRANCES AND BERNARD

Carlene Bauer

He is Bernard Eliot, a poet: passionate, gregarious, a force of nature. She is Frances Reardon, a novelist: wry, uncompromising and quick to skewer. In the summer of 1957, Frances and Bernard meet at a writers' colony. Afterwards, he sends her a letter, and with it begins an almost holy friendship. From their first, witty missives to dispatches from the long, dark night of the soul, Frances and Bernard tussle over faith and family, literature and creativity, madness and devotion — and before long, they are writing the account of their very own love story.

JULIA

Otto de Kat

From the moment he meets Julia, Christaan Dudok is dangerously close to love. But their first date is interrupted by S.A. Brownshirts storming into the cafe. It is 1938, and Germany is heading for war and fanaticism. Chris, a Dutchman, is both transfixed and appalled by the effect of Hitler's manic oratory on the people of Lubeck. The independence and freedom of thought that Chris finds so attractive in Julia lead her to emphatically reject the Nazi regime, and before long her courageous stance brings them both to the Gestapo's attention. Soon Chris is forced to make an impossible choice, the outcome of which he can only regret.